JOHNNY COOPER'S FIELD

a love story

Don J. Snyder

By the author of the novel, *The Tin Nose Shop*,
A BBC Radio2 Book Club Selection.

Also by Don J. Snyder

Veterans Park
From The Point
A Soldier's Disgrace
The Cliff Walk
Of Time & Memory
Night Crossing
Fallen Angel
Winter Dreams
The Winter Travelers
Walking With Jack
The Tin Nose Shop

Legend Press Ltd, 51 Gower Street, London, WC1E 6HJ
info@legendtimesgroup.co.uk | www.legendpress.co.uk

Contents © Don J. Snyder 2025
The right of the above author to be identified as the author of this work has been asserted in accordance with the Copyright, Designs and Patents Act 1988. British Library Cataloguing in Publication Data available.

Print ISBN 9781917163415
Ebook ISBN 9781917163422
Set in Times.

All characters, other than those clearly in the public domain, and place names, other than those well-established such as towns and cities, are fictitious and any resemblance is purely coincidental.

All rights reserved. No part of this publication may be reproduced, stored in or introduced into a retrieval system, or transmitted, in any form, or by any means electronic, mechanical, photocopying, recording or otherwise, without the prior permission of the publisher. Any person who commits any unauthorised act in relation to this publication may be liable to criminal prosecution and civil claims for damages.

Don J. Snyder was born and raised in America. He is the author of eleven novels and non-fiction books and wrote the movie *Fallen Angel* that starred Gary Sinise and Joely Richardson. He now lives in Scotland where he established the world's only caddie training school for soldiers, to try to help restore servicemen from around the world who are suffering from PTSD. His novel *The Tin Nose Shop* was published by Legend Press in 2022.

Visit Don at
www.donjsnyder.com

For Johnny, one true friend

Prologue

As I crossed the night sky at 33,000 feet on my flight across the Atlantic, I thought about how every love story has a beginning, a middle and an end, though they don't always come in that order. For many of us there is the beginning, then the end, and then the long march through the middle, trying to find what we once had that seemed to work so well, and that we somehow lost somewhere along the way.

On my left, an anaesthetist was trying to nod off, and on my right a retired salesman for some American company had just begun to explain that in the late 1940s you could order almost anything from the company he'd worked forty-one years for, including your house, when suddenly great flashes of blue lightning tore through the darkness around us. In an instant my existence and the story of my own life contracted to the space between me and the red *EXIT* sign I stared at as everything grew eerily still around us. And as the plane began to roll and pitch I bowed my head and focused again on the story of Johnny Cooper, whom I had left behind in Scotland tending his fir trees and giving thanks to God for the life he had been given. I thought it was my own life that was supposed to flash before my eyes at this point, but there was Johnny in his coarse woollen cap and the thick cable-knit jumper that he always left hanging on a peg above the wood stove.

He had been alone and lost in the world for a long time, yet he counted himself among the blessed because he had been loved and trusted, and what can ever be worth more than that? For years he had hidden himself away from the music of life, blind to his own essential goodness, but now he had reclaimed his belief that our lives are shaped more by the ways we love one another than by the forces that drive us apart.

I considered all of this and gave thanks for Johnny Cooper while the sky broke apart around me. Then my reverie was interrupted by the voice of the pilot on the intercom telling us that we were through the worst of a ridge of thunderstorms and though there might be more turbulence ahead, he had instructed the flight attendants to serve dinner.

The salesman, who possessed that irrepressible quality about him that I have always associated with Americans, picked up right where he had left off. 'The company shipped everything all over America by flatbed trucks in those days,' he said. 'Plumbing pipes, electrical wiring, windows. Even the bricks for your fireplace.' He had a soft and slightly modulated voice that I found reassuring.

We were buttering our rolls when the nose of the plane rose sharply, then dropped so steeply that everyone's dinner tray flew against the ceiling and people began to scream and swear.

The anaesthetist turned up the collar of her jacket and began to cry softly.

I looked at the salesman who calmly and methodically did up the top button on his shirt, straightened the knot of his tie, then looked at his watch as if he were about to present himself for an appointment. When our eyes met, he shrugged his shoulders as if to say, *Well, whatever happens, I'm ready, I've done all that I can do.*

I suppose that a salesman hears a thousand stories on the road, but he was exceedingly gracious when mine came pouring out as if we had known one another all our lives. I told him that not long ago Johnny had tried to remember every promise he had ever made in his life. He had sat beside a window one morning with a pen and written them down in the margins of a small Bible. Outside, there was snow falling into the sea at the first light of morning and he could see the wind race through the fescue grass across the hillside. This was at a time in his life when everything he hoped he would never lose had been swept away. He listed the promises from as far back as he could remember, from the smallest to the most important, then counted those that he had broken and those he had kept.

The salesman, though he looked puzzled as to why I was telling him this, nodded understandingly as the plane dived and rose again and a silver coffee pot bounced down the aisle like a cannonball. All around us, passengers embraced each other, fearing the worst. I turned towards the window and watched the wing dip low, then rise just as the cabin lights went out. When they blinked on and off again, I saw a man in first class lying on the floor, and a stewardess with grey hair drop to her knees and cross herself. I closed my eyes and no more words would come to me. I looked past the salesman to the window just as a heavy white cloud enveloped us. And then, a moment later, the plane regained its forward momentum and levelled off.

It was as though we all began to breathe again. The salesman brushed a piece of lint off his knee and said, 'Inventory. That fellow Johnny you were talking about, he was taking inventory of his life when he added up the promises.'

'I guess he was,' I said.

'It's all about dignity,' he continued. 'Each time we break a promise to someone, we lose some of our dignity. My mother taught me that. She never even finished eighth grade but that lady was the real deal, let me tell you.'

'You could be right,' I said.

And then the anaesthetist leaned forward, turned down her collar and asked, 'What happened to him?'

I told her that it was a long story. Then I reconsidered and recounted for both of them how Johnny had been a homeless man in Paris when he saved the life of a young woman. They fell in love but her wealthy father separated them. They married secretly and her father had the marriage annulled. She had their child and her father arranged for the child to be given up for adoption.

The salesman nudged me with his elbow and asked if they had ever got back together.

'No,' I said. 'Not yet.'

* * *

We landed an hour later and after the anaesthetist had stepped into the aisle, the salesman gave me his hand to shake and asked me my name. 'Rosie,' I told him. He asked me if this was my first time in America. I told him that it was and he wished me well and told me not to miss the Statue of Liberty and five national parks whose names I instantly forgot. Then he added, 'I hope you don't mind me saying this, Rosie, I know you can't be any older than your twenties, and you're a lovely young woman, but you look like you've had your own share of loss.'

I didn't lie to him.

He wished me good luck and then we went our separate ways inside the terminal and disappeared from each other's lives. Whenever I tell Johnny Cooper's story I think of how we are all in this life together just as the three of us were on that flight across the dark ocean. Maybe you and I are companions too, fellow travellers on a night journey, bound for where we can never be certain. Perhaps a place where we will finally be understood, and forgiven.

BOOK I

chapter one

mirror

I believe that anyone telling you the story of their life has a responsibility to tell the bad along with the good. Like Johnny, we have all done bad things which we are ashamed of, and those things must be revealed in a story like this one. But there are also the very bad things we've done or that have been done to us, things we've never told anyone. Those are our secrets and I believe they should be honoured as such.

And so all I am going to tell you about Johnny's youth, when he was known as Jean and spoke no English, is that he grew up in a small apartment in the 18th arrondissement of Paris, on the Rue de l'Abreuvoir, where rats raced inside the walls at night, and his father, a kind man but an alcoholic, drove a delivery lorry for a furniture store in the day and cleaned the warehouse at night until the winter he died a drinker's death when Jean was nine years old. After that, his mother, an irrepressible woman with startling green eyes, raised him on her weekly pay cheque from Le Bon Marché Rive Gauche department store where she worked for gratuities behind the lunch counter. They barely made ends meet, and Jean learned that poverty traps you inside its own cruel cage of tyranny where freedom and joy cannot thrive.

However, they could still dream. And it was in their apartment where his mother dreamed his future and returned home from work one night with a typewriter which she planned to learn to use so she could earn the money to send him to college.

The night she brought it home, he helped her set it up on a table beside her bed. He watched as she raised her hands to the keyboard, expecting her to tear into it with the same energy with which she approached everything. But she hesitated, withdrew her hands and let them fall into her lap, then just stared at the machine. She looked worn out and defeated. He had always thought of her as old, though she was only thirty-three or -four. While he watched her, she took a deep breath and put her hands out to her sides on the dark blue bedspread which would never completely lose the scent of his father's aftershave lotion and the ointment she had spent hours massaging into his father's chest in the weeks before he died.

She was silent for a moment and Jean saw something dark pass over her face. Then she raised her head and looked at her reflection in the mirror on the bureau across the room. She pried her shoes off with her feet as she stared at the mirror, thinking about his father, Jean supposed, remembering him in some way. He felt her sadness and so he called to her from the doorway. 'I'm going to be just like Papa someday for you, Maman.'

She looked up at him with a surprised expression and smiled bravely before she lay down on the bed as if all the energy had just drained out of her, and along with it, all her expectations. She drew the bedspread over her legs. 'Your father wouldn't want that, Jean,' she told him. 'Go to sleep now.'

He had just turned away when suddenly she sat up straight, swung her feet onto the floor, and pulled back her shoulders. Her hands were poised over the keys for an instant like a pianist awaiting the conductor's signal to begin. A band of moonlight fell across her legs.

She was still going at it when he got into bed. This was the first of countless nights when Jean would fall asleep to the sound of her typing, the little bell on the carriage ringing so faintly it seemed to be apologising to him each time.

chapter two

sermon

Their practice sessions when Jean dictated sentences to his mother, and she sat at the typewriter, the white cloth belt of her bathrobe tied around her head for a blindfold so she could not cheat, and her shoulders pinned back pertly to match some brochure picture of a proper secretary she must have seen somewhere, paid off for them. By spring she was skilled enough to answer a small classified advertisement that appeared in the newspaper one Sunday. The Protestant Faculty of Theology on the Rue Lhomond was looking for people to type sermons for the young men training there.

Students' handwritten sermons were dropped off at their apartment every Monday morning and by Thursday evening his mother had typed them onto three-by-five-inch index cards. Often Jean read the sermons aloud, dictating them to her, while she typed. They were terrible for the most part, long-winded proclamations about God and heaven, and their evenings were a hard test of forbearance until Jerry Hudson found his way to their door. A solitary man from America who had seen much of France during the war, spoke the language fluently, and had been determined to return there, he had a shock of jet-black hair and a lost look in his pale blue eyes. He had spent his youth travelling the world – compliments of the United States Army – and now seemed to be spending his thirties quietly dreaming about the places he had seen. He was the first person to call him Johnny instead of Jean, and he adopted that name for himself because it seemed to turn him into someone new. Jerry always gave him a mock salute each time he saw him, and he dressed in nothing but tan khakis top and bottom as if he expected he might be called back into service at any moment. His writing also had a dreamy quality to it, enriched by phrases of surprising luminosity.

In a lifetime we find and re-find ourselves many times ...

It got to the point where Johnny and his mother hurried through the other sermons each week just to get to his.

In the face of a stranger we might catch an unexpected glimpse of ourselves, Johnny read aloud one night. His mother stopped typing and silence filled the room.

'Read that again,' she said breathlessly. He did as she asked and when he looked up she wasn't typing at all, she was just gazing into the distance as if a voice was calling her.

chapter three

boathouse

They were married on a Tuesday, in the winter, the year Johnny turned eleven and had learned enough English from Jerry to dream in that language – which filled him with wonder and completed his desire to become someone he wasn't before. By spring Jerry had finished his coursework at the seminary and needed only to serve an apprenticeship before he could be ordained as a fully fledged pastor himself. When he accepted a position as assistant reverend at Eglise episcopale libre at La Seyne-sur-Mer, a small town on the Riviera, they travelled the ten hours by train, taking with them nothing but their clothing and the typewriter.

The church provided them with living quarters: three rooms in a parsonage where they stayed for just a year before Johnny's mother had earned enough money working as a secretary in a maze of offices at the Toulon naval base to buy a house of their own.

Really it was a boathouse, not a house for people. It stood on the mudflats in a protected cove on the south shore of Falcon Bay, four nautical miles from where it spilled into the Mediterranean Sea. Their front door rolled on iron wheels and opened to a ramp where boats had once been launched on the incoming tide. You could see the blue-green sea water through the cracks in the planked floorboards of their living room before they stuffed the cracks with strips of felt. They divided the loft into two bedrooms and repaired the old lead-paned windows that faced the sea. They replaced the sagging sills and patched the hip roof and built a screened-in veranda where the three of them spent hours watching the slow parade of fishing boats passing through the channel each morning, and stars reflected on the water as if they were drowning in the bay at night. The real magic of the place was in the room they transformed into their kitchen. There, a trapdoor in the floor opened to a rope ladder and a waiting rowing boat below, lashed to the cedar posts that served as their foundation. In the evenings when the bay was flat calm, the three of them would climb down the ladder into the boat and, bent low with their heads bowed, slip beneath the underpinnings of their home out into the cove. Johnny would be at the oars, his mother in the bow with an oil lamp lighting their way across the dark water, and Jerry in the stern with a torch, reading his next sermon aloud to them. Eventually those sermons gave way to discussions, always in English, about what was happening in America. The race riots, the assassinations of Martin Luther King and Bobby Kennedy seemed to be breaking Jerry's heart into pieces. Johnny would always remember his sorrow when he spoke about the little girls who were murdered at Sunday school in a church bombing. It seemed to Johnny that if these terrible things were happening in a country as great as America, then the whole world could be torn apart at any time. He didn't know it then, of course, but those nights in the rowing boat out on the bay would stay in the core of his memory for the rest of his life.

Johnny was at school the afternoon his mother and Jerry were drowned when the boat capsized in a freak squall that swept through the bay with wind gusts of seventy knots that had apparently originated on top of Mount Etna in Italy, just over a thousand miles away.

Their deaths, more than his father's before them, made

Johnny feel temporary about himself and seemed to strip him of his belief in life's possibilities, so that by the time he was old enough to walk out of the Orphanage Saint-Philippe in Paris, he went into the world looking only for a place to hide.

Most likely because of the way Jerry spoke to him about how the army had transformed him from a boy into a man, Johnny joined the French Foreign Legion when he turned eighteen, signing up for five years on the very day he met that minimum age requirement without having to provide authorisation from a parent or guardian. He was hoping, of course, to discover that he was brave and reliable, as he was certain Jerry must have been in his time at war, but when he was dispatched with the Legion's 2nd Foreign Parachute Regiment to the Battle of Kolwezi in Zaire to rescue 2,000 Europeans who had been captured and were being held as hostages by local rebels, and the fighting turned to hand-to-hand combat, he was so terrified that he dropped to the street among the fallen and pretended he was dead. Afraid to open his eyes, he waited until darkness fell and then managed to disappear, buy trousers and a jacket to replace his uniform, and his first bottle of whisky which, from his first swallow, made him feel like he had finally found a way home, though he had no idea what home really was.

Thanks to Jerry Hudson, he still dreamed in English, and he discovered that the dreams he had of dying were the most reassuring. He knew that he would be punished severely for desertion if the Legion ever managed to find him, and so he disappeared in Paris where, for a while, he was given a chance at a real life by a procession of young women, girls really, who seemed to want to save him from himself. Those were the days when his physical beauty opened doors for him that he always ended up closing and hiding behind so no one would see that, though he was trying for all he was worth to outrun his father, he was already following in his footsteps. He had already developed the capacity to drink enough on any given day so that he had no memory of that day when he woke the next. In some way it was like he was being reborn each day into a world where he did not know a single person and no one knew him. After the last girl gave up on him he ended up living on the streets where he discovered a marvellous sense of freedom. He begged for money to eat, he slept in doorways and under bridges. There were so many bridges over the Seine to choose from. Pont Alexandre III. Pont de la Tournelle. Pont de Bir-Hakeim. Pont des Arts. And his favourite, Alma's bridge, that took its name from the famous Battle of the Alma in the Crimean War when the Russian army was defeated. He was aware that he was not only a deserter from the Legion, but also from the real world. He was Johnny to his fellow deserters, and to further conceal his past, he spoke only English and when pressed claimed to be American, adopting the city of Jerry's home – Boston, Massachusetts – as his own. 'Home to Paul Revere,' he would often add, to underline his deceit.

They say there are some things we cannot hide from, but I know this to be untrue. If you're frightened enough, and you turn your fear to cynicism, you can hide from everything. Whenever Johnny saw a rich man walk by he muttered to himself, 'Fine, in the next life he'll be a beggar in Calcutta.'

That was the kind of man he became, living on the streets of Paris among the hopeless and the hidden. Not at all a man like Jerry. Not at all the kind of man he had wanted to become. If you were to have asked any of the millions of people in the city who had passed him on the pavements or ridden with him shoulder to shoulder on the Métro if they had ever seen him, none of them would have. He had become invisible.

chapter four

girl

The girl whose life, against long odds, would coincide with Johnny's, perhaps because of fate alone, began as all our lives begin – with a single cell. Though it was so small that it was only visible under a powerful microscope for the first twelve hours of its solitary existence, this single cell contained all the information required to form the girl who would create and possess something that could never be taken from her – her story. The cell floated in a fluid membrane surrounded by hundreds of protein molecules that set off a chain of reactions. After thirty hours or so, it divided from one cell into two. Some fifteen hours later, the two cells divided to become four. And at the end of three days, perhaps while her mother was painting her nails, the fertilised egg cell became a berry-shaped structure made up of sixteen cells as round and mysterious and unfathomable as the first atomic bomb at the Trinity test site in America, with its plutonium core whose isotopes split apart and divided cataclysmically when they were struck by neutrons. During the first eight or nine days after conception, the cells that would eventually form the embryo continued to divide. At the same time, the hollow constellation in which they had arranged themselves was slowly carried towards the uterus by tiny hair-like structures down through the dark tunnels of the fallopian tubes. Though no larger than the head of a pin, it was now composed of hundreds of cells and it would perish and foreclose on the life of the girl if evolution had not bestowed upon this cell the unwitting knowledge that it must bury itself against the side of the mother's uterus for the nourishment it would need to prosper. Over the next ten days, while the girl's mother did her shopping, drove to the dry cleaners to pick up her pale blue cashmere coat, her blood supply was beginning to form the placenta that would transmit the vital oxygen the girl needed to survive. After those ten days the cells had increased in numbers to around 150, each containing the combined DNA of the mother and the man whose sperm vitalised her egg. Soon blood vessels began to develop. By the eighth week the heart began to beat, organs began to form and the neural tube emerged in the wet darkness along the back of the embryo, soon to be transformed into the spinal cord and brain. The next week the strange tail of the foetus disappeared and it began to resemble a human being. Our girl became a girl between the ninth and the twelfth weeks. And soon after, something went terribly wrong despite 6 million years of evolution to perfect this process, something that would, in time, grant this girl the inestimable gift of completing someone else's story.

chapter five

agony

The mother's name was Donna and she named her baby daughter Elizabeth. This was the only child she would ever have, not because she didn't want more children, but because her husband, Martin – who grew up a member of the privileged sperm club and parlayed his exclusive American education at Choate boarding school and then Harvard into one stunning success after another in the world of academics on his path to becoming the youngest head of the department of mathematics in the Sorbonne's celebrated history – could not bear to take another chance on another baby after Elizabeth came into the world with her right leg almost two inches shorter than her left. This was the first setback he had ever had to endure. A man who walked through the rain without getting wet, he cursed the God he did not believe in for his defective child.

What condemned Elizabeth was the combination of her father's obdurate sense of entitlement and her mother's religion. A devoted Christian Scientist, Donna believed that all real healing was achieved through prayer alone, and that because the body was not real, sickness could never truly exist and was, instead, only an evil illusion, a condition of flawed thoughts. She rejected the surgery to shorten Elizabeth's longer leg as barbaric but at Martin's insistence reluctantly agreed to an only slightly less barbaric series of treatments at the Pitié-Salpêtrière hospital designed to stretch the femur of the shorter leg until she could no longer bear to hear her daughter howl in agony and she begged her husband to please make it stop. 'Our daughter's life is in God's hands,' she told Martin again and again which, in time, gave him the excuse he needed to wash his hands of his daughter's imperfection – and effectively of her life as well. This was quite easily accomplished because he had something that almost no women had in those days – an office to escape to. And his office was a place where he could take refuge in the respect of his colleagues and the adoration of his young students, especially his female students, still referred to as coeds in those days. There seemed to be an endless procession of these girls making their way to his office for extra help with the complex problems of statistics or probability he assigned them, each of them somehow more beautiful and perfect than the last. In other words, Martin had it made. And like many men, he only returned home to sleep, to be fed and to be sexually satisfied by his compliant wife who had been made even more compliant by her religious belief that it was her duty to please her husband.

Donna was no fool, however; she knew herself well enough to comprehend that it was a terrible flaw in her own psychology that rather than resent her husband for his absence and his indifference, it made her long for him terribly, and undertake a feckless campaign to make him happy. She knew he was ashamed of their daughter and she took the blame for this along with whatever quantities of Valium and vodka were required to get through the hours of each day which often felt interminable. She was trying to be a good mother and yet she knew that her first priority was just to survive. She also knew that without Martin she and her daughter would be cut loose from the security they needed desperately. She possessed no resources of her own being so far from her home in San Diego, California, only those that her husband provided. But this did not fully explain her dependence on Martin. It ran deeper than that. For a reason she would never have been able to explain to anyone, the less attention her husband paid her, the more she craved it and the harder she tried to win back the affection he had for her before Elizabeth was born.

She knew that it was a terrible thing to think, but there were days when she admitted to herself that she would have given away her child just for the chance to have her husband want to hold hands with her again. She hated herself for this, but she was so desperately lonely. Her loneliness had become a trial, an illness, and because she believed that only Martin was the cure, she made the conscious decision to choose him over her broken daughter.

chapter six

latin

And so at the same time Johnny spent starlit evenings in the rowing boat with his mother and Jerry out on the bay while it seemed that Jerry's America was falling apart and that the world was more fragile and transient than Johnny had ever imagined it could be, Elizabeth was isolated in a kind of solitary confinement in her own tilted world. At Martin's insistence she had been homeschooled by tutors in their house at Jardin des Plantes ever since she was of kindergarten age. He told her that she would thank him for this one day, for paying for her to be educated privately the same way Queen Elizabeth had been across the Channel when she was a young princess.

One of her tutors was the brilliant Sara, twenty-six years old and in her final year at the prestigious Cours Florent drama school where she had mastered five languages, among them English with a broad repertoire of American accents that ranged from Brooklyn to Cajun. She had been called unstoppable by those who knew her best. She had an energy about her and a most pleasant disposition, and calloused hands from the hours of volunteer work tending communal vegetable gardens for immigrants in Île-de-France. Martin hired her to teach Elizabeth Latin which she did with great forbearance, and a fierce determination to introduce her pupil to some of the childhood experiences that she had been deprived of. One morning she arrived with a skipping rope. It took three weeks before they came up with a way for Elizabeth to compensate for her shorter leg and so to triumph. They played hopscotch together. Sara even showed her to cast a fly rod exactly as her own father had taught her so she could fish with him in the Hautes-Alpes. In all of these enterprises Sara's principal objective was to persuade Elizabeth that she was entitled to a life of dignity and purpose. To this end she also taught her Latin phrases meant to empower her.

Esto quod es. Be what you are.

Vive ut vivas. Live so that you may live.

And, most important of all, *Non ducor duco.* I am not led, I lead!

'You must not ever be led,' Sara told her. 'You have the power to lead.'

'Where does this power come from?' Elizabeth asked her.

'It comes from within.'

'But I don't feel it.'

'What *do* you feel?'

'Lost. Blind. Hopeless. Lonely. Confused. Abandoned. All of those things, though not necessarily in that order. And frightened. Yes, most of all frightened.'

'What are you most afraid of, Elizabeth?'

'I'm not sure I can tell you.'

'Why not? Why should there be anything that you can't tell me?'

They were sitting on Elizabeth's wicker bed. Sara took her hand gently into her own and an understanding passed silently between them. It was an understanding that changed Elizabeth's world. Or, more accurately, prepared her for what transpired beyond the boundaries of her known world.

'You mean sex,' Sara said, matter-of-factly.

'Yes.'

'And your mother hasn't told you anything?'

Elizabeth bowed her head and shook it slowly. 'I heard my father telling her that they should put me in a convent, to become a nun before I get up to mischief with boys.'

This made Sara laugh faintly, but then she apologised. 'It's just that your father's choice of words – *up to mischief* – well, that's certainly one way of putting it.'

Elizabeth told her that it made her angry, not knowing anything. 'I mean, since the survival of the species depends upon it, you'd think we would be born knowing what to do. And how to do it. The way animals are.'

This made Sara smile. 'You're such a bright girl. You can be whatever you want to be in your life.'

'I don't want to be a nun, I'm certain of that. I don't know if I even believe in God.'

'Then don't be a nun. Don't be anything your father wants you to be unless it's also what you want to be.'

Elizabeth suddenly felt brave enough to ask. 'What kind of mischief will boys want to do with me?'

'I can tell you,' Sara said reassuringly. 'And I can show you. But only if you want me to.'

'How does it begin?'

'Well, it should begin with a kiss, but from my experience, it usually begins like this.' With that she placed a hand on Elizabeth's breast. They looked into each other's eyes as clouds passed the window and turned the light in the room. And from that first touch they went on.

chapter seven

birdhouses

Elizabeth would not have chosen to inherit her father's genius for mathematics that had brought her mother – and therefore her – so far from home to Paris. She would have preferred to be a poet or a cobbler. Anything else, really. But it turned out that she experienced great comfort in numbers and finding solutions to complex problems. The first time she attempted to solve the Riemann hypothesis, one of the world's most significant and unsolved maths problems whose solution had eluded not only her father but any number of Nobel laureates, she felt like she had been transported, that the molecules inside her had been rearranged and that she was no longer disabled. She began working on it night and day, with barely any sleep or food, with the door to her room locked. Whenever her mother knocked or called to her, she found that she could not break her concentration to speak. She was suddenly mute. Unable to say a word. After seven days and eight nights of this, her father pried open her door with a crowbar and summoned an ambulance that took her to the Sainte-Anne hospital in the 14th arrondissement, where she underwent electroshock therapy against her will, her arms and legs strapped to the table by leather belts, a rubber wedge clamped in her mouth to keep her from swallowing her tongue. After five sessions she could not remember how to write the number four. She spent whole days sitting at a barred window writing rows and rows of numbers, only vaguely aware that the four was always missing.

It was determined that she had suffered a psychotic episode, so serious that the doctors in charge told Martin and Donna they were lucky to have brought her back. Elizabeth herself, still mute, had no memory of any of it once the storm had run its course, and she was back in her room with Riemann's hypothesis, picking up her work where she had left off, and unable to understand why her father had dispatched her tutors which left her no interaction with anyone from the outside world – and made her feel like she was an unwelcome visitor in her parents' house. Late at night she often stood outside the door to their bedroom, listening to them discussing what should be done with her. This was when she began to save her urine in her mother's long-stemmed wine glasses that she had had shipped all the way to France from California. She covered the glasses of urine with aluminium foil and hid them on the shelf in her closet.

One night she snuck out of the house and walked for hours until she ended up at a McDonald's in Créteil, a suburb about eleven kilometres from her home, where she discovered that Sara was right. The boy from behind the counter who could only take her order when she wrote it down for him took her virginity half an hour later up against a green iron rubbish bin that reeked of pickles and onions, not bothering to kiss her before he went for her breasts. It was over in minutes and he hurried back to work, straightening the paper hat on his head while she watched for a moment and then ran all the way back home, back to her room, convinced that there was a pattern to the pimples on the boy's chin that would supply the missing piece to Riemann's that she had been searching for.

* * *

Two days later, after Donna had found stains on her daughter's underwear, Martin took Elizabeth to the office of a doctor friend he played golf with who performed a dilation and curettage surgical procedure scraping the walls of her uterus with a curette as a precaution against pregnancy, while she kept her eyes closed and thought of the time Sara told her that she could be anything she wanted to be in her life.

Martin didn't drive her home. Instead he returned her to the Sainte-Anne hospital where fourteen sessions of electroshock therapy left her wondering if whatever was wrong with her was something that she had done to herself, or if someone else had done it to her. She spent most of the time sitting at a round table where she silently painted in pastel colours the birdhouses that her fellow inmates built. Most of the birdhouses were poorly constructed. Lopsided, exactly how she pictured herself.

chapter eight

sara

At the front door Donna didn't want to let Sara in because she knew that Martin would disapprove but there was such concern and sympathy in the young woman's eyes when she said that she had not been able to stop worrying about Elizabeth since... 'Since I was banished,' she said.

'I don't think my husband would concede that he *banished* you.'

Sara shrugged and asked, 'What would you call it then?'

'My husband—' Donna began to say, but Sara cut her off.

'I'm not really interested in what your husband thinks. But I am very interested in what *you* think. Do you allow anyone to come see your daughter?'

Donna averted her eyes and Sara could tell that she was ashamed.

'I've tutored a lot of students in Latin but I've never had any of them pick it up as quickly as your daughter. Your beautiful daughter. Beautiful in every way.'

Sara looked past her, across the corridor to the kitchen where there was a highball glass with ice cubes in it and a bottle of vodka or gin standing on the counter.

'No one is perfect,' Sara said.

This seemed to stun Donna for a moment. Then she replied,

'I think Elizabeth would love to see you,' as she swung the door open wider. 'But she hasn't spoken a word in months. The doctors at the… the hospital call it selective mutism.'

* * *

Elizabeth talked to Sara from the moment she saw her. They talked genially for a while. They even laughed like schoolgirls when Elizabeth described how the paper McDonald's hat the boy was wearing nearly slid off his head just as he finished. 'He thanked me before he ran back to work,' Elizabeth told Sara.

'Well, that was thoughtful of him,' Sara said. 'And how about you, how did you feel?'

'I didn't feel disabled,' Elizabeth replied immediately.

This troubled Sara but she didn't have time to dwell on what Elizabeth had said – or on the thousands of sheets of paper with numbers and equations scrawled on them that were scattered across the bed and floor – before she followed her to her closet and was shown the wine glasses filled with urine.

They said nothing for a moment and then Elizabeth spoke. 'What do you think it means, Sara?'

How could she answer this question? Nothing in her life had prepared her to answer this question in a way that would not reveal her alarm.

She was trying for all she was worth to invent a lie when Elizabeth let her off the hook and said, 'I guess we all have our troubles, don't we?'

'We do,' Sara hurried to say. 'When I was your age I was lost. And afraid.'

'What were you afraid of?'

'Oh, I knew that I was different from all my female friends who couldn't wait to meet Mr Right, get married, have babies. I knew that would never work for me.'

'What are you saying?'

'You don't know?'

'No.'

'You can't guess?'

'No.'

'If I do get married it won't be to a man.'

Elizabeth took this in her stride. 'And you knew that when you were how old?'

'Thirteen, I think. But before that I knew that I was different. We're all different, Elizabeth. We're all different in some way.'

Elizabeth raised one hand and gestured to the wine glasses on the shelf. 'But some of us are more broken, aren't we? Do you think I'm too broken to be fixed, Sara?'

Sara took her hand and said no.

'What will fix me?'

'The same thing that fixes each of us.'

'What is it?'

'Love. I think it's love. That's what everyone is looking for. Searching for. And meaning. We're all longing for meaning.'

'Meaning? What is meaning?'

'Meaning is whatever fills our soul, Elizabeth. You'll find something that fills your soul, and then you'll know. And you'll heal. It may take time but it will happen.'

'Time. If it takes too long my father will put me back in the loony bin. I can't go back again. Do you know, I couldn't even remember how to write the number four? It's barbaric. And the patients there… some of them will never leave. They'll never get to live any kind of real life. I don't want to end up that way.'

'You're not going to, Elizabeth. Trust me. You must trust me.'

'I do trust you. But do you still believe that I can be anything I want to be?'

'I do. I'm certain of it.'

chapter nine

shoes

And then, against long odds and like a key turning in a latch it was cut for, their lives coincided. Fate was not a good enough explanation for Elizabeth, whose mathematical mind compelled her to consider that because there was not an infinite number of ways to cut a key, nor an infinite number of locks in the world, there existed the very real probability that the key anyone held in her hand to unlock her front door would also unlock countless other doors. And so, she would always believe that what took place on the Christmas Eve of 2001 was a miracle.

Johnny was forty-one years old, panhandling outside the Théâtre de la Ville on Place du Châtelet where the coloured lights on a big tree decorated for the season were shimmering like the liquor bottles on an illuminated bar, and out on the pavements whenever a plane crossed the sky overhead on its way to Charles de Gaulle or Roissy, people would stop and look up and hold their breath with dread for a few moments, wondering if what had happened in New York City might happen here next.

He got to his feet from the granite steps where he had been sitting in the cold for hours with his blue cap beside him. His bones felt as fragile as glass and he had just begun walking to get himself a warming cup of coffee when he spotted a young woman with black hair and wearing a long blue coat standing on the pavement with her head bowed. As a bus roared up the street three blocks away, she raised her head and glanced at it with her shoulders pitched forward slightly, and Johnny was quite certain it was a bus she was waiting for that would take her somewhere splendid. But then she did the oddest thing. She took off both her shoes and lined them up precisely before stepping to the edge of the pavement. He looked at the shoes just long enough to discern that they didn't match exactly – one was higher than the other – before he understood what was about to happen as the bus picked up speed, and he ran to her and hauled her to safety just as she was stepping into its path.

She was like a rag doll in his arms as he led her away from the edge of the pavement. 'Where do you stay?' he asked her.

'I don't understand,' she answered with a soft voice just above a whisper.

'Where is it you live?' he asked.

'With my parents,' she told him. 'But I can't live there any longer. I can't live anywhere.'

A gust of bitter wind made Johnny's lungs contract. Above him stars hung in the sky; they were pierced with light and seemed brittle enough to crack and fall to the ground. It was then that he looked down at her feet and saw that they were bare. He dropped to his knees and put her oddly unequal shoes back on as he looked up into her eyes. She seemed so lovely to him, he could not imagine why someone so beautiful would want to end her life in such a violent way. In that moment he unbuttoned his coat, took off his St Christopher necklace and placed it in her left hand. He rose to his feet and picked her up and began carrying her in his arms. She was the first person he had been this close to since he last felt young, and though he had lied, cheated and stolen his way through the years since then, he promised whatever God was watching and listening that he would never take anything from this girl.

* * *

She was reluctant but she gave him a telephone number to call, and it wasn't long before a car with a driver dressed in a coat and tie and black cloth beret came for them. And instead of spending that Christmas in the homeless shelter in Nanterre, Johnny found himself in the most different circumstances imaginable; the driver took them to a mansion in the seaside town of Honfleur, over a hundred miles from Paris. Johnny was shown by Martin and Donna to a wood-panelled room with a Persian rug beneath his feet and a pale-blue-painted tin ceiling above his head stencilled with boats under sail, their hulls different colours, a room with windows that faced the Channel. A room where they welcomed him to spend the night. 'It's the least that we can do,' Donna told him. 'It's too cold outside to be wandering the streets.'

He thought about this, and about how awful he must look for this woman to just glance at him and ascertain that he had no home.

Elizabeth, who Donna told him had just turned twenty-eight, slept upstairs while Johnny ate a sumptuous meal with her parents at a long mahogany table beneath a crystal chandelier. Martin wore polished gold glasses. He had thick black hair and though Johnny guessed him to be in his late forties or early fifties, his face bore no lines and he appeared much younger. Donna had a pleasant smile but there were dark shadows below her eyes that made Johnny wonder what kind of despair she had endured. She spoke softly, holding her husband's hand through much of the meal, as she told Johnny all about her daughter's struggle with her mental health. All the hospitals they had placed her in. All the treatments and medications which seemed to work for a while. 'It's a chemical imbalance that has baffled some of the best psychiatrists in the world,' was how she explained it. 'And it's been there since her childhood. When we still lived in America,' Donna said as she bowed her head.

Her husband reached across the table and placed his hand on her shoulder. 'Now, now,' he said with a condescending tone in his voice as if he was trying to placate a child. 'You must not dwell on those things.'

Just as they were finishing their meal, Elizabeth came into the room, wrapped in a blanket, with her dark hair falling over her shoulders. In the candlelight, her hair looked so black it made her eyes the deepest shade of blue Johnny had ever seen. To him, she looked even more beautiful now and it took his breath away.

Before she sat at the table she walked over to him and kissed the St Christopher necklace he had given her, then placed it in his hand and thanked him.

In front of him, on the table, was a long-stemmed crystal glass filled with wine but he never reached for it. And that night he fell asleep sober, with moonlight glancing off the Channel outside his window, wondering how far down the hallway, how far away from him, Elizabeth was sleeping. And then he dreamed about a future for the first time in years.

chapter ten

key

The next morning they all sat around the Christmas tree exchanging gifts. Elizabeth, wearing her blue cloth coat as if she might dash outside into the cold at any moment, was beside Johnny on a white couch. Every time he looked at her, her eyes met his.

Johnny had nothing to give them, of course, but Martin handed him a box wrapped in gold foil paper. Inside there was a phone small enough to fit in his pocket.

'I want you to stay in touch with us, Johnny,' he said. 'And don't worry about the bills, they'll come to me in Paris.'

That was when he told Johnny that he was provost of graduate studies at the Sorbonne and that they only used this house at Christmas and for a week in the summer each year.

* * *

This time the driver took Johnny back into the city with Martin. They said goodbye late in the day outside the shelter for the homeless at Nanterre where Johnny promised reluctantly to call him if he ever needed his help. He had walked two blocks when the phone rang. 'Thank you again, Johnny,' Martin said. 'And the best of luck.'

When Johnny put the phone back in his pocket he felt the scrap of paper Elizabeth had slipped into his coat with an address in Paris, and beside it the key to their house in Honfleur that he had stolen earlier that morning, and was so overcome with shame he could barely take his next step.

Still, he could not help himself. When the weather turned brutally cold in late January, Johnny went back to Honfleur. He lived in the house for almost a month, staying in one room, careful not to disturb anything and moving about at night without putting on any of the lights. Each day began the same way. He would get out of bed just after sunrise, shave and take a shower, then he would stand inside Martin's dressing room in a thick burgundy monogrammed bathrobe, before trying on his suits and ties, pretending he had a life and a job to go to. He was polishing his wingtip shoes one morning when the gendarmes knocked at the front door. One of them put handcuffs on him while the other left the room and went back outside to call Martin in Paris. He returned a few minutes later and apologised to Johnny. 'The owner just told me that he gave you a key to the place and invited you to stay here,' the man said irritably. 'Why didn't you just tell us and save us all a lot of trouble?'

Johnny looked right at him and asked, 'Would you have believed me?'

* * *

Later, Johnny stood outside on the porch watching clouds gather over the Channel, with his phone to his ear. There he heard Martin say, 'After what you did for my daughter, you are welcome to stay in the house until you've found a place of your own, Johnny. But my hope is that you will do your best to make something of yourself. We all have that responsibility. Do you know what I mean?'

Johnny didn't really know, but he said, 'Yes, sir. And thank you.'

As though he understood this, Martin went on, 'What I mean is each one of us has the duty to achieve our full potential in this life, Johnny. That's the only way the world ever gets any better.'

And with those words etched firmly in his brain, Johnny somehow convinced himself that though the man's daughter was from a different world, he might somehow become a man that Martin and Donna would approve of. Perhaps a man whom Elizabeth might come to love, because, in truth, he already felt something for her, something he could not define or put a name to. It was as if they had known each other in some other life, some other world, and had both been moving unwittingly, all their lives, towards the moment they met on the pavement.

chapter eleven

print shop

Wearing her father's dark grey slacks and a blue cotton shirt under a cream-coloured sweater, he took the bus to Le Havre and found work in a small printing shop where the owner, an assassin in the French Resistance, operated one of the last Linotype presses in France, printing out fine stationery and business cards and invitations to exclusive parties, and certificates of membership in private clubs in Paris. The Saint James Club, Manko and Matignon. His name was Henri Bernard. He was a gregarious man in his mid-seventies who worked with ink on his hands, a small cloth towel attached to his belt by a clothes peg, and with his sleeves rolled up high so he could proudly display the elaborate tattoos on both arms that were a riot of colour though they had faded across the years. His mother would have killed him for these tattoos, he told Johnny, but he was drunk when he got them done on his twentieth birthday, never expecting to survive the war and therefore face his mother's wrath.

Aged seventy-five, Henri's eyesight was failing. What he needed Johnny to do was cut out each steel letter, line them up properly into the words they were meant to compose, then lock them in a wood frame that Henri clamped to the press that thundered and shook the room violently with the sound of a freight train as he fed blank paper into one end and which came out the other end printed handsomely in black ink. His routine never varied: he printed just a single piece of paper, asking Johnny to shout the words back to him above the sound of the press, before he shouted back the same thing each time with great satisfaction: 'Now we're cooking, Johnny!'

They worked well together and with each word Johnny built he was vividly reminded of the days of his boyhood when his mother typed out the sermons for the young students at the seminary, one letter at a time. He had never really placed much value on words before. It had always seemed to him that people talked constantly and often thoughtlessly, even when they had nothing actually worth saying. And that words were only words, and were worth far less than actions. But now, creating the words, one letter at a time out of steel, assigned a kind of permanence and importance to them and filled Johnny with a sense of purpose he had not felt since he was a boy transforming the boathouse into a home with his mother and Jerry before they were drowned.

Along with his employment, Henri had provided Johnny with a place to stay in a room above the print shop.

In that room there was a window that looked out on to the harbour, where the steel masts of sailing boats glistened in the first slanting gold light of dawn as Johnny sat there writing letters to Elizabeth in Paris, summoning the courage to declare his desire to care for her for the rest of his life. The words seemed to be coming to him from somewhere far off in the distance, already formed, so he merely had to transcribe them. He felt so connected to something inexplicable racing through him, that he often wrote with his hand trembling as if some great power source in the universe had been channelled through his heart and soul.

> *I know that I am unreliable in matters like this, Elizabeth, but I have watched people everywhere, and I have come to believe that at the end of our time*

*on this earth all of us are going to regret the same
thing, that we didn't love each other better when we
had the chance.*

He addressed the letters to the place written on the scrap of paper she had given him. Though he was quite certain that she would never write back, still he wanted beyond hope and dreams to be with her again. He was a man who had walked for a while in shoes that he had stolen from her father, and yet he allowed himself to believe that his life and Elizabeth's life had intersected for a purpose, and that one day they would be together. He was not fully aware that he was building a world of dreams around this girl he didn't really know at all, or of the danger inherent in such an enterprise.

With each letter he wrote, each word really, he felt himself returning to the world, stepping out from the shadows and the fears that had concealed him. He discovered that if he took the time to choose his words carefully and only put them down on paper when he was certain of them, a calm silence with the weight of sunlight, a kind of surrendering, descended upon him and he could write for hours. He wrote with absolute conviction, believing that there was always the chance that his words might make some difference. He kept telling Elizabeth how certain he was that their lives were meant to join as they had. *You and I were brought together along one narrow path of the stars,* he wrote to her once.

Each letter was really a promise that he would love her and care for her for the rest of his time if she were to trust him and try to love him in return. In each letter he tried to make her believe in herself and in the fulfilment of a life shared with him.

*Please remember, Elizabeth, that you do not deserve
to be alone in this world. So even if you and I never
see each other again, please do not close yourself
off from the chance to be loved by someone who will*

cherish you, because you deserve to be loved in the best possible way. I swear this is true. I think what I want most of all is for us to share a dream and to let that dream lift both of us above the darkness that has haunted us, into the light.
Love, Johnny.

To improve himself for her, he began attending AA meetings three nights a week, shyly showing up just after everyone else had taken their seats so he could remain the stranger at the back of the room who made coffee for everyone before he slipped outside during the break so he wouldn't have to reveal anything about himself. He kept his silence until the end of each meeting when they recited the Serenity Prayer together.

'God grant me the serenity to accept the things I cannot change, the courage to change the things I can, and the wisdom to know the difference,' he repeated beneath his breath one night before he rose slowly to his feet to share something with the group for the first time. He felt like he was back at the lycée, having just learned to tie his own shoes, standing at the front of the classroom with a name tag pinned to his shirt pocket. He had been writing to Elizabeth for eight months from February until September and though she had never written back to him, he had remained sober the whole time so that he could be certain he would choose the precise words he wanted in the twenty-two letters he had written her. 'I live each day to write those letters,' he told the group at AA. 'I write them slowly. Sometimes I take two weeks to finish each one. And when I post them, I am always filled with hope. I have begun to believe again that we must never give in to despair.'

He looked briefly at their encouraging expressions, then told them the whole story of how he met Elizabeth on Christmas Eve, leaving out only the part about stealing the key and breaking into the house in Honfleur and helping himself to her father's clothes. As he talked, he grew more animated. He spoke of fate and destiny and how writing to Elizabeth had given him strength and optimism for the first time across so many years of deprivation. They smiled back at him and nodded thoughtfully and he went on and on until he had finished and they all bowed their heads and prayed for him. As they were leaving, one woman came up to him and said, 'If there's any justice left in this forsaken world, you will find the love story you deserve.' She smiled at him then, and looked deeply into his eyes as Johnny thanked her, before she turned and walked away.

This gave Johnny the confidence to tell Henri his true story at work the next morning. It felt like he was making a confession and the whole time he was speaking he wondered if the day would ever come when he would be making the same confession to Elizabeth. 'I've told a lot of lies, Henri,' he said. 'After all that you've done for me, I never should have lied to you.'

Henri shrugged this off and related how he and his confederates in the Resistance lied constantly in order to live to fight the Nazis another day. 'We loved our country and lied without guilt,' he said. And then the tone of his voice changed and he was deadly serious when he warned Johnny to be careful whom he told his true story to. 'No matter how many years have passed, Johnny – or Jean – the Legion will still lock you up for desertion if they ever manage to find you.'

chapter twelve

bell

It was only three days after Johnny had made his confession to Henri that the bell above the print shop door rang and Elizabeth stepped inside. The press was thundering and Johnny was leaning over the table where he built his words so he was not aware of her presence until Henri came up from behind him and yelled above the noise, 'Someone is here to see you!'

Johnny was stunned, of course, too stunned to even move. And yet he had played out this moment again and again in his imagination for so many weeks and months that her presence seemed providential. She smiled at him and took his hand and led him outside so they could hear each other. Johnny's first impression was that there was an incandescence about her; she seemed to be lit from within. She put her arms around him and pulled him close. A hundred questions raced through his mind as he watched her kneel down on the pavement and open the wheeled suitcase she had brought with her. But he asked only the one that mattered most to him, 'Are you well, Elizabeth?'

'I am, Johnny. I am well,' she said as she stood up to show him a coffee tin with a plastic lid. When she removed the lid, there were all the letters he had sent her, folded neatly. 'They kept me alive, Johnny,' she told him. 'You saved my life a second time. Look.' She pulled up the sleeves of her coat and showed him the horizontal pale white lines, first on the right wrist, then on the left. 'I would have kept trying if you hadn't written to me,' she said.

'Oh no,' he heard himself gasp.

She took his arm, gripping it tightly, and assured him that it was okay, everything was all right now. 'Really, I'm well,' she said, looking into his eyes.

He wanted more than anything to believe her.

'When we left after Christmas, my parents put me back in that hospital,' she continued. 'That's the address I gave you and that's where I read your letters. But now I'm free from all that. Look at this.' She took a plane ticket from her suitcase. It was a ticket to New York. 'My father thought that a trip was what I needed most after all the concoctions of medication and the electroshock treatments had worked their magic and he declared me restored. He dropped me at the airport with enough money to live like a princess for months. Here, look.' She reached into the case again and pulled out two handfuls of hundred-dollar bills. Johnny couldn't remember ever seeing so much cash in one place and he couldn't keep himself from wondering immediately how much it added up to. 'But I came here instead,' Elizabeth said softly. 'I came here to be with you, Johnny, because of these beautiful letters. I felt that I belonged with you.' She took both his hands in hers and smiled at him reassuringly. 'Are you glad to see me?' she asked, her eyes opening wider as she anticipated his response.

He told her honestly that he had no idea what to say. 'It all feels like a miracle to me.'

'Let's believe it is a miracle then,' she said. 'I think we should believe in miracles. It was a miracle that we met. At least that's how I think of it.'

'I do as well,' he rushed to assure her.

They stood there in silence for a while before she asked him if he was still staying in her father's house in Honfleur. 'My mother told me you were there,' she said.

Johnny pointed to two windows three storeys above them and explained that he lived in a room there now.

'I think we need to be by the sea,' she said. 'Don't you, Johnny?'

He wanted to be sure what she meant by this. 'Are you going to Honfleur?' he asked.

She smiled demurely. 'Not without you,' she told him. 'No one will even know we're there. We'll live like millionaires while my father pictures me shopping at Tiffany's in New York City.'

'If you come inside, I'll show you what it is I do here.'

Elizabeth put the coffee tin back inside her suitcase and followed him into the shop, the bell ringing above their heads as he pushed open the door for her.

He introduced her to Henri as an old friend. 'A long-lost friend,' she added as she shook his hand.

Henri turned off the press and let the room fall into silence before he spoke to her. 'A long-lost friend,' he said with a wistful expression. 'Do you know, I lost twenty-three of them in the war. Young men and young women who were my close friends and then were killed before the war ended, and so became my long and lost friends. But that's a long time ago. Old men talk too much. Let me stop talking and get back to work.'

He started the press up again and when he left and it was just the two of them alone at the desk, Johnny pulled a chair up beside his and gestured for Elizabeth to sit down. He showed her how he stamped out each letter, one at a time. He placed the first one in her hand. It was the letter E. It only took a few more minutes before he placed the rest of the letters of her name in the palm of her hand. Her eyes filled with wonder and he watched as she closed her hand around the letters as if they were something priceless. 'I'll keep them forever,' she told him.

The whole time he was making the letters, thrilled by her delight and the miracle of being close to her again, he was confused as to why she had given him the address of a hospital, and why she had tried – again – to end her life. But he thought that all of his questions would have been lost in the noise of the printing press and, besides, he didn't feel he had the right to ask them.

She whispered in his ear that she needed a piece of paper and a pencil. He took them from a drawer in his desk and watched her write down these letters:

A C W H I T E M O E T S E O E M T H

'Can you make them for me?' she asked him.

He got right to work and when he had finished he spread them out on his desk. She was as excited as a small child. 'I've composed a secret message for you,' she said. 'But I'm too impatient to wait for you to figure it out.'

And she lined the letters up for him in the words that she had chosen:

C O M E T O T H E S E A W I T H M E

chapter thirteen

hands

She went on to Honfleur ahead of him and after he had finished his workday and washed up, as he was saying goodbye to Henri, the old man remarked that the way Johnny had met this girl by stopping her from stepping in front of a bus was a hell of a way to begin a love story. 'You don't want to go through this life without a good woman who loves you. Trust me on this. I had a wonderful wife. We met during the war. We fought side by side. We had the same nightmares for years. We went on to love each other for forty-nine years before she died. Do you know that every single night I came home from this shop she would clean the ink from under my fingernails with turpentine? And when she took her baths, I would always wash her hair for her. If that's not real love, I don't know what is, mister.'

* * *

Johnny travelled by bus for just over half an hour, out to the house at Honfleur, with his own steel letters for Elizabeth in an envelope inside his coat pocket. He kept his eyes closed most of the way as if he was afraid he might wake up from a dream. *It's only a dream,* he kept thinking to himself as he felt the world roll under him through the soles of his feet and watched the fading light glance off the darkening Channel. He tried to look back over his life and name what was real, among all that he had only imagined to be real. The time he shared with Jerry and his mother in the boathouse was real. He could still hear the sound of their oars splashing gently in the water as they rowed out into the bay. The time he spent as a soldier with the Legion was real. But those things happened so many years ago that they no longer counted in his estimation. All that counted now was what was in front of him. And because the bus to Honfleur seemed to take an eternity to cover the twenty-four kilometres, he became filled with anxiety that when he got to the house Elizabeth would not be there at all. That this day, what had transpired had not been real at all.

* * *

But it turned out to be very real. She was waiting for him at the door. Waiting and smiling and taking him into her embrace, exactly like a long-lost friend. That was what it felt like to him.

She whispered in his ear, 'I've made us dinner, but first there is something we must do.' She stepped away from him and walked to the far side of the room while Johnny stood still, confused and wondering. When she reached the wall she knelt down and took off her shoes exactly as she had on the pavement when he first noticed her. Then she walked towards him, swaying from side to side until she was standing at arm's length from him. 'Look down,' she told him. And when she stood up perfectly straight with one hand on his right shoulder to balance herself, he saw. 'I was born this way,' she told him. 'The Leaning Tower of Pisa.' She smiled at him when he told her that he had always wanted to go to Italy. Then he took off the shoe on his right foot and slid his foot under hers. When she let go of his shoulder, she was perfectly balanced. She took him in her arms again. 'It's a perfect fit,' she said. 'You have my missing piece. That must mean that we were made for each other.'

Johnny was too overwhelmed with gratitude to say anything.

She had prepared a dinner of haddock that she picked up at the fish market, seasoned with basil. And small red-skinned potatoes that she cut in half and baked in the oven. And a crisp salad of greens and tomatoes, celery and walnuts and goat's cheese. He honestly could not remember the last time he'd eaten salad, he told her, which made her laugh out loud.

After dinner they took a walk along the shore. And when he felt her reach for his hand and take it in hers, it all began to feel impossibly real. He could feel her pulse through her hand, the pulse she had tried to still when she slit her wrists in the hospital. *Thank God she failed,* he thought.

She told him that she had planned her escape carefully. She had agreed before Christmas to go back into the psychiatric ward after the holidays and to endure more treatments, only after her father promised her a trip to New York when she was better. 'I never intended to go to New York,' she confessed. 'When your first letter reached me, I knew that I would come to find you as soon as I was released. That first letter almost arrived in time. Just two days after I tried to end my life. There was a wonderful young man there, an orderly named Peter. I called him Saint Peter. I told him that I had suffered these spells which the doctors called psychotic episodes since I was six years old and that I simply couldn't endure them any more. Saint Peter, it turned out, needed five thousand francs to buy a used car to replace his old Volvo that had died. I gave him my debit card, told him the PIN so he could retrieve the money from a cash machine, in exchange for a double-edged razor blade, with the promise that no one would ever know where it came from. He didn't want to do it for me, but I finally convinced him by adding up all the months I had spent in psychiatric hospitals. It came to a total of three and a half years. "That's no way to live," I told him. He understood and obliged me with a way out of all the suffering and the humiliation. Saint Peter risked a great deal to help me, Johnny. Can you understand?'

They stopped walking for a few minutes and watched the waves rolling in. 'I can't really understand,' he told her. 'I mean, you are a grown woman.'

'No. Just a silly girl,' she insisted. 'Twenty-eight years old.'

'Still, you couldn't be admitted without your consent, could you?'

'You don't know my father,' she said. 'He always gets what he wants. He doesn't ask anyone for consent. And besides, the bargain we made – the trip to New York – was my way of escaping him, and coming back to see you.'

'Why have you come back to see me?'

'Oh, Johnny, to thank you.'

'Thank me for what?'

'For making me feel alive. When you put my shoes back on my feet and picked me up and carried me, I felt whole for the first time in my life. I felt like I mattered in some way. Wait...' she said. 'I want to say this properly so that you understand. Just give me a moment to find the words.'

For a while they just stood there by the dark blue water with the dull concussion of waves breaking onto the shore. She never let go of his hand.

Then, at last, she began. 'I have a feeling deep inside that I will be saying this to you again and again, Johnny. But here it is. I sensed that you had been broken in some way. I mean, in those moments on the pavement, with me in your arms and you carrying me like a wounded soldier, I knew. I knew that we could only see in each other what the rest of the world could not see in us, and what we could not even see in ourselves. *We saw that we each have value.* Both of us have value and we deserve a chance. Will you remember me telling you this?'

He promised her he would. And then he rushed to add,

'But maybe we'll have the rest of our lives together so you can tell me every day. Especially on the days when I don't believe in myself and you don't believe in yourself.'

'Wouldn't that be wonderful?' she said. And then she kissed him on the mouth for the first time. A long kiss that conveyed meaning and promise.

* * *

It was late when she led him upstairs to the room she had prepared for them. A room with twin beds, separated by a small white wicker table with a blue satin shade set upon a lamp. Johnny was both disappointed and relieved. It had been so long since he'd been with a girl, so many years, that he wasn't even sure he would know how to go about it the right way. And he wasn't sure that he wouldn't end up disappointing her. And he was almost certain that he was not entitled to be that close to her. That making love to her would be a violation of some code of honour.

They talked in the little room, holding hands between the space that separated their beds that were covered with pale yellow duvets. And just holding hands was more than enough.

'Maybe this is how old couples fall asleep,' she said. 'How wonderful.'

That was the last thing she said to him. He listened to her breathing and then she took one last deep breath as if she was about to go under water before she fell asleep.

When he was certain she was sleeping he got out of bed and knelt down below the windows with their diamond-shaped panes of glass and gave thanks for this miracle that had come to pass. This miracle he felt completely unworthy of.

chapter fourteen

bicycle

Johnny would remember this time as a procession of sunlit, unhurried days, though while he was at work he always had the gnawing fear that when he returned to Honfleur, Elizabeth might be gone. He went home to her at the end of each workday, walking as fast as he could, even running to catch his bus. Henri had offered to give him some time off but he declined because he wanted Elizabeth to think of him as someone who could hold down a job and bring home a steady pay cheque, the way his father did and then his mother after his father died.

Riding the bus in and out with the congregation of men in suits, reading their newspapers and looking so businesslike, he tried his best to see himself as one of them, living out the same daily routine of going off to work so they could provide security and reassurance for the people they had pledged themselves to, and then returning home to the gratitude of those people they cared most about. Wasn't that intended to be the fundamental structure of a man's life and the basis on which he measured his value? And how deeply satisfying it was to Johnny.

Each day before he finished at the shop, he stamped out steel letters like he was composing a secret code, then placed them in an envelope, sealed it and put it in his coat pocket for the journey home.

The words never comprised more than one sentence:

STAY WITH ME FOREVER

I WILL TRY TO NEVER DISAPPOINT YOU

I AM THANKFUL WE FOUND EACH OTHER

Elizabeth opened each envelope eagerly and spread the letters out on the mahogany dining room table, beneath the crystal chandelier, pushing them around in different sequences – like someone trying to come up with a winning word in a game of Scrabble – while they slowly ate the dinners that she had prepared.

Each evening Johnny watched her struggling and kept offering to help, but she insisted on deciphering every message on her own. And when she finally had it, he could see that she was pleased with herself.

One night she told him he must write his whole life story for her. 'One steel letter at a time,' she said.

He laughed and told her that he would have to fill a room in this house with the letters.

'I could take the rest of my life to fit your story together,' she said. 'What better way to learn someone's story? One letter, one word, one sentence at a time. I'll have white hair by the time I've finished. And wrinkles. And I'll need you to help me get up from my chair.'

She laughed at this in a self-deprecating way. But Johnny carried to some deep part of his comprehension this satisfying picture of her growing old in his company.

* * *

One night, when he returned home from work, she presented him with a bicycle she had bought at a second-hand shop. She sat side-saddle on the crossbar while Johnny pedalled them along the beach at low tide where the sand was dense enough that the tyres didn't sink in. There were no other people for as far as they could see. It was as if they had discovered this part of the world and were its only inhabitants. 'May I ask you something?' he said as they rode along.

'Of course. Ask me anything,' she told him.

'These episodes? Can you tell me about them? Just so I can understand a little better.'

She answered him slowly and thoughtfully. 'Well, when they come on, I don't know where I am, or who I am, and I can't feel my feet on the ground beneath me. I'm sort of hovering above my body. Drifting. Fading away. I can't really feel anything, Johnny, or make sense of anything and I think they're more disconcerting to the people around me than they are to me. I can hear their voices but something has switched off in my mind and their words don't make sense. They're sort of like when I spread your steel letters out on the table. Only I can't make sense of them the way I can your messages. And by the way, I just was thinking earlier today that I could be the only person in the world who waits for a man to bring her letters stamped out of steel, that turn into sentences. Isn't that amazing, Johnny? I mean, doesn't that make us so unique. So...'

As she searched for the right word, he found it for her. 'Special,' he said.

'Yes. Special,' she said.

'And blessed,' he added.

'Yes. And blessed,' she agreed.

* * *

'But why?' she asked him that night as they lay in their twin beds and held hands across the narrow space that separated them. 'Why have we been blessed this way, Johnny?'

He told her that he wasn't sure.

She explained to him her father's theory that all of life came down to nothing but luck. 'Good luck and bad luck, he's said to me so many times. That's all. Nothing is ordained. Nothing happens for a reason. Everything is no less arbitrary than a roll of the dice, he once told me. He's such a practical man. It's enough to drive you crazy,' she said without a trace of irony in her voice. 'But my mother is different. She lives inside his prison made of gold and pearls, but she has a wider vision of the world. What's the word, Johnny… wait. Just give me a second. *Ontology.* Yes, ontology. The nature of the metaphysical. She always spoke of the mystery of life. She told me that we are all blind and so it takes us most of our whole lives to learn our own story. We're living that story each day, of course, but we don't know it, because it isn't really about us. It's the part we play in someone else's story that defines us. And so we often have the feeling that with each passing day the world is becoming a stranger and stranger place. A place we can no longer comprehend. A place where we feel like we do not belong. And that's because we believe we know what life consists of and we cannot see that one day we will fight as hard to hold on to some beliefs as we do to let go of others. What we perceive, we think is truth, Johnny. My mother told me that this life of ours is only a shadow of another life. Perhaps a life where time moves in the opposite direction and things fall *up* in the air. Just think of it – we inhabit a mystery, Johnny. Atoms in our bodies trace to the remnants of exploded stars. And we can't even look up at the sky and say how far it goes.'

He listened so intently that for a moment he forgot where he was. And it seemed to him that no one had ever said anything to him that made more sense, and that satisfied the deep longing he had carried inside him since his father died.

'Your mother passed all that on to you?' he asked.

'Yes, like a map I could follow,' she said. 'And before I close my eyes I have to tell you something. I thought of it on our bike ride when you asked me about my episodes. We used to have a bird feeder outside our kitchen windows. I remember this one sparrow that couldn't fly. She just sat on the porch and ate the seeds that fell from the feeder. That's me, Johnny. I'm a bird with broken wings.'

chapter fifteen

mistake

There was a late September afternoon, a day exactly like any of the other twenty-three days Johnny and Elizabeth had shared, when he returned home and found her gone. She was not in the kitchen where he expected her to be preparing their dinner as she normally would. She did not call his name to him through the empty rooms. And he was seized with a panic that, at first, paralysed him so that he could not move, and then sent him running from room to room, the envelope of steel letters in his right hand tearing open when he collided with a coat rack in one room, tripped and fell, hearing the letters scatter across the black and white tiled floor. He was so terrified that he had lost her, he could not get back to his feet and for a while he crawled along the corridor calling her name while he grew more certain each time she failed to answer him that the source of his greatest joy was now turning into the source of his greatest sorrow. He had to concentrate to keep breathing. Something was preventing him from swallowing, and a freezing cold numbness spread through his limbs. Finally, he made it up the stairs and saw her things were still there which steadied him to some degree so that he could look out of the windows to the beach, where he hoped he might see her walking. But there was no one except two small boys chasing after a black dog.

It wasn't until he came back down the stairs and out onto the front veranda that he noticed the bicycle was missing. 'Thank God,' he heard himself exclaim. 'Thank you, God.'

He sat down in one of the rocking chairs and let his head fall back so that the lowering sun fell across his face, until he remembered the steel letters scattered across the floor.

That was where she found him, down on his hands and knees gathering up the letters. 'Just a little accident,' he said. 'How are you?' He was trying hard to keep his voice steady and to appear calm. 'I was in such a hurry to get home that I forgot to seal the envelope. Did you have a good day? Tell me, how was your day?'

She told him that it had been a splendid day. She had discovered a lane that ran through a field of wild roses. 'It went on and on for miles, Johnny, and I just couldn't stop and turn back. I don't think I've ever felt healthier or stronger in my whole life. I was pretending I was an Olympic athlete, racing around an oval track on the bicycle and that I was no longer disabled.'

He told her how pleased he was to hear this and he held his composure through the rest of the evening while they made dinner and sat together at the long table in the last burst of pale pink light off the Channel.

It wasn't until they were lying in their beds, the windows across the room filled with bright autumn stars, that he told her how frightened he had been. 'I thought you had left me,' he said.

She apologised and told him that she would never leave him. 'These days with you have been the best days of my life. We have something, Johnny. You and I have something that will go on and on. It's like a light that can't be extinguished.'

But the light was dimming. Johnny could see this. Something was wrong. Something had changed. At the dinner table a few hours earlier for the first time she could not decipher his sentence of steel letters without his help.

I will love you until the end of my time, were the words he had stamped for her that day.

Before she fell asleep, she promised him that the next time she left the house for a long ride she would leave a note in the mailbox so that he wouldn't have to worry.

* * *

And that was where he found the note one week later. It read:

> *I made a terrible mistake, Johnny. I forgot that my father would be following the credit card charges. I never should have used it. He has sent people to take me home now. I will beg them to let me say goodbye to you in the print shop, but in case I can't see you, please know that it will only be a matter of time before I make my escape again to be with you. I will always find you in this world, Johnny. No matter what. And this time I will stay with you forever. Love, Elizabeth.*

What alerted him to the mailbox was the sight of the bicycle lying on its side like a wounded animal by the front porch. Inside the box was the Maxwell House coffee tin with the neatly folded letters that he'd written to her. He tried not to ask himself why she had left them behind.

* * *

She didn't stop by the print shop. And all her things were gone, along with her suitcase. If it weren't for the words she'd written in the note, he might have walked into the sea and not stopped until he was out of his depth.

Instead, he returned to his room above the print shop, where each day Henri seemed to look more frail, as if he was the one who had been abandoned and heartbroken.

chapter sixteen

ashes

And then one day, as another Christmas grew near and the trees in Le Havre were decorated and lit up for the season, she wrote to him. Just a short note, saying that she and her parents had moved back to America. Along with these few words was a plane ticket for him to San Diego to visit her. He was beside himself with joy and so was Henri, who told him to take as much time as he needed. 'I'll manage on my own until you return,' he said as they shook hands. 'But that girl of yours… bring her back with you, and don't ever do anything to lose her. Find the strength to fight for this.'

Johnny had no way of knowing that he was asking Henri the same question Elizabeth once asked Sara. 'Where does it come from, Henri?' Johnny said. 'The strength, I mean.'

'It comes from within you,' he replied.

* * *

On the plane Johnny sat alone, staring for a long time at the picture on his passport which had been issued to him during his last year in the Legion and was his only piece of ID. As he began to recall those days, his hands started to shake and he almost asked for a drink.

Then, to calm his nerves, he looked at the note Elizabeth had sent him with the ticket. He read it over and over. It was only a few words, but the more times he read them, the more there seemed to be something there, some mystery that nagged at him. The alcoholic could lie, cheat and steal with the indifference and efficiency of a spider tearing the wings off a moth in its web. Lies were his currency. His compass. Place him inside a dark house of lies on a moonless night, and he would make his way from room to room without knocking into the furniture. He was such a thorough liar that he could not be tricked by a lie. Only the truth could deceive him.

Perhaps he did not see the trick at first, because during the month with Elizabeth his hope had dulled his wariness.

They were high over the Rocky Mountains when Johnny finally realised that the handwriting on the note with the ticket did not match the writing in the note that Elizabeth had left for him in the mailbox.

He knew then what had happened and what awaited him in California, and though he knew that a better man, a man with real courage, would not be afraid, he was afraid. Those mornings when he had stood in Martin's dressing room choosing what to wear, he had sometimes pictured Martin and his wife as two people in the world who were not so far above him. Now he felt like he didn't belong in the same world they inhabited. And this made it difficult for him to take his next breath. He had brought with him just a small duffle bag and the coffee tin with the letters to Elizabeth. On the long flight to California, it troubled him again that she had left them behind.

* * *

Just as he had suspected, Martin was waiting alone at the gate inside the terminal. He seemed to have aged ten years in the months since Johnny had last seen him, and he might not have even recognised him had Martin not called his name. During those months Johnny had cast him in a luminous moment in his memory of the Christmas morning they shared in the big house in Honfleur. But now he looked like he had walked miles through ashes since then. His shoulders were stooped. The light was gone from his eyes. His hair had lost its lustre.

They sat in a bar and after Martin explained that it had been time for him to retire from the world of academia and return to America to manage his investments, they talked about the love Johnny had for Elizabeth and the love she had for him and the time she had spent in psychiatric hospitals fighting for her life before Johnny met her and the resources she would need in the years ahead, and the ways Martin had tried to be a decent father and the times he had given up on her and how truly grateful he was that Johnny had saved her life but how certain he was that it would never work between them. Martin ordered them both some Scotch. Johnny had been sober for a year, but now when he felt like he was going to choke and his hands began to tremble, he took his first drink to steady his nerves. And it worked. He immediately felt himself begin to disappear. After his second drink he was hovering above the table, looking down at two men he did not recognise. Much of what transpired between these two men would remain unclear in Johnny's memory, as if it had happened under water.

The next thing Martin told him was that as a father he had to do anything he could to keep his daughter from marrying a homeless man who was thirteen years older and would never be able to give her anything resembling a secure life.

Johnny was listening, but he was also looking past Martin to the busy streets beyond the airport. Long ago it seemed now, in the days after he deserted from the Legion, he used to take the same walk every day, late in the afternoon, along the Seine to a small hotel that stood on the bank of the river. It took him forty minutes to reach that place. He always walked as dusk was descending. It was a freezing cold winter. And he always began each walk telling himself that this time he would step into the river and then curl up under some trees in his soaking wet clothes and be dead from hypothermia by morning. He lacked the courage, but the desire to end his life had been deep in him then as it was now, sitting in the airport bar with Elizabeth's father.

'I have a job,' Johnny told Martin, as if this might change things.

'I've heard that,' Martin said. 'But I have to ask you to promise me, I mean give me your word that you won't write to my daughter again or try to see her. She's in a different hospital this time. There's a doctor there trying out a new concoction of drugs.'

Johnny assented by nodding his head. And Martin thanked him.

'What about the phone?' Johnny asked.

'Oh, I cancelled the contract,' Martin said. 'I was afraid she would call you. You probably would have done the same thing if the tables were turned.'

Johnny was silent, and it seemed it would all end right there, but there was still the fact that he had saved this man's daughter and for that Martin wanted to repay him.

A few more drinks and they stumbled along like drunken sailors, like long-lost comrades, like Elizabeth when she was barefoot, through the families and lovers with suitcases, to the departures hall where Martin put him on a plane that evening for Scotland. He knew a man there who would give him work at a golf course and a place to live, and a chance to start over. Before he turned to leave, he gave Johnny a roll of British banknotes. 'If you're going to start a new life, you need a little cash,' he said.

Johnny put the money inside the coffee tin with his letters to Elizabeth and clutched it to his chest as the plane took off.

That night he slept in the sky with the stars and a half-moon, as he crossed America and then the Atlantic before he awoke as morning was breaking in Scotland where his real life would begin at last.

BOOK II

chapter seventeen

value

The tall fescue grass in the sloping hillsides along the shore of the North Sea in the village of Elie was still the colour of honey in the last light of day and the dunes threw their great dark shadows across the mounds and hollows of the ancient ground that comprised the golf course. He had been in Scotland only three weeks but he had written to Elizabeth every day, addressing the envelopes to the hospital where he had first written to her across the months after they met.

And then he saw her standing in that light one afternoon as he made his way up the beach towards the whitewashed cottage just beyond the thirteenth fairway where he had been given living quarters. She ran into his arms. The letters he had written her were stuffed in the pockets of her coat and some of them fell onto the beach as they kissed.

When he knelt down to pick them up, the St Christopher medal swung free from his wool jumper. She took it in her hand when he rose to his feet, and she told him once again that they had seen in each other what everyone else had missed. 'Do you remember me telling you this, Johnny? How we can't even see it in ourselves,' she said, 'only in each other.'

'Our value?' he asked.

'Yes, our value,' she said.

She wouldn't let him ask her any questions about what her parents would do if they discovered she had come to meet him here. All she had brought with her in her green backpack was a small sketchbook and a wedding dress that had once belonged to her grandmother.

They were married within the month by Father Sutherland, a former RAF officer from Montrose, in an apple orchard on St Katherine's Hill. They picked apples after the ceremony so she could bake Johnny a pie. Even as he watched her roll out the crust in the cottage, waiting to take her in his arms again, he was already remembering the sight of her standing below him, holding out her white wedding dress to catch the red apples he dropped to her through the branches. It was a picture so pure and perfect that even as he was in the midst of it, he felt it belonged to someone else's life, not his.

His cottage was little more than a restored shed that stood in the tall grass of the ancient golf course where Johnny had been hired to work as a groundsman. Each morning before he left for work, he sat at the low table in front of a window and wrote Elizabeth a letter in the first light of morning, holding his St Christopher necklace in his left hand the way he always had when he wrote to her before in France, and placing the letter on her pillow as she slept.

These were the finest days of their lives, like their unhurried, sunlit days in Honfleur when they had felt blessed from morning until night. He sat on the porch with his shirt off and she trimmed his beard with kitchen scissors. He washed her black hair in the old porcelain tub. They repaired a bicycle and rode it across the beach at low tide, she sitting side-saddle again on the crossbar. They flew a kite with a red tail along the green fairways. One afternoon they walked together to the local pub and the deli that sold spirits where Johnny shook hands with the proprietors and left a handwritten note asking them never to sell him any alcohol under any circumstances, even if he begged them for it, or threatened to burn down their establishments.

At night they lay in the tall grass, naming the constellations above them, knowing that they shared the kind of love where you ask for nothing more. Love that was enough.

It lasted six days and then one morning after Johnny had left for work, the phone began to ring. She wasn't going home, Elizabeth told her father. She wasn't ever going to leave Johnny again. But when she told Johnny about the call, he convinced her that she had to return to tell her parents that they were married and to ask for their blessing. 'I think we both owe them that,' he said. 'And we owe this to ourselves. And now that we are married they will understand.'

He helped her pack. She wanted to take the letters he had written her since she arrived so she could show her parents the depth of his devotion to her. She folded them inside her backpack along with her passport and their wedding documents.

On the way to the bus the next morning they walked to the orchard and she made him kneel in the grass with her as she held his hands in hers. 'You have made me happy, Johnny. You alone. I want you to say this with me. Word for word. Will you?'

'Yes,' he said.

'I have been loved here,' she said. Then she waited as he repeated her words before she went on. 'And no matter what happens...'

'And no matter what happens...'

'I will remember what it was like.'

'I will remember what it was like,' he said.

She drew his hands to her lips and kissed them. He took the St Christopher from around his neck and placed it in her hand.

'Keep this until you come back,' he said to her.

At the bus stop he did't want to let go of her when she turned to walk away. But for some reason he felt strong as she climbed on board and smiled at him through the window.

He went to work, then walked back to the empty cottage at dusk. Off in the distance there was snow now on the hilltops and he made note of this, telling himself that as soon as Elizabeth returned, they would hike there together.

Each day she was gone he lost a little more of his resolve. Though his phone remained silent, he thought she might call him at any moment, and he kept it with him everywhere he went. He spent most of Sunday praying in a church with the phone beside him on the pew.

* * *

He thought maybe he would regain some strength and hasten Elizabeth's return by going to the shop the next day after work to buy some of her favourite things. Ovaltine. Chocolate-covered digestives. Frosties. He was walking up the beach to the cottage with his groceries in a cardboard box when he saw a man standing at the door, smoking a cigar.

It was Martin's lawyer. He did't want to go inside. After Johnny set down the box, the lawyer opened his briefcase and took out a blue folder with typed pages in duplicate inside. He placed the pages on the box and gestured to them as he explained that it had only taken him two hours to learn that Johnny was still officially a deserter from the French Foreign Legion. 'That could be a problem for you,' he said.

He had a document for Johnny to sign.

'What is it?' Johnny asked.

'It's an annulment agreement between yourself and Elizabeth Stoddard,' he said.

Johnny felt something cold and dull pass beneath his ribs. 'I have to talk to her,' he said. 'And her last name is Cooper now, not Stoddard.' Johnny was barely able to lift his voice above a whisper.

The lawyer pointed to where Elizabeth had already signed. 'There's nothing to be discussed,' he said.

Johnny heard him explain that in addition to his problem with the Legion he could also be prosecuted for taking advantage of someone who was unstable and undergoing psychiatric treatment.

As he said this he raised his eyebrows and shrugged with a satisfied expression.

This is how my life is going to end, Johnny thought. He could feel himself growing weightless, rising from the earth, a slight pressure against the soles of his feet. Soon he was up in the branches of the tree and Elizabeth was below him holding out her white wedding dress to catch the red apples.

chapter eighteen

waves

After that, Johnny Cooper became one of those drunks who somehow still manages to get up every morning and go to work. There was no strict prohibition against drinking on the job. Plus he lived in a place now where you could go on a bender for three or four days and feel like you were in good company and would not offend anyone or be looked down upon. Not a single self-righteous glare from a neighbour. In fact you felt like you had earned your place in a solemn fellowship of the disappointed and the disheartened and that you would be looked after until you were back on your feet. This enabled Johnny to go about his tasks at the golf course with a humming inside his brain that accompanied a gathering confusion. He was still a young man, of course, only in his forties, but he didn't feel young, and no amount of whisky could completely eradicate the picture he carried in his head of walking into the sea and ending his life as he had dreamed of doing in the Seine when he had been so lost before.

Every day at work while he walked in straight lines behind the mower, cutting the greens and fairways, he glanced at the beach where waves broke evenly along the shore and imagined his body crossing the North Sea and then somehow the English Channel before ending up on the beach at Honfleur where he and Elizabeth had spent so many happy hours. Though he had lacked the courage to step into the Seine, now that he had had so much taken from his life, he began to revive that old plan. He would wait until some night maybe a week or a month from now, while it was still winter, and he would walk into the water, then lie soaking wet in the dunes and let the cold take his life from him as he drifted into sleep.

He set his imagination upon this plan, working out each detail with such precision that it all began to seem more real to him than the real world. Sometimes at work he concentrated so deeply on his death that when someone called his name or appeared in front of him he was surprised to find them speaking to him as if he were still alive.

One morning he was deep in his daydream of death as he used a hot-air blower to melt the early frost on the eleventh green when one of the boys from the maintenance crew drove up in a buggy and told him there was someone looking for him at the clubhouse. He took Johnny back with him and when the first tee came into view, he saw Elizabeth's mother, Donna, standing there.

'I was hoping you might take a walk with me, Johnny,' she said pleasantly as she shook his hand.

He was too stunned to move. 'Is Elizabeth okay?' he asked desperately. 'I just need to know that she's all right.' By now she had been gone for weeks.

'She is,' Donna said, taking him by the arm.

And with that, they set off down the fairway together into the sunlight slanting low off the water.

She told him that he looked well. 'A light still shines on you, Johnny,' she said, though of course he couldn't see it himself. 'And I'm proud of you for putting together a life here.'

While they walked she told him that when she and Martin were first dating he had often spoken about this place. He'd discovered it in college and had told her if he ever made a mess of his life, this is where he would come to start over.

'His plan in those days was to take the money his father had given him and try to make his first fortune in the real-estate market,' she explained. 'Each time he bought another piece of property he would say to me, "Well, Donna, if this one goes south, there is always Scotland."'

Recalling this made her smile, but only briefly. Johnny watched something dark pass over her eyes.

'We were lucky though,' she went on. 'Everything Martin touched seemed to turn to gold. And his brilliant mind for mathematics opened every door. We were very lucky. Until Elizabeth was born. By the time she turned eleven she just stopped smiling. She seemed to have the weight of the world on her shoulders. There is a lot of sadness in the world if you're tuned into it, and she began to see it everywhere. In everything.' She told Johnny the story she had told him once before about the man who ran the Ferris wheel at the fair. 'All she could talk about that night when we got home was the sad little man who worked there, how his glasses were held together by tape. And I hadn't even noticed him.'

Johnny just listened. When they stopped to watch two golfers up ahead, she told him that Martin had played the game with his father, who had been an international businessman.

'He was the one who opened the door at the Sorbonne for Martin. He knew people in high places everywhere. And golf wasn't just a sport for him, I can assure you,' she said. 'He used the game to humiliate his business opponents. He would drag them onto some fancy-schmancy course and then beat the stuffing out of them. He always played his important matches with a hole in the right pocket of his trousers and rather than take a penalty for a lost ball, he would sneak another one from his bag into his pocket and let it fall down inside his pant leg. Imagine wanting to win at anything that badly.'

'Do you think I'll ever see her again?' Johnny asked when he could no longer keep silent.

'I don't know,' Donna said, not unsympathetically. 'It's a long life, Johnny, we never can be sure of what will happen.'

'What would I have to become?' he asked her.

She looked into his eyes and pushed her hair back from her face. 'I came here to talk with you about love,' she said. 'Elizabeth was telling me that the two of you have the kind of love where all you ask is to be together in a room. That is all you need to be happy. I told her my therapist told me long ago that that isn't love; it's infatuation or something else, but it isn't love.' She paused and Johnny watched her look off into the distance as if the next thing she wanted to say was out there somewhere. 'Don't ever go to a therapist to discuss such matters,' she said.

'It *is* love,' Johnny told her.

She nodded and said, 'Maybe. Maybe it's the only kind of love worth fighting for.' She smiled at him and promised that she would work on Martin. 'He may come around in time,' she said. 'Elizabeth is still so young. But when she's forty and you're fifty-three, the age difference won't matter so much, right?' Donna stopped and turned to face him. She looked straight into his eyes and put both her hands on his shoulders and said, 'Please remember if you ever have children of your own someday. Remember me telling you that whenever they disappoint you, you must only see the good in them, and never judge them harshly. Because the rest of the world will always see their shortcomings and the things they do wrong, so you have to take their part, no matter what. Will you remember, Johnny?'

Johnny was just about to tell her that he would remember this when she exclaimed, 'Prince Charles and Princess Diana. Weren't they thirteen years apart as well?'

chapter nineteen

hill

Eventually they walked back to the modest clubhouse and she took Johnny inside to order lunch. 'You don't look like you've been eating enough,' she told him as she looked over the menu. She decided on a club sandwich and a double Scotch with a side of water. The thought of eating anything turned Johnny's stomach but he knew that she was testing him and so he ordered sausages and mash, the first thing he spotted on the menu.

'Nothing to drink?' she asked as she placed the napkin on her lap.

'Just water,' he said as calmly as he could manage.

Soon after their food arrived she decided that she didn't really want her whisky. 'I forgot it's only five a.m., my time at home,' she said. 'Why don't you have it, rather than let it go to waste?' She pushed the glass to his side of the table.

Suddenly he was aware of the waitress and the bartender watching him and as he declined her offer they both looked relieved.

She seemed satisfied and began to eat her sandwich. 'Why don't we say this, Johnny,' she began. 'Why don't we say that you and I will become friends someday and that years from now we will look back at this morning and decide it was all meant to be.'

'I'm not sure I understand,' he said.

'What I mean is, what were the odds that my life and yours would ever come together like this? You grew up in France. I grew up in America, in Fort Collins, Colorado. I was going to become a social worker or a nurse and I had no desire to ever go very far from home. I drove to the airport one night to pick up a friend and I saw Martin standing outside the terminal, looking up at the stars. His plane had been forced to land there because of bad weather and as I walked to the doors behind him he said, "You don't see stars like this where I come from." That was it for me. And then, almost thirty years later, our daughter almost steps in front of a bus to kill herself in Paris and now you and I are having lunch together in Scotland. Isn't it just amazing and crazy, the way life goes, Johnny?' She opened her bag, saying, 'I suppose our lives are really only a collection of moments. Of course we live for years and years, but the shape of our lives is determined by just a few moments.'

For some reason this made sense to Johnny in a way nothing else ever had.

* * *

She wanted to see where they were married and so Johnny walked her up St Katherine's Hill to the orchard. Tears filled her eyes as she stood there looking down on the village.

He thanked her for coming then she looked at him for a long time in the silence that fell between them. 'Johnny,' she said, softly, 'you're going to be a father.'

The sky above his head began to turn in one direction and the ground beneath him in the opposite. He almost reached for her arm just to take hold of something to keep himself from falling.

'This wasn't supposed to be just a social visit,' she said.

'I have a piece of paper in my purse that I'm supposed to get you to sign so that you'll never have any legal claim to the child. But from what I've seen today, there's no need for that. You'll have to trust me to go home now and try to make things right for you. Will you trust me?'

'Yes,' he said.

'I'll call you, Johnny,' she promised. 'You still have the phone?'

He told her that he did, but that her husband had deactivated it.

'Don't you worry about that,' she said.

* * *

If Johnny ever needed a reason not to kill himself in the deep cold of winter and to stop drinking, he had it now. While he waited for word he began writing to Elizabeth every day at a new address in California that Donna had given him, setting down words to make this impossible miracle seem real. And before the ground was frozen he obtained permission from the golf club to plant a stand of Douglas fir trees in an open field on a promontory beyond the thirteenth green. He planted five trees in honour of the people he had lost – his father and mother and Jerry, and two more for Elizabeth and their child she was carrying. It was not the right time of the year to plant anything, but he needed to do this. He needed to do something. Each sapling was only ten inches high with a slender trunk no more than half an inch in circumference. As he held them in his hands they were almost weightless and seemed to stand no chance at all against the elements. When he set them in the black soil of Scotland's ancient ground over which clans had ridden on horseback a thousand years before, he had the peculiar sense that someone was watching him. Twice he paused and looked around across the open fields where it seemed a figure had been outlined against the sky just a moment before. He listened to the wind rush through the tall grass and in the momentary silence that followed he heard his father's voice calling him for the first time since he was a young boy. This startled him so profoundly that for a moment he didn't know where he was in the world. A great storm of confusion encircled him. His breathing became shallow and forced. When he tried to stand, he found that he could not raise his body up through gravity and the weight of light. He looked into the empty blue sky above him, and then at the rich soil on his hands, and waited patiently until his equilibrium returned. And with it came a new understanding of his place in the world. *All that we know*, he thought, *everything we comprehend and conceive and remember and long for through our lives does not end when we are laid into the ground, but become reference points set in the new landscape that we will cross wherever we go next*. This thought calmed him and gave him hope. After he planted his trees he covered them with baskets that he had lined with burlap and straw for protection through the months ahead, and on the clement days that winter, when the wind was from the south over land and the sun was bright, he would stop in the field on his way to work and tip over the baskets so that the light could reach them.

chapter twenty

blankets

From the time I first heard Johnny's story and began to understand what his life must have been like in those days before we met, I thought of all the difficult things that we all have to get through on this earth. The illness and disillusionment that mark anyone's life. The constant journey from hope to despair and then back to hope once more if we can manage. But I wonder now if there is anything more difficult to get through than time itself. Those expanses of time when each empty hour slowly pours itself into another hour. Time when you are alone, waiting for your life to open for you.

Stack enough of those hours on top of each other and you begin to feel like you are losing your mind. And so it was for Johnny until he decided that the only way he was going to keep his sanity was by preparing for Elizabeth to arrive with their child.

He obtained permission from the owner of the cottage to turn the attached small potting shed into the baby's room and this occupied all his free time. He had only been a boy when he worked with his mother and Jerry fixing up the boathouse, but the skills Jerry had taught him with a hammer, chisel and saw returned to him with surprising clarity. Borrowing tools from the maintenance team, he cut a square from one exterior wall and installed two beautiful antique windows, each with twelve small panes of glass, six on top of six, and crown-moulding trim. He stuffed cloth between the studs for insulation, and put up plaster walls. Over the plywood floor he nailed down wide pine boards which he varnished a warm pumpkin colour. He painted the ceiling the same shade of pale blue as the room with the twin beds he had shared with Elizabeth when they slept in Martin's mansion in Honfleur. The last thing he built was a bookshelf below the windows. Then, after he returned all the tools, he began to furnish the room, enlisting the help of a woman he had come to know as a friend in AA. Her name was Eleanor Lind and though she lived alone now in reduced circumstances in a room not much larger than a broom cupboard at the local boarding house, she had once resided in the largest house in the neighbouring town of Anstruther, which she and her husband had filled with five children. 'We had five babies in six years,' she told Johnny proudly the first time they talked about his new life which was about to begin. 'It still fills me with wonder to say that — five babies in six years! And because my husband earned plenty of money, I was always buying something.'

She helped Johnny choose curtains for the baby's room and a beautiful braided wool rug and rocking chair to get started. Now that he was no longer spending any of his pay cheques on alcohol, he seemed to have plenty of money for the first time in his life, and they began taking the 95 bus to St Andrews on Johnny's days off to buy from a bewildering assortment of baby things from Marks & Spencer, which they carried back to his cottage together.

'We're making the nest, Johnny,' she would proclaim each time he kicked open the front door and they stumbled inside with more packages. They bought so many children's books that Johnny needed to build more shelves. 'Reading to your baby,' she told him, 'is the very best thing you can do.'

'My baby,' he said. 'That will take some time to get used to.'

'You're sure to grow into the job,' she assured him.

They bought cotton bath towels and silk embroidered receiving blankets, and Eleanor appeared one morning with a doll she'd bought at a charity shop so she could teach him how to properly wrap an infant. He was all thumbs at first but gradually caught on.

'Nice and tight,' she said. 'Babies aren't as fragile as we think. And when they fuss it's usually because they're bored. You need to learn all the little tricks. Like when you hold your child, you want to hold him facing out every so often so he can see his world as you're seeing it, instead of looking back over your shoulder. My third baby would not let me hold her facing in. I remember that now.'

It took Johnny a long time to ask her the one question that plagued his mind. He told her how his father had died when he was still small, but he knew that he was an alcoholic too. 'I guess I'm scared I may have passed it on in the blood,' he said as they lined the books on shelves in the baby's room.

'You can worry yourself sick about a million things,' Eleanor replied. She changed the subject so quickly that Johnny knew it would be impolite to push. 'Let me show you how to sterilise the bottles and mix the baby formula,' she said, walking towards the kitchen sink.

He followed her, then asked her as delicately as he could if any of her children were struggling with the disease.

'My oldest is still only fourteen,' she said with a great sadness in her voice. 'So it's too soon to know anything. But I've always told myself that if one of them has my sickness, I'll be there for him through thick and thin. And that's more than some healthy parents can say.'

Johnny waited a moment then asked, 'How do you know, Eleanor?'

She turned slowly and looked into his eyes. 'When you hold your baby for the first time, you'll know. Trust me.'

And he did trust her.

* * *

The cottage was soon adorned with a small enamel bathtub that sat on four scrolled mahogany legs, a wicker changing table with shelves for nappies, a high chair made of maple for when the baby was old enough to sit at the table, and a white canvas bassinet with a linen canopy.

Finally, they assembled the baby's crib – which she told him the Scottish called a cot – together one afternoon and above it hung a mobile of little stuffed cloth fish in pastel colours that swam through the air in a circle to the accompaniment of the Beatles' 'Yesterday'.

When they had finished, they both stood looking down at where the baby would sleep. Eleanor took his hand. 'There's nothing in the world more gratifying than caring for your baby, Johnny,' she said. 'I've made a mess of my life, but in the darkest moments I remember how they looked up at me with their clear eyes, how they smiled at me and patted my face as if I were the most special person in the world. They made me feel adored. You'll have this too, Johnny. And you deserve it.'

BOOK III

chapter twenty-one

apology

We are blind where love waits for us, beyond our persistent fears, at the far edge of our loneliness where dreams and memories converge in the stillness. In a small, old-fashioned town like Elie, people know one another's sorrows, and everyone knew Johnny's story, how he lived alone in the whitewashed cottage with the reminder of what he had hoped for and lost. The baby's room set up and waiting, month after month, year after year. For twenty-one years now. The children's books gathering dust on the shelf below the window. Sunlight fading the pastel fish made of cloth that swung on the mobile above the empty cot.

After fourteen years his field was filled with trees and some had grown tall enough for him to cut one down at Christmas every year and pull it on a sled into the town square where the people who cared about him waited to help string coloured lights on it for the season. They knew his troubles and wished the best for him. They understood why he had accepted his fate and why he had never gone to America to claim his wife and child. In his mind Elizabeth and her family had decided in the end that he was unworthy, and because this was something he had always believed about himself, he did not oppose them.

People understood this and yet they couldn't see him anywhere in town without wondering if he was still waiting.

In truth his waiting changed one morning. Snow along the shore of the North Sea is rare, but one March morning Johnny awoke to find the countryside blanketed in white. Through all the years he had heard nothing, and still he kept Elizabeth's letters in the coffee tin beside his bed, until he finally carried it across the narrow hallway and set it on the shelf with the children's books, closing the door to the baby's room behind him as he left, and knowing that it was an act of surrender. Some kind of surrender.

Of course he never stopped waiting, and that was why he never drank again. He told me that the closest he came to giving up was when he walked to the edge of the sea with the phone one night, planning to throw it out into the water. Somehow he looked up at the stars and turned away from his plan, not for a reason he could name at first, but walking back to the cottage he acknowledged that the feeling he'd had when he'd swept Elizabeth from the path of the bus, the feeling that their lives had coincided for a purpose, was still with him even after all the years of silence. Had he been some other kind of man, say a successful man with prospects for the future or a history of progressing from one bright achievement to the next, the silence would have been merely unacceptable and he would have renounced it with resentment, or at least indifference, and gone on with his new life. But though it was unbearable for Johnny, he accepted it nonetheless as a kind of punishment he deserved, and he carried on, sometimes because the girl he loved and their child were still out there somewhere in the world, other times because he was quite uncertain they had ever existed at all, except in his imagination.

How strange it must have been for him to look up from his rake and see Martin standing in front of him, a elderly man whose dark hair was now white as snow. Johnny was speechless in his shock and so he said nothing, didn't even move. 'With all this white hair I would have preferred to look like a wise old sea captain, but God is punishing me, I guess,' Martin said. 'Making me look more like a cheap department-store imitation of Santa Claus.'

He strode purposefully towards Johnny and gave him his hand to shake as if they were two opponents absolving all hard feelings at the end of an athletic contest, a tennis or golf match.

'Do you hate me, Johnny?' he asked when their hands dropped free. Johnny was still unable to utter a word, but Martin didn't seem to be waiting for an answer. In any case he had already turned away to take in the landscape. 'Johnny,' he said with a solemn tone, 'my God, the whole world has gone mad, but this place is the same. So beautiful. So still. I was seventeen when I came here with my father. A golfing expedition. We played all the famous Scottish courses. It was a rite of passage. When my father sent me to Europe as a graduation present, I came back here. I drove from Sweden; he'd bought me a new Volvo that was waiting there for me, and I picked it up in Stockholm and drove it all over Europe, then he had it shipped home from Edinburgh. That was in nineteen seventy-one. The world was crazy then too. The war in Vietnam. Enough nuclear missiles to kill everyone ten times over. People forget, you know, Johnny.'

When he bowed his head he looked so vulnerable that Johnny asked his question. 'Why is God punishing you, Martin?'

Martin looked up. His eyes widened. 'For being a snob, I guess,' he said. 'That's what Donna has been telling me for years. We've had a good marriage all along, and the only thing we've argued about was me believing that I was better than some people. I like good wine. I like to play the best golf courses. Why not? If you're going to go out for a meal, why should it be anything less than perfect? Do you see what I'm saying?'

'Not really,' Johnny said.

The snow had melted quickly and because it was spring,

the golf course was busy and they had to walk down along the shore to find a place where they could be alone. Martin had a lot to talk about. 'I'm not trying to defend myself,' he went on. 'But even while Donna and I waited for Elizabeth to be born I already wanted her to grow up a certain way. I signed her up for the best private schools, and then the best piano and dance teachers, and the best tutors for maths. I knew the way we just know some things that she was going to inherit my mind for maths. I had this picture of her coming to visit me in the faculty lounge, prepossessed and beautiful, impressing my colleagues with her intelligence and charm. I used to worry about her not getting into a top-flight university. Maybe Oxford or Cambridge. That was my biggest worry until she began cutting herself with my letter opener.'

Now he paused and looked off across the sea for a long time before he continued.

'So, God punished me, Johnny. Instead of worrying whether Cambridge or Oxford would accept my daughter, I begged every psychiatric hospital in France to take her in. But I still worried about what my colleagues at the Sorbonne would think. I did, Johnny, I admit it. As sick as Elizabeth was, I still worried about that. So I guess Donna is right. I guess I am a snob, and always will be. And that's why I couldn't let her marry you.'

He turned and looked at Johnny's eyes as a gust of wind blew his hair back from his face.

'We did get married, Martin,' Johnny reminded him.

'I know you did.'

Johnny placed the flat of his hand against his heart and said, 'I've been married to your daughter for twenty-one years, in here. Nothing you did ever changed that.'

Martin nodded.

'Why have you come back now?' Johnny asked. And even before Martin answered he allowed himself to think that maybe this was the end of his waiting, and that soon Elizabeth would be reinstated here, walking along this beach with him again.

'Are you still drinking?' Martin asked.

'No.'

'Too bad. I could use a drink. It would make this a little easier.'

'Just tell me,' Johnny said, expecting the worst.

'It's cancer, Johnny. Donna doesn't have long to live. She asked me to come see you, and to apologise for both of us. Will you accept our apology, Johnny?'

Even though he knew that he would now lose Donna, the one person he believed might still have helped him share a life with Elizabeth again, Johnny was so relieved that nothing terrible had happened to her that he accepted Martin's apology gratefully and began to breathe again.

chapter twenty-two

past

I've no idea really how much of my own story even matters. But I have to explain how I happened to be on the plane that night with the salesman and the anaesthetist on my way to America. I had grown up on the Strathairly estate where my father was a gamekeeper just a few miles from the golf course in Elie. We lived in a small stone cottage and I walked the fields with him during lambing season, shotguns over our shoulders from the time I was eight years old, shooting the crows who ate the eyeballs out of the baby lambs while the bleating ewes looked on helplessly. My mother had died soon after I was born, so it was just my father and me until I met a Royal Marine from up the west coast in Arbroath and spent most of my time there where we got engaged just a month before he was deployed to Afghanistan – and I promised to be there when he got back so we could get married. I would have kept that promise happily, but Liam was killed just two days before he was due to return to Scotland.

Every day for most of a year I felt like I was slowly falling down a dark flight of stairs, and I think the only thing that got me through the despair were the long walks I took each morning and each afternoon no matter how poor the weather, across the estate, up the side of the hill at Shell Bay and down the other side to the Elie golf course where I almost always saw Johnny Cooper out working. Often in the freezing gales and lashing sleet storms it seemed like he and I were the only two people left in the world, and because I knew his story, I wondered if, like myself, he needed to be battered by the weather to be reminded that there was still some strength left in him and that some part of him was still alive. Despite the stories I'd heard about him for years, I was afraid that if the baby's room with the empty cot didn't really exist it would not be because it was no longer there, but because it had never existed at all, which would mean that his story had just been something he'd invented in order to make some sense of his past. I don't know; maybe we all invent our past. Maybe I was already inventing mine. And anyway, until we've had enough torn from our lives, we don't really have a past at all, do we?

But of course it was real. And the afternoon he invited me to his cottage and sat listening patiently to my story, I still had no idea that our lives had coincided for a purpose. It wasn't until another Christmas came and my father and I stood in the town centre helping string the coloured lights on one of Johnny's trees from his field that I began to believe I might have been put on this earth to join the broken ends of his story together.

It was very late that night when I put on all the warm clothes I owned and started out for his shed with a torch that painted a cone of light along the path I knew so well I could have walked with my eyes closed. From high on the hillside I could see smoke rising from his chimney into a sky swept with stars, and one lamp lit at a window.

He apologised that all he had to offer me was tea.

We sat for a long time in front of the peat fire. He had heard about my fiancé's death and told me how sorry he was. 'I know how it feels to lose people you love,' he said.

'I know you do,' I said.

'Two people were taken from me,' he went on. 'One of them I never even met. You probably already know my story.'

Still, when he asked me if I wanted to see the room he had prepared for the baby, I said I did.

When we stood looking in at the empty cot it was the first time in my life I was quite certain that I would never marry or have children and that I would live a solitary life as he had.

'Do you have any idea what happened to them?' I asked him.

'I have one letter,' he said, and I watched him turn and walk to a small table where he pulled open a drawer. 'I was thinking about something tonight in the town square when the tree was being decorated,' he said to me. 'I was remembering when I planted the first trees. Twenty-one years ago now. I can't believe I've managed for so long. And you? Are you looking after yourself?'

'Trying,' I said.

'You're young. You must try as hard as you can,' he said. 'Someone told me once that when we add up all the things we've lost in this life, or that were taken from us, we are also adding up all that we once possessed and can be thankful for. That doesn't help you now, I know.'

I interrupted him and told him that he was right, and that I was thankful for the time I'd had with this boy I'd loved.

He handed me the last letter he had received from Martin Stoddard a year earlier. It was written on thick pale blue paper with the name – *The Homestead* – embossed in gold letters across the top, just above an address somewhere in California. Before I could read the letter, Johnny asked, 'What was his name? This soldier you were going to marry?'

'Liam,' I told him.

He took hold of my hand very gently and said he was certain that there were many worlds and that I would see Liam again. I looked into his eyes and nodded.

The letter was just a few lines long.

Johnny, I believe every man deserves to drive some good wheels. I've done some research and you should be able to buy yourself an Aston Martin in Edinburgh for around 150,000 pounds sterling. That is approximately 173,000 US dollars which I am enclosing as stock options through my broker. Drive her as fast as you can and enjoy every minute on the wrong side of those crazy roads! All my best. Martin.

It made me smile and, when I looked up, Johnny was smiling too. 'The bond is still in the envelope,' he said.

And so it was.

'I guess you didn't fancy yourself behind the wheel of such a car,' I said.

'I've never driven here – it would still feel like I was on the wrong side of the road. I haven't had a driver's licence since I lived in France, and that was… well, a long time ago.'

'Well,' I told him, 'you might have cashed in the options and bought yourself a nice wee cottage.'

'I'm fine here,' he told me.

'Yes, I suppose this suits you well,' I said.

Before I folded the letter and slipped it back into the envelope, I took note of the name of the town. And in order to lift myself above Liam's death which still haunted me, I realised I had to do something bold. I knew that then. Something so unlike the girl I had always been and wanted to leave behind. And so it was that I flew to California to find this man who had considered himself a better man than Johnny Cooper.

chapter twenty-three

california

The Homestead, where I found Martin, was what Americans called an assisted living village. I'd never seen anything like it really, with its lighted ornate fountains and life-sized bronze sculptures of Greek gods and goddesses and perfectly manicured hedges and walkways of crushed seashells. Martin's large and sumptuous room was adorned with the same elegance right down to the cut crystal bowl of fresh fruit on his bedside table. The door to his walk-in wardrobe was open and I could see glimpses of tailored silk shirts and suits made from the best cloth, and fine leather shoes no doubt imported from Italy. His surroundings stood in such sharp contrast to the man himself, that it all seemed fraudulent, as if it had simply been created for a film set that would, in time, be torn down and carted away. A stroke had left him paralysed on his left side, with his mouth frozen half open so that he had to keep wiping the drool from his chin with a white handkerchief embossed with his initials in hand-stitched burgundy thread.

When he spoke, he hid his mouth behind the handkerchief so that his words sounded like they were coming across a long-distance phone call with a poor connection. It was impossible to imagine that this man had ever determined Johnny's life in the way he had.

When I told him that I had come all the way from Scotland to meet him, his bright blue eyes lit up instantly. He raised his right hand and motioned for me to come closer. 'I have a friend in the village of Elie,' he told me straight away.

'That's why I've come,' I said. 'I need to help him find his wife and child.'

With this, his eyes closed and then he bowed his head as if he were praying.

A moment passed before he raised his hand and pointed to the window directly across from his bed. 'There,' he said. 'Bring it here.'

I was confused at first. And then he gestured towards the window again and I saw a small photograph in a silver frame standing on the sill.

And there he was. Johnny's son. I knew it couldn't be anyone else. I saw him in his son's face. But that wasn't what struck me at first. He was wearing an army uniform and he looked so much like my Liam with his deep-set eyes and long lashes, the sharp widow's peak in his black hair. Even the cast of his shoulders matched Liam's. I felt my knees buckle and I reached for the arm of a chair to steady myself. He looked lost. But he was beautiful in that way few people really are when their beauty is matched by an equal measure of mystery. For a moment I felt like I was sailing across time and memory, back to the last moment I held Liam in my arms. I could feel the bristles on his face against my cheek, and the palms of his hands resting on my breasts.

When I turned and looked back at Martin, tears were running down his face. It was obvious that he had placed the photograph precisely where he could gaze upon it when the first light of morning reached the room until it disappeared in the darkness of night. So that it was the first and last thing he gazed upon as another day turned past him.

'Does he come visit you here?' I asked him.

He shook his head. The handkerchief fell from his hand to the floor. I picked it up and, quite to my surprise, found myself wiping away his tears with it before I placed it back into his hand.

He patted the bed, indicating that I should sit beside him. We were both staring at the photograph when I noticed something that startled me. In the boy's eyes there was the same look that I had seen in Liam's eyes before he left for war. It wasn't the look of fear, or even apprehension. It was far more complicated than that. It was as if there was a silence blowing through him, as if all the sound in the world had been replaced by a silence that inhabited him. It makes no sense, I know, but that is what I saw in the photograph. And something more. It was the same way I felt whenever I looked at photographs of Liam, wondering just how we could be so alive in this world and then suddenly gone.

'Is this Johnny's son?' I asked and I heard my voice rising with defiance.

He nodded his head slowly and sheepishly.

'Where is he now?' I asked.

He motioned to the drawer in his bedside table. I didn't wait for him to nod his consent before I opened it and found a letter inside. The address at the top was of a police department in a place named Iowa City, somewhere so foreign to me it might as well have been the name of a distant galaxy. I read the words below: *We're picking your boy up too often, Mr Stoddard. Fighting. Drinking. Gambling. If the prosecutor didn't have a soft spot for soldiers, he would already have been transferred to the state prison. I advise you to get him some professional help.* It was signed, *Deputy Morse*.

'And what about his mother?' I asked forcefully. 'I need to find his mother.'

He shook his head and told me he didn't know where she was. 'She doesn't write to me,' he said.

'And have you ever told this boy about his father?'

He shook his head and looked back at the photograph.

'His name?' I asked.
'Billy,' he said.
'Billy,' I repeated under my breath.
I had nothing more to say to him.

chapter twenty-four

jail

I suppose I was already falling in love with Billy Cooper before I met him, though at that point he didn't know me or even that his last name was Cooper rather than Stoddard, the name that Martin had given him. People are always making fun of young lovers, diminishing what they share as infatuation or obsession. Dismissing them as silly dreamers. But I wonder if young people in love are the possessors of the most real kind of love there is because they are most open to it, most vulnerable and eager and susceptible. And unafraid. Somehow they know its real value. Their whole world is defined by what they share because all they share is each other. Because they have nothing, their love becomes everything. From the time I fell in love with Liam while I was still at university I began to study older couples. Everywhere I went I watched them and wondered why they no longer held hands or touched. How could they bear to live that way, when there was nothing I wanted more than to touch Liam and to be touched by him? My whole world was circumscribed by our physical touch. Nothing of any value existed beyond the dimensions of whatever room we were in. Even when we were apart that was all I thought about. And I was convinced that the older couples I watched – many of whom no doubt had accumulated so much... houses, cars, cottages by the sea, stacks of money in the bank – had not forgotten what they once had and had lost. Lost or given up, or just tried their hardest to pretend that they didn't remember. And I counted them all as beggars compared to Liam and me. Compared to what we had. Shakespeare knew this and gave the words to Juliet for her to describe: *They are but beggars that can count their worth. But my true love is grown to such excess I cannot sum up sum of half my wealth.*

I was just another beggar now since I'd lost Liam and what we had shared together. I think Billy saw this. He was in a small cell, dressed in slippers made of cardboard, and prison-issue trousers and shirt. The man in charge had kindly provided me with a small wooden chair, which reminded me of the ones we had used in primary school. And when I told him that I had come from Scotland and intended to take Billy back with me and that I would find him work there so that he could begin a new life, he seemed quite astonished and also pleased to hear this. 'He's not a bad kid,' he said. 'Just mixed up. Maybe it was what the war did to him, I don't know. But I can speak to the prosecutor. He's a friend of mine. He might agree to drop any further charges and allow him to go in your custody. He's got a passport issued by the army. It's among his things in a locker upstairs. I'll tell you what – Scotland would take him far enough away from the people he's gambled with and owes money to. The crowd he's been playing poker with aren't known for being merciful.'

I conveyed all this to Billy. He seemed to take it in with a distracted curiosity. 'I can hear Scotland in your voice,' he told me.

'You've been there?'

'No. Never,' he said. 'But I served with two guys from there. Scots Guards.'

'They were your friends?'

'Yes. We were close.'

'Well, if you come to Scotland with me, you can look them up.'

There was only silence for a long moment.

'They're dead,' he said eventually. 'All my friends from the war are dead.'

Well, I thought, *that's our common ground then. We've found our way to common ground in five minutes' time.*

'What kind of country is Scotland?' he wanted to know. I told him it was one of the last places on earth where humility was still a virtue. This made him smile. 'You mean unlike here. America, I mean.'

I told him that I didn't know anything about America outside what I heard on the news.

'Actually,' he said, 'there were some special forces soldiers from Great Britain and Canada assigned to our unit in Afghanistan. I know what you mean about humility. I saw it in them. So, what, will it mean that I'll be in your custody?'

'I'll get you a place to live. It won't be fancy. I'll get you a job.'

'What kind of job?'

'There's a golf course there. I know the man in charge of maintenance.'

'Working outside?' he asked.

'Yes, in the worst weather you can imagine. But you're young and strong.'

He smiled again, and said he didn't feel young, or strong. 'How did you find me?' he asked.

I hesitated, then said, 'I met Martin.'

He smiled. 'Good old Martin. What a piece of work he is, huh? He didn't want me to join the army. He pictured me working on Wall Street.' He shook his head, still smiling. 'He raised me,' he said. 'My parents split up and took off right after I was born.'

'For where?' I asked.

'God knows where,' he said without a trace of self-pity.

'You've never tried to find them?'

'They could be dead for all I know. Anyway, Martin and his wife were all the parents I could take.' He laughed pleasantly at this, then went on. 'They spoiled me rotten. Summer jaunts around Europe with a personal nanny who used to hold my undershorts out for me to step into. I had my own sports car by the time I was sixteen. I never thought once about who my real parents were. Those things happen, you know. People get married when they shouldn't. And have kids when they shouldn't. We all make mistakes, right?'

'That's true, Billy,' I said.

That first time I spoke his name it was like a door swinging open into a room filled with doors. I wondered who had given him his name. I wondered why Martin and Donna had never even bothered to tell Johnny that he had a son named Billy in this world. He must have wondered whether the baby that he was never permitted to even lay his eyes on was a boy or a girl. He might have wondered for years. He might never have stopped wondering. Or maybe he had somehow made himself stop.

'And you?' he said.

'Me?'

'What's your name then?'

'Rosie.'

His eyes narrowed as he thought for a moment before he told me he didn't think he had ever known a Rosie. 'What do you do when you're not talking to drunks in jail? I mean what are you?'

I answered without hesitation though it was the first time I had ever spoken the words. 'I guess you could say that I'm half a widow,' I told him.

He looked at me until I knew I was blushing. I turned away and then looked back to find he was still looking at me.

'Liam and I were engaged to be married when he got home.'

'It doesn't seem to fit you,' he said. 'Half a widow, I mean.'

'In my mind I was already married to a soldier,' I told him.

'I guess that had to be the explanation,' he said sorrowfully. 'Where was he killed?'

'Afghanistan.'

'What province?'

'I'm not sure,' I confessed. 'I suppose I should know though. I really don't know anything about the circumstances of his death. I didn't want to know.'

'I understand,' he said. 'But someday you will.' Then he told me something that caught me off guard. 'I wish it had been me,' he said. 'Instead of your fiancé. When I was in Afghanistan I used to have these dreams of dying. They were the best dreams I ever had.'

chapter twenty-five

rules

So then what brought us together was what we had lost. What had been taken from us. Though I knew the full extent of my loss, he was blind to all that had been taken from him. And that was just the beginning. There was Johnny, a father who had lost the woman he loved, along with their child. A child who had become this young man. And the mother who might have waited every day of her life for this child she had lost to come home to her. From that first time I saw Billy, I imagined what calm it would bring to both Johnny and Elizabeth to know at least where he was and that he was well. I imagined his mother taking his face in her hands and looking across the years that had separated them, looking into his green eyes that she would see at once so perfectly matched Johnny's. The boy's father. The young man she had loved. Her husband. I had to remind myself of this. They had been husband and wife, though they were never acknowledged as such by the world. And for what reason? Who had the right to separate them? What rule had they broken? And who made these rules? *Husband, father, wife, mother...* did these words count for anything at all in this broken world? I had always thought of them as a kind of promise. And like the salesman on the plane that night, I think I also believed that each time we broke a promise, some of our dignity was surrendered, or stripped from us. But I was just a young woman, so what did I know of such things? I was so briefly a fiancée that I never had a chance to grow into the definition of that word. Perhaps I would have failed miserably as a wife, having never had a mother to properly prepare me for what my husband would expect of me. From me. And what would have been expected? Loyalty? Attentiveness? I had no idea then, and in truth, I still have no idea.

I also had no idea if I had any right to interfere in Billy's life. It was a risk. But what worthwhile thing does life ever present to us without risk? Without taking a risk perhaps we miss the thing worth most to us. The thing worth everything in the end. It's about overcoming our fears, I suppose. Looking back now I see what I was most afraid of. I was afraid that Billy would be just one more person I came to know and then lost.

It only took another day before Billy was released after the prosecutor had declared that his passport and our plane tickets from Chicago to Edinburgh were in order. I was filled with hope, even though I'd had sufficient experience in my life of knowing what hope can cost you. I'd already built one world upon hope and should have been reluctant to build another. But when you're young there is always possibility.

All the same, this new chance felt like it was receding from me when Billy paid a visit to duty-free at the airport, and then on the plane, when he took surreptitious swallows from the bottle of whisky when the flight attendants weren't looking. Again and again he offered to share it with me and I kept refusing simply because I'd never cared for the taste.

'Are you one of those people who believe that everything happens for a reason?' he asked.

I answered as honestly as I could. 'I don't know, really. I think it's probably something I might have once believed. But I think I have the right to ask if my Liam was killed for a reason.'

'How was he killed?'

I told him that I didn't really know. 'No one told me anything and I didn't want the details anyway. It was too painful.'

'Well, you have a right to know,' he insisted as he took another furtive gulp from his bottle. 'If you know the names of the men he was serving with, they'd tell you the truth. They wouldn't hold anything back. Was the casket open or closed?'

When I didn't answer right away he apologised and said it wasn't his business.

'Closed,' I said finally.

He turned his head away to the dark oval window as if out there in the blackness he could see something no one else could see. He was still looking away from me when he said he did think there might be a reason for some things happening. 'War, for example. It's all about damned fear. One country fears another country. One ruler fears another ruler. But what happens to a soldier like yours in a war – it all comes down to luck. Good luck or bad luck. You take one step to the left instead of the right and you step on a mine and—' He stopped suddenly and stared at me. 'Do you want to know how I afford my medicine?' he asked, nodding to the whisky bottle. I'm not sure how I would have answered him even if he'd given me time to answer. Instead, he leaned over and took off one of his shoes. He snapped on the light above us. 'Have a look here,' he said. I saw that all the toes were sheared off his right foot. 'This plus the migraines puts eleven hundred dollars into my bank account every month.'

I managed to tell him I was sorry, though I felt like I had just stepped off the window ledge of a tall building and was falling and falling into another universe where a coincidence as strange as this one was commonplace. A mother and son who could be standing beside each other and not know whom the other was, were marked in the exact same place. *What kind of world is this?* I thought to myself. *Do we all live inside these mysterious coincidences without even glimpsing them? Are we all blind to the real shape of our lives?*

I was still dazed and lost in my own thoughts, and when he spoke again his voice seemed to be coming from further away.

'Don't feel sorry for me, please,' he said. 'I'm one of the lucky ones.' While he was putting his sock and shoe back on he asked me, 'How far will my eleven hundred a month go where we're headed?'

'With that, and what you earn working—' Before I could finish, he interrupted.

'What kind of work is there at a golf course anyway?'

'Well,' I said, 'the fellow I know mows the greens every morning at dawn.'

'Even in the winter?'

'Yes, year-round. You'll be amazed how green it stays in the dead of winter when we only have six hours of light each day. And filling in divots is endless.'

He smiled. 'Martin tried to get me to take up golf. He tried endlessly. I'd hack up the course. I was hopeless. Plus golf to me is just a bunch of spoiled men with big bellies, riding around in carts.'

'Buggies,' I said.

'What?'

'We call them buggies in Scotland. But there aren't any at the course in Elie where you'll be working. And you won't find any spoiled blokes with pot bellies. It's a working-class course and it's owned by the town. We get the odd tourist in the summer. Golf in Elie is a way of life, really. It's the daily walk that matters. Dogs are welcome too. They're trained not to interfere with the match. You'll be amazed. It was America that turned the game into an enterprise of privilege and exclusion.'

He asked me if Liam had played.

'He did,' I told him. 'He worked at the course from the time he was twelve years old. He worked for the man you'll be working for. He's in charge of groundskeeping.'

'Did you play with him?'

'No, but I walked beside him. We had some of our best conversations walking round the golf course. That's where we fell in love,' I said.

'What was it he said to you?'

I told him honestly that I wasn't sure. 'It's often far too windy to hear above the gales. Maybe it was just the silence, the silent spaces while we walked. When neither of us felt we had to say anything at all. I remember thinking that I never wanted to take another walk without him at my side.'

'So, that's when you knew you loved him?'

'I think so, yes.'

'I've never had that,' he said. 'I prefer to be alone.'

'Why would you choose the army then?' I asked.

'I joined the army to piss off Martin, really. I wanted to do something hard after a life showered with privilege. But it was all a waste. The war was a waste.' He looked away again before he went on. 'We've left and turned the country over to those bastards. They knew we would. All they had to do was wait us out.'

This angered me, perhaps more than it should have. 'Don't say that,' I told him forcefully. 'What you and Liam and the other soldiers did there gave freedom to a whole generation of girls and women who were being brutally oppressed. You changed their world, Billy. You and Liam helped change their world. You gave them the chance to learn to read and to write. Don't ever forget that.'

I could tell he didn't believe this.

'We land in Dublin with a few hours to wait for our flight to Edinburgh.' I said. 'If there's anyone you want to call, just to let them know, you can use my phone.'

He declined my offer with a simple shake of his head. 'There's no one,' he said.

He put his head back and closed his eyes then. I looked at him a long time and wondered how he spent his days with no one who mattered to him, or to whom he mattered. Just like Johnny, I thought. They've been living the same way. Separated by an ocean and a continent, but living the same solitary existence. Alive but not really living.

His eyes were still closed when he said, 'I'm sure I would have been honoured to serve with your Liam.'

I closed my eyes and before I nodded off I wondered what, precisely, was required to turn *being alive* into living?

chapter twenty-six

lies

At Dublin Airport we drank coffee that he topped off with what was left of his whisky. It was just after five in the morning and a dark rain lashed against the big glass windows.

'I'd like to know more about this fellow I'll be working for,' he said. 'Johnny Cooper, right?'

'Yes.'

'How old is he?'

'Mid-sixties, I would say.'

'And you know him well?'

'Quite well, yes.'

'And how does Martin know him?'

A lie, I thought. *I need another lie that will pass for the truth.* 'I believe Martin made many golf trips to Scotland and that's how they met. A long time ago, I think.'

'And Martin wrote to him and he sent you to come find me?'

'Yes. He thought you might find yourself in Scotland.'

'Find myself? I'd rather lose myself there. That's what I'm hoping for.'

'Fair enough,' I told him.

* * *

By just a little after nine o'clock he was sitting on the couch in my flat while I cooked him a proper breakfast of eggs, bacon, beans, toast, tomatoes and black pudding. He had barely touched his supper on the plane and so he'd had nothing but whisky and coffee in the last eighteen hours. I was chattering away to him while I stood over the stove. The last thing he said to me was that he had to be back in the States by December 17 so he could lay wreathes on the graves of his three friends at Arlington Cemetery in the annual ceremony that took place there before Christmas. I didn't answer him because now that he was here, no more than half a mile from his father's cottage, I couldn't bear to think of him ever leaving.

As I brought his plate of food to the table I saw that he had fallen asleep in the chair. He had taken off his shoes and the empty part of the sock on his injured foot filled me with a heaviness that made me sit down and just stare at it for a long time, and wonder how Liam had been broken when he was killed, wonder what parts of him were missing in his coffin.

I covered Billy with a blanket and went to find Johnny. All sorts of sentences were lining themselves up in my mind. There were so many things I wanted to tell him and I was rehearsing them all as I walked across the golf course. I found him down on his knees, laying bricks of sod into a scarred patch of ground, and as I got close enough for him to hear me, I called his name. And when he turned and looked up at me I asked him this question. 'What is it that turns *just keeping alive* into *really living*?'

He smiled at me with a curious expression. 'Just one thing,' he said, as if he'd never been more certain of anything before. 'Love.'

'Are you sure?'

He thought for a moment. 'Well, work helps too. But labour without love isn't much more than brutality.'

I nodded.

'You know what I mean, Rosie,' he said. 'You had that with your Liam. Whenever I saw the two of you together, I knew. You're much too young to remember the old Beatles song, "All You Need Is Love", but they got it right. My mother used to sing that song to my father when I was a boy. She sang it with conviction too, as if she meant it.'

'How long has it been since the girl you loved was here, with you?'

'The girl I loved and married,' he said.

'Yes, the girl you married.'

'Twenty-two years, four months, and seventeen days as of this morning,' he said.

He smiled at me when he said this, for my sake, I think. Because he didn't want me to feel sorry for him. It made me ashamed that I hadn't kept track of the days since Liam and I were last together, before he had left for the war. Johnny must have sensed this because he told me that the passage of time was different when you've grown old, when there is more of your life behind you than out ahead.

I asked him if I could help him roll out the new turf. We were both down on our knees when I told him that I had been to America and that I'd seen Martin. He was amazed at this.

'You saw Martin?' he said.

'I did. He's had a stroke, but he's still thriving.'

'How did you find him? Why did you go see him?'

'I wanted to know where she was. The girl who loved you and who you loved so completely.'

He looked at me and narrowed his eyes as if he was searching for something in my face that he had not seen before. I lowered my eyes when I told him that Martin had no idea what had become of Elizabeth.

He bowed his head for a moment. I watched his hands pressing the sod into place. 'I want to get this finished before it rains,' he said.

I looked up at the dark clouds sailing in from the west, across the Firth of Forth. 'You must be so tired of this weather,' I said. 'We should all be living in California under warm blue skies.'

'Maybe so,' he said. 'But my work is here. And to be honest, standing up against the bad weather makes me feel strong. It's an illusion, I'm sure. But I take satisfaction from it.'

'You've put so much of yourself into this ground, Johnny.'

'Do you want to know why?'

'Tell me.'

'Have you looked at the monument in town by the church?'

I told him that I'd passed it a thousand times but never stopped to read the names until Liam joined the army.

'The boys who left here for the First World War,' he said. 'The Great War. There are thirty-seven names on the memorial. Thirty-seven from this little village. And did you see how they put their occupations beside their names? Many of them worked on this golf course. Groundskeepers. Club makers. Caddies. I always think that maybe this ground was the last place they ever felt safe. There was no danger here. They might have taken their last walk here with their sweethearts before they got on the train to a boat that crossed the Channel and swept them away, into a storm, and they never came back. Everyone in this town knows my story, but I don't know theirs. I don't know anything about any of them. They would have left here over a hundred years ago. All the people who waited here for them to return are lost and gone now.'

He stopped suddenly. The wind fell off as if to deepen the silence between us, and it was quiet enough for me to hear waves breaking along the shore where the lighthouse stood at the end of the pier.

'They want to buy me one of the fancy sit-down mowers,' he said.

'Perhaps you should take them up on the offer,' I said.

'I prefer to walk. To keep fit.'

'That's because you're still hoping, isn't it?'

He looked into my eyes.

'You're still hoping that what was taken from you will be returned.'

He didn't answer, just looked away and said how tragic it was that all those boys from this village had been lost in the war.

I told him that the world was filled with young boys who were lost.

'More now than ever probably,' he said. 'I mean, given the way the world has become such a mess.'

'Well, I found one of them.'

'In your Liam, you mean?'

'No, that's not what I mean.' I wiped the dirt from my hands. 'I found your son, Johnny. I wanted to find him for you. I went to America and found him.'

A long time seemed to pass before he spoke. 'Where did you find him?'

'A place called Iowa City.'

'Iowa City?' he said disbelievingly. 'What is he doing there?'

'He's not there any more. He's here, Johnny. I brought him back with me. He's asleep on my sofa.'

chapter twenty-seven

names

A soft rain started to fall as we walked back to his cottage. I had decided it would be best to leave him alone, but when he pushed open the door, he gestured for me to go in ahead of him. I looked at his things. The burgundy chair with its stuffing showing through the arms. The coffee table where he had mended a broken leg. The small black iron stove where he was already down on his knees starting a peat fire.

'I soak these little sticks in kerosene,' he said. 'Never fails.'

I asked him if I should put the kettle on.

'Please,' he said.

From where I stood at the little counter covered in pale yellow lino I could see into the baby's room. While the water was boiling I walked to the threshold and just stood there looking at the cot that seemed to have been freshly painted in a coat of white gloss.

I didn't hear Johnny come up behind me and I was surprised by his voice. 'It's not my museum,' he said. 'It's my altar where I pray each day. I kneel at the cot and pray for our baby. Then at the little daybed, I pray for Elizabeth. I can remember when I put the daybed there because a woman at the church had told me that the most important thing for a new mother was to be able to take little naps with the baby beside her.'

My heart was splitting apart as I listened.

We were sitting in front of the fire, drinking our tea when he asked me what he was called. I was confused for a moment. 'The boy,' he said.

'Billy. His name is Billy.' Then I said it. 'Johnny, your son's name is Billy.'

I listened to him repeat the name before he said he wondered who had chosen it for him. 'Do you think it was Elizabeth?'

I was considering how I might answer his question when he went on.

'I always wanted to think that they got the chance to spend time together. Wherever they were in the world, whether it was a son or a daughter, I wanted to believe that. I needed to believe that.'

I told him that I understood.

'Do you understand? Can you understand?' His voice fell off to just above a whisper. 'I mean, to live for so long knowing that you weren't good enough.'

'You're right,' I told him. 'No one can ever understand another person's pain.'

'It's not the pain,' he said. 'I grew used to the pain a long time ago. It's the time. The time that's been lost. We can never get time back, can we?'

I shook my head.

'What's he like?' he asked.

'Billy?'

'Yes.'

'Well, we've spent less than twenty-four hours together but he seems like a nice enough young man. He's been in the war in Afghanistan.'

'The army?' he asked.

'Yes. He lost some good friends there. He told me that he's

visited their graves. I think that says a great deal about him, don't you, Johnny?'

He asked me what it was that he had failed to see all these years. 'Can you tell me that, please? I think about it constantly. Was there something more I could have done? Something that I should have done?'

I told him it wasn't his fault. 'They were taken from you.'

'Yes, but I could have gone after them. I could have flown on a plane like you just did. I could have searched for them.'

'But there was Martin,' I said.

'Martin,' he said softly. 'I could never measure up to a man like him. But it's not on him. He's not to blame.'

'Maybe no one is to blame,' I told him.

'Well,' he said, 'the honest truth is I wanted Elizabeth to come back to me. I promised her that I would always be here waiting for her. And I made my decision that if she came back here, if she found me instead of me finding her, then it would mean that she loved me. Truly loved me. As I loved her. Does that make sense?'

'It does. It makes perfect sense,' I told him. 'And you've kept your promise, Johnny. And now you have your son, just across the way.'

He didn't acknowledge this, perhaps because it couldn't possibly have seemed real to him.

We were sitting at his kitchen table when he asked, 'What have you told him about me?'

'Just that you're an old friend of Martin's and that you could always use some extra help working at the golf course.'

'You haven't told him who I am?'

'Oh, Johnny, I wouldn't ever have done that. It's not my place. That's up to you.'

He wanted to know why on earth Billy had agreed to come to Scotland in the first place, and I explained that he had been in some kind of trouble with the law.

'For what?'

'Gambling, I was told.' I left out the drinking part to spare

Johnny. 'I think he's just one of those people who is searching for something.'

Johnny got up then and walked into the other room. When he returned he had the envelope with Martin's letter and bond inside. 'He'll need some proper clothes if he's working with me. Everything waterproof. A good waxed coat. It's the only thing that blocks the wind. I'll put this money in the bank today. Something tells me that I'll be spending some of it to buy him a ticket home.'

'Maybe,' I said. 'Maybe this is just a fool's errand on my part.'

He looked into my eyes again. 'What's he searching for that he could possibly find here?' He asked this with such sincerity that I knew I would always remember wanting to give him the answer he needed to hear.

'Maybe himself,' I told him.

He nodded. 'Maybe,' he said. 'If it was me, I would run as far from this place as I could run. But maybe he's not a coward like his old man. Maybe he's got some courage in him that I never had.'

'Courage, Johnny? How many people could have endured and kept hoping the way you have for so many years? Maybe what Billy will find here is his home. The home you prepared for him here, a long time ago.'

He listened and then told me that he had often made up names for his baby to try to make him seem real. 'I tried a lot of different names for the baby. Names for boys and for girls. I'd try one and keep it in my mind for a while, to see how it felt to me. And then I'd try another. I tried all sorts but I never tried Billy though. I wonder if it suits him. Do you think it suits him?'

'Yes, very well,' I said. And when I said it I hoped against hope that it was his mother who had given Billy his name.

chapter twenty-eight

possibility

I saw them walking side by side for the first time through Johnny's field of trees. Billy in his new olive-green waxed jacket and black waterproof trousers and dark blue wool cap and black wellingtons from the shops in St Andrews. It was August but a freezing gale had been blowing from the east for three days and three nights and I was taking my morning walk wearing four layers of clothing, everything I owned really. I kept my distance and felt so privileged to be bearing witness to these moments. *What a mystery life is*, I thought again as I had on the plane when Billy showed me his wounded foot. Here was a young man standing beside an old man with no idea that man was his father. Two strangers meeting for the first time, with no way of knowing if all their lives they had been preparing to meet this way, in this place. It was perfect really – the two of them standing among the mature trees that Johnny had planted when he lost Elizabeth, and the younger ones behind them in perfect rows and spaced at equal intervals, with this young man who had been their baby more than twenty years before. Across the years Johnny had spent thousands of hours clipping and trimming the branches so that the shape of each mature tree matched so perfectly in height and form they looked like a painting that had been pasted against the dark, threatening sky.

During the first three days and nights I stayed at my father's cottage so that Billy could have his privacy at my place. I took him shopping for the clothes he needed and made a point of checking in on him at least twice each day, finding him sleeping on the sofa where I had left him. The only sign that he had awakened and walked to the deli in town was the next bottle of whisky on the floor beside him.

Now, while I stood there watching them, I was looking for some sign that Billy knew. That Johnny had told him in their first hours together. What kind of sign I wasn't sure. Maybe Johnny's hand on his shoulder? I have always been a hopeless romantic, always seeing in people what I needed to see rather than what was there in front of me. Never willing to admit that life was more about making accommodations than reaching dreams. More about finding some way to manage in the space between how we dream our lives will turn out and how they actually do. What was it I wanted? Simple. I wanted to believe that Johnny's years of longing had come to a close and that being in the company of his son would make him believe again in life's possibilities for him as he once had in his days with Elizabeth in France.

While they walked among Johnny's trees I began to imagine that it was Liam there with him. Not Billy. I suddenly felt something cold moving through me. And then I was filled with anger. It made me realise that I was still grieving, and that there was an emptiness in me that someone else's happiness might never fill. I hadn't been angry before, but now I wanted to march across the golf course, up the side of the hill, and scream at both of them not to waste another minute. I would never have Liam again. But they had each other. There they were, only a few steps apart. I could have screamed at them from where I stood – *Take a good look at each other! Acknowledge who you are to each other! Something valuable has been returned to you in this world where we cannot count the ways we can lose the people we love best!*

The longer I stood there watching, the more certain I was that I had to get away for a while. And by the time I had climbed the hill to meet them I knew exactly where I needed to go.

'So, which one for Christmas this year?' I asked.

'I'm not sure,' Johnny answered.

'They all look the same,' Billy said with such a cynical indifference I immediately regretted bringing him to Scotland. I managed to scowl at him in such a way that he couldn't miss my disappointment. I took a step towards him and was close enough to smell the whisky on his breath.

'How do you ever decide, Johnny?' I asked. 'They're all so perfect.'

'I leave it up to the moon,' he said. 'On the first clear night in December when the moon is full and it casts a band of light across the field, I always choose the tree it strikes first. And that's not something I've ever told anyone else in town.' He smiled at both of us.

'My lips are sealed,' I said.

We both turned to Billy, who shrugged and reminded us, again with disinterest, that he didn't know anyone in the entire country to tell. It was then that I realised just how wide the distance was between him and Johnny, and I stood there believing with some certainty that if Billy didn't make the first step, if he didn't put his heart and soul into this chance, a chance whose dimensions he couldn't possibly measure, the distance would never be narrowed.

chapter twenty-nine

window

On a sun-struck morning I took a coach to Dundee and then a train to Perth, and then another train to Inverness where I planned to stay for several days and to let Johnny and Billy find their way on to some common ground without my interference. But something happened on my trip that I felt I very much wanted, and needed, to share with them.

When I returned, Billy's things were gone and I feared he had left and gone back to America. I walked across the golf course and saw no sign of either of them, until I found Johnny outside his cottage, leaning against one wall trying to block the wind so he could light his pipe. Before I could say anything he told me that I had made a mistake. 'I've been dragging him from the pub at all hours,' he said. 'One night he didn't come home at all. I found him passed out in a bunker beside the eleventh green. It's a wonder he didn't die of hypothermia.'

'You've told him?' I asked.

'Told him? No, I have not told him. I wish you hadn't brought him here. Not everything that's broken can be fixed, Rosie. You're too young to know that.'

'Too young to still have hope, you mean?'

He just looked at me.

'Johnny, you're not exactly the person who should be

condemning me for hoping. Look at yourself. You've held on to hope as long as I've been alive.'

He smoked his pipe in silence for a minute. 'You're right,' he consented, 'I shouldn't be lashing out at you. It's just that he's my son all right. I see myself in him. He drinks to kill his pain just as I did. He's got no self-control when it comes to the drink. Just like me. I know the drill, Rosie. I know where he's headed.'

'Only if you give up on him,' I said.

'What kind of man will he become?' he asked with utter hopelessness, and though I was sure he was putting this question to himself, I intruded.

'Maybe a man as fine as you,' I said. 'I want you both to come to my place for tea tonight. Be there at six.' And then I turned and walked away.

I'd only taken a few steps before he called to me. 'I've been lying too. Whenever he brings up Martin.'

'You'll be forgiven,' I told him. 'But when the time is right, you must tell him who you are.'

'Who am I, Rosie?' he called to me.

I turned back. 'You're a man with someone to walk beside you,' I called to him. 'That's who you are now.'

'And what's at the end of the road for us? For Billy and me?'

'I don't know the answer to that question,' I told him.

* * *

I made our tea. We sat at the table quietly over our food. Billy was shovelling it in like a starving man. 'I could get used to this,' he said. 'What do you call it again?'

'Mince and tatties,' I told him.

It wasn't until his plate was nearly empty that I interrupted the meal and said that I had something I needed to share with them. They both turned to me and waited thoughtfully.

'I took the train to Inverness,' I began.

'Where's that?' Billy asked.

'North from here. A lovely place. That's where Liam and I went. I stayed in the same hotel we had stayed in on our last night together. The Royal Highland Hotel. I asked for the same room. Room one-two-four. I slept in the same bed.'

They both were no longer looking at me. They had their heads bowed over their plates, embarrassed for me, I supposed.

'It's all right,' I reassured them. 'I need to tell you this.'

When they were looking at me again I went on.

'That night, our last night together, I lay awake listening to Liam breathing. I think I believed that if I stayed awake I could keep the night from ending. And I was filled with dread when I saw the first light of dawn at the window. I closed my eyes and fell asleep. When I woke, Liam was dressed in his uniform and combing his hair. I'm telling you this, both of you, for a reason.'

I stopped and looked at Johnny's face and I could see he was anxious about what I was going to say next. He must have thought that I was going to let it all out. All the truth. But I didn't. I knew that wasn't my place. Instead I told them that we all needed to remember that life is not nearly long enough and that we must do our best, our very best, to fix whatever we can in the time that we have. 'We must do our best for love,' I said slowly. 'Love endures all things. Love bears all things. Love believes all things. Love hopes all things. That's all I have to tell you. Nothing terribly profound. But there it is.'

It was then that I saw Billy smile for the first time. It was such a lovely and sincere smile, filled with understanding. He nodded slightly to reassure me, I was certain. And for this I was suddenly terribly grateful.

chapter thirty

belonging

I know they often argued. Johnny complained to me that Billy had a chip on his shoulder and on most days he kept to himself and barely said a word to him. You could always tell his silhouette in the distance whether he was mowing or raking, when he stopped every so often, took a flask from his pocket and tipped his head back like a man blowing a trumpet.

I think maybe two weeks had passed when I found Johnny burning brush in a pit by the shore. While the fire burned he was carefully taking apart the baby's cot and laying the pieces gently on the flames.

'I'm not going to tell him,' Johnny said to me when he saw me approach. 'What good would it do to make his life more complicated than it already is?'

I didn't argue with him. Instead I waited for him to get it all off his chest.

'God knows what he's been through in the war. He's entitled to drink as much as he wants, as far as I'm concerned.'

'Have you spoken to him about it?' I asked.

'Spoken? Try getting five words out of him. Walk past the pub some night and you'll see him sitting by himself with his head down. He might as well have a sign hanging around his shoulders saying *Don't bother me!* You'd have to be blind not to see that he's a loner. He doesn't belong here.'

I told him that most of us don't know where we belong. We stood in silence for a long time. Long enough for me to think about love. About how you can make love, or take love. You can find it and lose it. You can pray for love and search for it. Or curse it. It can last. It can vanish. You can marry for it or cheat for it. You can pay for it and sacrifice for it. It can be destined or doomed. Celebrated. Ridiculed, or renounced. Or squandered. But in order for it to count, I mean *really count*, and be real, it must be given. It has to be given.

'Maybe he just needs your love,' I told him.

He seemed to consider this for a moment. And then he told me that he didn't possess the courage. 'Not for this,' he said.

'Love makes us courageous,' I told him. 'Remember, all you need is love, Johnny.'

I thought there was no more that I could possibly say. But then he asked me, 'How do I go about it, Rosie?'

At first I wasn't sure how I could answer that question. I'm still not sure I said the right thing. But I reminded him that his son who was lost to him for so long had now been returned. 'Just go back now,' I said. 'Maybe that's all you have to do. Go back to the day you set up the cot you're burning. Your baby's cot... and began waiting for his mother to return with him. Retrace your steps, Johnny. And I believe those steps will bring you to *now*. And *now* is all that matters.'

It seemed to me at the time to be a simple proposition. I suppose what I was trying to make Johnny see was that it was not the chance that mattered most. But what he made of the chance. And, of course, not everyone has the kind of chance he had. Billy had told me that surviving a war was nothing more than a matter of luck. Good luck or bad luck. Taking a step to the left instead of the right. We have choices but often we have no idea of the consequences. Johnny had not chosen to live without the people he wanted most. But other choices he had made earlier in his life had set him on his solitary journey. He had paid a steep price for the poor choices he had made. What worried me most of all was my persistent fear that perhaps we cross lines in our lives and, once we cross them, we can never cross back.

* * *

They had worked all day in the rain rebuilding a stone wall along the edge of one green on the course that was only a few paces from the sea when the tide was in, starting just at sunrise, mixing cement in two wheelbarrows and finishing as the sun dropped beyond the sea. I had watched for a while from a distance. I had seen Johnny resting and smoking his pipe while Billy worked with his shirt off under the warm, empty blue sky after the rain had passed and it became a day so unlike most days here. One of perhaps twenty in a year when there was no wind. I had walked a thousand times along the coastal path that ran beside that crumbling rock wall. With my father when I was small. Alone most of the times. And maybe a dozen times with Liam when I realised that I never wanted to take another walk without him at my side. As I had told Billy – that was when I knew I was in love with him; it was a new definition of love for me, and though I never shared this with Liam, I was hoping he felt the same way.

When Billy came to my cottage that evening when the first stars were up, he said something to me so unexpected that it took my breath away. He sat at my table and said, 'I don't think I realised how lonely I've been until now.'

I sat down, across from him. 'Since the war, you mean? Since your friends were killed?'

He shook his head slowly, then bowed it, pouring whisky from his flask and stirring it into the black tea I had made us. 'Since long before that,' he said.

I asked him what it was that made him realise this.

'I don't know,' he said. 'Maybe it's the wind that sounds like thunder when it races across the roof of Johnny's cottage.'

Johnny's cottage, I thought, *not my father's cottage.*

'Or when the wind falls away,' he went on. 'And it's so quiet I can hear the sea rattling the pebbles on the beach. I can hear them from my bed when it's that still. I never took notice of stillness before.'

Home, I thought. *He knows he's come home. Some part of him knows.* Perhaps that is where loneliness ends for someone who never knew where home was. It made sense to me and I wanted to keep him there, waiting for him to say more.

'People know his story,' he said, looking straight into my eyes. 'People in the pub. The woman in the bakery.'

'Katherine,' I said.

He told me that he hadn't known her name. 'The baby's crib that was in my room. He had a wife and a baby, people say.'

I was lowering my teacup and when he asked me what had become of them, I couldn't stop the cup from rattling against the saucer. He took notice of this and asked me if I was all right.

'Fine,' I assured him. 'I'm fine.'

'He won't let me pay him rent for my lodging.'

'*Lodging*,' I said. 'That's a word I haven't heard in a long time. Is that what you are then? A lodger?'

'Not if he won't let me pay him. I'm a bum.'

'Don't say that about yourself.'

'A beggar then. Does that sound better?'

'A lot better, yes. We're all beggars, Billy. Each one of us is begging for something.'

'What do you mean?' he asked me.

'Well, we beg for understanding. Forgiveness. Love. I'm five years older than you, so I can tell you these things and you have to believe me.'

He smiled at this. Then he asked, 'Do you know anything about his wife and baby?'

I shook my head and lied. 'Only the stories. The same

stories you've heard. The same that my father told me after I'd grown up. I was a child myself when Johnny lost them.'

'How does a man lose a wife and baby?' he asked. 'What does he have to do wrong?'

'I don't think you can count the ways, can you?' I said. 'I mean who can count the ways we can lose the people we love best?'

'They must have had a reason to leave him,' he said. 'If you were a child when it happened, then I was just a baby. Right?'

'Yes.'

'I wonder what the world was like back then. The millennium. The end of a century that had seen two world wars and the fighting in Korea that killed another sixty thousand American soldiers. God knows how many innocents. Sixty million people dead from the two world wars, they say. At least that many. Probably many more. They never get the counting right, you know. Pieces of people put into sacks and buckets by someone with a shovel. Everything is just an estimate. A figure that someone puts on a piece of paper and then it becomes the truth. And maybe another two million innocents killed from our bombing in Vietnam. We dropped more bombs on that sorry country than we did on Japan and Germany combined.'

At some point while he was telling me this he seemed to no longer be conversing with me but delivering a monologue that had long been gathering meaning and force inside him somewhere.

'Do you know what Martin Luther King said about America?'

I said I didn't have any idea. He filled his teacup with whisky again, then told me. 'America is the greatest purveyor of violence in the world.'

'Well,' I said, 'the British Empire isn't exactly blameless.'

I watched him drink the contents of his cup. Then I slid my own cup across the table and asked him if he could spare some for me. He picked up immediately on my sarcasm. He poured some from his bottle and apologised. 'I should have offered,' he said.

I took a swallow and felt it burn my throat all the way down.

'Your mother,' he said suddenly. 'How old were you when you lost her?'

I told him that she had died from complications of childbirth sixteen days after I was born.

'You and Johnny have that in common,' he said. 'You both lost people who were important to you. I'm sorry.'

'At least in my case, I never knew her. And I had my father to look after me. For Johnny it must have been much more difficult. I've felt sorry for him.'

Billy nodded and then held up his bottle. 'He told me it was because of this.'

'He told you?'

'Yeah, he told me that his wife left him because of the booze. She took the baby and just left him. He kept the baby's crib up, hoping she would change her mind. But she never did. My drinking bothers him, I can tell.'

'Maybe it reminds him of what it cost him,' I said.

'Maybe. I worked with some vets after I got home,' he went on. 'These were guys who had it a lot worse than me. Brain injuries. I found that I was a good listener. I could draw them out of their pain. But first I had to kill my own. Or drown it.'

'Do you still feel the pain?' I asked him.

'Not if I drink enough of this,' he said, with such a warm smile, so filled with compassion and humility, that I felt drawn even closer to him.

chapter thirty-one

restlessness

A love story, one that is true in every aspect and pierced with the light of desire, is its own country, its own continent, its own constellation spread across the night sky. It owes nothing to convention. It ignores the world's expectations. No one can trace its boundaries. No one can measure its dimensions or calculate its value. It creates its own memories that travel across time and all that is taken from us as weightlessly as shadows, and captures us in all our glory, and marks the holiness of what we shared. I believe Johnny had this with Elizabeth. I can tell you honestly that I was just beginning to learn some of this with Liam, and it was Billy who taught me the rest. I felt us drawing closer over the summer but I denied it until the first chilled mornings of autumn arrived. I can go back now and tell you how many cups of tea it took. Tea that I had with milk and sugar. Tea that he had with his whisky. The long talks over our cups of tea will stay with me for the rest of my life because even as we sat at my table or in front of the turf fire, I could feel myself moving. Moving so slightly that it was barely perceptible. But now I see that I was moving from the past into the present where my soul was alert once more to the beauty around me. And to his beauty.

And I should say this about his drinking, I saw it as an act of benevolence; he was numbing his own pain so that he could listen to me pouring out mine, as he had the veteran soldiers he'd tried to help. And the more I spoke about the pain of losing Liam, while he listened and the deep green in his eyes seemed to encourage me not to stop, but to keep telling him, to give him every detail of my pain and to hold back nothing, the more I forgave him for the nights when he drank somewhere alone and didn't come over my threshold. On those nights I lay awake waiting for him. Wanting him to touch me, for I believed that his touch would truly end my pain.

And so what of his drinking, I would ask myself. Johnny had told me that Billy never once showed up late for work, and that his drinking seemed to leave no mark upon him. In summer it is light in Elie from five in the morning until ten thirty at night. Billy often worked all those hours without taking a break to eat anything, Johnny told me. His hip flask that he kept in the back pocket of his trousers was all the sustenance he needed. I marvelled at this. At his physical strength. In truth, I marvelled at every single element of him. Whatever molecules he was comprised of, I wanted to incorporate into myself.

One night he told me that he loved his work because it burned away the restlessness that had haunted him his whole life. As a boy he said he had driven Martin and Donna crazy. He never slowed down. Never walked when he could run. He told me that he had gone to war hoping to die there just to finally put an end to the restlessness that never left him. 'I used to look at people who could just put their feet up and read a newspaper and I couldn't understand how they managed it. I've never read a single book from cover to cover. I only got through school because Martin pulled strings with the headmaster. I was eight or nine when he told me that he and Donna had adopted me. By then it was pretty obvious that they had no particular affection for me. Having Donna hug you was like having someone throw a wet blanket around you. She was a tough cookie, let me tell you. Don't get me wrong, they gave me everything. I have nothing to complain about. I was certainly not deprived.'

'Of course you were,' I told him forcefully. 'You were deprived of love.'

'Well, who isn't?' he said. 'Whoever gets enough of that?'

I wanted to tell him then that his mother and father would have loved him endlessly. But I said nothing of that. That was Johnny's story to tell, not my own.

* * *

'I'll never be a real man,' he told me the first time I held him. He was standing at the door and I just marched straight across the room and wrapped my arms around him, laying my head on his shoulder. He didn't move. He was in such shock that he kept his own arms outstretched at his sides as if he were frozen in place.

'Why would you say such a thing? You're already a man.'

I felt him shake his head.

'Well, then what is a man, anyway? Tell me that,' I said defiantly.

He had a simple answer: 'A man puts on a suit made of steel in the morning while he listens to news from the Tokyo Exchange, rides a train to an office and makes money for the people he has pledged himself to.'

'Are you sure he doesn't tend the ground on a golf course?'

'That's just a worker, not a man. A worker who can be replaced by another worker.'

'So the real man then, why is he real?'

'Because he has people at home depending on him. People he doesn't want to let down. I knew I could never measure up to that. At the last bell I would prove myself to be…' He searched for the right word. 'Inadequate,' he said.

That was when I took hold of his hands, one at a time, and wrapped his arms around me. 'You're far more than adequate,' I told him.

There was a brief silence before I asked him if Martin had ever told him anything about his real mother and father.

'Nothing,' he said.

'Where did Martin and Donna find you?'

'I have no idea. I suppose through one of those high-class adoption agencies. But you have to understand that we were never close. There were always summer camps and boarding schools which suited me fine because they have one philosophy at those places and that's to keep you so busy you don't have time to get into any trouble. I loved being busy.'

'Didn't you ever want to know who your real parents were?'

'Not really. Well, that's not entirely true. When I went to war I had this half-baked, romantic notion that I might do something heroic and they might read about it in the papers or something. But that was foolish.'

'Were you scared?' I asked him.

'No. Not at all. There's a secret; maybe your Liam knew it as well. You just have to tell yourself that you're already dead. Then the fear evaporates.'

'Hold me, please,' I said. 'Hold me so I'm not afraid.'

He did what I asked. When I felt the stiffness leave his arms and his body coming to rest against mine there was that feeling again, a feeling I had nearly forgotten. The feeling of being small, and cared for.

chapter thirty-two

bread

There was a lovely bench made of mahogany on the fourth fairway where Johnny and I often sat in the evenings after the wind had fallen off. From there we could see in the big glass windows of the pub and watch Billy sitting alone with his head bowed.

'It's his church,' Johnny said. 'The way he bows his head, he could be praying.'

'What do you think he's praying for?' I asked.

'Who knows? Maybe just to forget.'

I told him that I had never prayed before Liam left for the war. 'I began praying as I watched his train leaving the station though. And while I was waiting for him to return I prayed that the time would go fast. I was aware that I was wishing away a part of my life and I promised God that once Liam returned I would never wish time away again. I would make the most of every day. Every hour and minute.'

He told me that it was different for him. After Elizabeth was taken from him he prayed that time would go slowly so that when they were together again they would still be young and strong, and the memory of what they had shared would not have dimmed in his mind.

'So we both believed the same thing then,' I said. 'We

both believed that it was only a matter of time before our lives would start up again.'

He nodded silently and said, 'I wonder if God forgives us for being so foolish.'

'Were we foolish? We just dreamed, Johnny. Dreams are never realistic unless someone else makes them real. Liam would have made mine real. Elizabeth would have made yours real. There was nothing foolish about our dreams; it's just that the people we depended upon couldn't...' I struggled for the words that would fit both Liam and Elizabeth. '... help us.'

'It was not your Liam's fault,' he said quickly. 'He wasn't to blame. And I have never felt that Elizabeth was to blame either. Her father – Martin – was such a force.'

'Well, he's not a force now,' I assured him. 'He's a weak old man. And so it's just a matter now of finding the person you've waited for all these years. She didn't simply vanish. She has to be out there somewhere, just like your son was.'

'Out where?' he asked.

'I don't know.'

'Out there somewhere married to someone for twenty years now? Someone who has taken care of her this whole time I've been here doing nothing but waiting. Someone who made her forget long ago what we had here. It was only a matter of days, you know.'

'Yes, I know. I know, Johnny.'

He pointed to the pub. 'Everyone there knows. Every person in this village knows. My story seems to have captured people's imaginations.'

'Their hearts,' I said.

He shrugged a kind of consent.

'They care about your story, Johnny, because, like you, they are still hoping that it will end with some happiness for you. They care about you. They admire you for never giving up. Giving up your hope. Your dream.'

'However foolish it might be?' he asked.

'Yes. Absolutely. And you should know that Billy knows

your story as well. He's heard it. He just has no idea that he's part of it.'

Johnny turned and looked at me, waiting for me to face him. 'You want me to tell him, I know, Rosie. And I know that you're right. But I just don't know how to do it. If I tell him my story he has every right to say that Martin was right. I had no prospects. I had nothing to give his mother.'

'Except love,' I reminded him. 'Unending love. What could ever be worth more than that, Johnny? What could ever have more value than that? Billy will have the great consolation of knowing that he was carried into this world on a real love story.'

He thought about this for quite some time. It was dark now and above our heads the first stars were taking their places once more across the sky.

He began slowly and I was aware that he was not choosing his words at all. 'I never lost her,' he said, barely above a whisper. 'This is something that no one in the pub knows. Elizabeth has always been with me, at my side. Three mornings a week I take her by the hand and we walk down Library Lane and up High Street to the bakery and I ask her what kind of bread she would like. Some mornings she says wholemeal. Some mornings she prefers sourdough. Then we discuss whether to have the bread sliced in the shop, or take it home and slice it ourselves. Usually she asks me to take it home to slice. We talk about the day ahead while I make my coffee. I tell her about the weather and she helps me on with my coat before we leave the cottage. When I mow, I ask her to tell me if my lines are straight. When I climb down into the bunkers with my rake she is beside me, making certain that my work is in good form. I speak to her the whole time. We talk like old friends.'

He stopped for a moment to light his pipe, and then went on.

'In all these years, Elizabeth has been here. Beside me. We often sit out under these stars. And before I close my eyes each night I say the same thing to her that I say to God. I ask her to forgive me for the ways I've disappointed her, and I ask for her help.'

'What kind of help, Johnny? What kind of help do you ask for?'

'I ask for the help not to give up.' Some thought amused him and made him smile. 'I'd be ashamed to have her see me now,' he confessed. 'So old. Looking so terribly... well, just plain old. But I see her as she is now. And I love the lines on her face. I love her grey hair. I've never told anyone this before.'

Now his smile was gone and in the silence I took his hand. He must have read my mind.

'She's not a ghost,' he said, as he raised his head and turned to look at me. 'You might think that I live with a ghost. But she's real. To me she is real.'

chapter thirty-three

wind

As a rule Billy didn't take days off but he was making an exception so he could take me sailing because I had told him that I had never sailed before and that I hoped one day to learn. He had arranged to rent a small boat. 'That shore I've been staring at across the water for three months now,' he said, 'as we walked to the pier. What is there?'

'North Berwick,' I told him. 'A lovely village.'

'Good,' he said. 'Then that's our destination. I'm judging six nautical miles. On this wind from the west, we'll sail on a broad reach and be there in three hours.'

We climbed from the pier into the boat which was made of wood painted pale green. He threw a canvas bag into the front of the boat.

'What's in there?' I asked him.

'Everything we need,' he said as he walked to the bag and opened it. He showed me the contents. 'Sandwiches for our picnic. Two wool sweaters. You call them jumpers, I believe.'

'Yes, jumpers.'

'And fuel for the skipper,' he said as he took out his bottle of whisky.

We sat in the back of the boat.

'I'm going to teach you to sail,' he said. 'That line right there.' He pointed.

'The rope?'

'We call them lines, not ropes.'

'This one?'

'Yes.'

'Un-cleat it. That's good. Now pull on it.' When I did, the sail at the front of the boat rose slowly. 'Keep pulling,' he said, 'until the sail reaches the top of the mast.'

I watched it rise to its full height until I couldn't pull it any higher.

'Now cleat it as it was,' he said. I did this improperly and he got up and helped me. 'You want to make a figure of eight like this so that it's well secured. You see – it's tightening against itself. But it can be quickly un-cleated if you need to get the sail down in a hurry. Now take that line and do the same and we'll have our main sail flying.'

When I had finished, both sails were filled with sunlight and he untied us from the dock so we were floating free.

'Watch this,' he said. 'Right now we're just drifting because we haven't pulled the sails tight enough to create any resistance against the wind.' He took one line attached to the small front sail and another attached to the large sail. 'These we call sheets. The jib sheet and the main sheet.' As he pulled them in I felt the wind begin to tug at the sails and suddenly we were moving steadily through the harbour, ploughing through the water.

'It's like magic,' I said. 'No sound. No nothing.'

'But you can feel it,' he said. 'Here, give me your hand.' He placed my hand with his on the tiller, a narrow length of wood, sanded smooth and varnished, and I felt the wind's power through my palm. 'It all happens here,' he explained. 'The tiller is attached to the rudder beneath our stern. That's how we steer her. Watch. When I push the tiller away just a little the boat turns into the wind and we stop moving and our sails begin flapping.' It happened just as he said it would.

'This is called being "in irons". You can't sail straight into the wind, Rosie. You must sail across it at various degrees. We're heading there,' he said, pointing to the far shore. 'You take the tiller and keep us on this course. Pick out something you see in the distance and hold the bow of the boat on that point.'

As we cleared the harbour and could see all of Elie behind us, he was staring at Johnny's stand of trees on the promontory just along the western shore.

'The only trees in the whole village,' he said, sounding slightly amused.

'Well, it's what we call links land,' I told him. 'The narrow band of land that links the sea and the farmland. The ground is mostly sand and it's too salty to grow anything. So all over Scotland they built golf courses and cottages on that links land, to save all the arable land for farming. The grass is fescue and it grows year-round in the sandy soil.'

'Why the trees?' he asked.

'Why did he plant the trees? It's where the town gets its Christmas tree each year,' I told him. 'You must have heard this before.'

He didn't say anything. For a long time he just looked off into the distance as Johnny's trees receded from us.

'Where did you learn to sail?' I asked him.

'A summer camp that Martin sent me to. A place called Camp Robin Hood. All rich kids from around the world. The sons of princes and these despicable tycoons who spent their lives stuffing their pockets. Profiteers who, by the way, got rich off the war that took your Liam. I hated the place. But I learned to sail there. You were supposed to use the buddy system and never sail alone. But I always sailed by myself. Whenever the coastguard posted the small craft warnings and all the boats headed for shelter, back into the harbour as fast as they could, I headed out. Alone. Into the storm. The worse it was, the better. Waves breaking into the boat, wind whistling through the shrouds. I'd be down on my knees bailing with one hand, the other on the tiller and this…' He reached inside his shirt and took out a medallion and placed it between his teeth. 'I'd be biting down on my St Christopher to steady my nerves. He never let me down.'

My God, I thought. *Where did he get that? Could it possibly be the same one his father gave to Elizabeth the night he stopped her from ending her life on the street in Paris? The same one he placed in her hand when she left Scotland to tell her parents that she and Johnny were married?*

'So you believe in St Christopher then?'

'The patron saint of travellers,' he said. 'And we're all travellers, aren't we? On some journey.'

Finally I asked him where he got the medallion.

'My mother,' he said. And this took my breath away until he went on to say that Donna had given it to him. 'On my ninth birthday. She told me that it had belonged to my real mother who had given me up to the adoption agency. It was the only thing she sent along with me. I wore it to war. As I said, it's never let me down.'

He let me steer us out into the bay. As we left Elie behind us I explained how every Christmas Johnny cut down one tree and the whole town decorated it on the village green, always on Christmas Eve. 'The youngest child in the village gets to climb the ladder and place the star at the top,' I said.

He took a long swallow of whisky from the bottle and said, 'There's something beautiful about that, isn't there?'

chapter thirty-four

home

I looked into the canvas bag then, and found an empty chopped-tomato tin. 'What's this for?'

'In case we get caught in rough weather and I need you to bail,' he said with a wide grin. 'Take a look what else is in there.' I rummaged around and found a small square box made of wood. 'Open it,' he said.

Inside there was a compass.

'Are we going to get lost?'

He smiled at this and asked me if I knew how to use one. I told him I had no idea. He knelt down beside me, our faces practically touching. 'It doesn't do any good to have a compass in your boat if you don't take a reading before the fog moves in. See, when the red hand settles on the red N for north, then take a reading for the harbour at Elie that we just sailed out of. That's our heading on the way back. So no matter where we are out at sea, we turn the compass in your hand until the red needle is at N and then we sail for the reading we've taken. Now you know everything you need to know about reading a compass.'

I thanked him. I could tell that he was enjoying himself. He told me that he used to teach the younger boys at camp to sail and he loved it.

'You never forget who teaches you to sail,' he said. 'It's like the first person you make love with.' He looked away, out at the distant shore when he said this, and I realised that he must have felt as awkward saying this to me as I felt hearing it.

When he looked back and our eyes met I knew what he was wondering. 'We were waiting until we were married,' I told him. 'It was Liam's idea. He had made a promise.'

'To whom?'

'To God.'

'He believed in God then? He was a religious man?'

'Yes.'

'And that was all right with you?'

'I loved him.'

'I understand,' he said. 'But every war that's ever been fought was fought in the name of one man's religion or another. Take away religion and there's no war. Like John Lennon said. Imagine no religion. That got him into a little trouble. I've made my religion of the stars. I learned to navigate by them. If the sky is clear tonight I could sail us back to our harbour without the compass. You can use the satellites instead of the stars if you prefer. Your smartphone could take us all the way to America.'

'I think I'd prefer the stars. Maybe you could teach me.'

'It would take some time,' he said. 'I'm thinking of leaving.'

'Going back to America?'

'No, there's nothing about America that I've missed. Not a single thing. What I'd like to do is go up into the Highlands. The Outer Hebrides maybe. And just disappear.'

'For how long?'

'I don't know. Long enough to forget and to be forgotten.'

We were nearing the shore now. We could see a row of cottages.

'You've sailed us all the way across,' he said. 'I have to teach you how to stop. When we get ten metres from the beach, push the tiller away from you gently, and turn the bow into the wind. The sails will be empty and I'll take them down, and we'll drift the rest of the way.'

I listened to everything he told me, but I was really somewhere else. I was disappearing in the Hebrides with him. Until he had said it, I hadn't realised that it was exactly what I wanted most. Just to disappear.

* * *

We sat in the dunes and ate the picnic lunch Billy had prepared. 'Tuna fish and sweetcorn sandwiches,' he exclaimed proudly. 'We don't have these in the States but I gather you folks are quite fond of them. So am I. In fact, I'm fond of everything in this country of yours.'

'Even the weather?'

'Especially the weather. The way it changes constantly. California weather is a bore. Same sunny sky every day.'

I told him that I could get used to that.

We both fell asleep in the sun for a while. I woke first and was startled to find him lying next to me, so close to me. I propped myself up on one elbow and watched him sleeping for a long time the way I had watched Liam sleep through our last night together in the hotel. And then I leaned over and kissed him on his lips. His eyes opened. I apologised as fast as I could.

'Don't be sorry,' he said. 'That's just about the nicest thing anyone has ever done for me.' He took one look at the dark clouds gathering in the west, moving over the water on a strong breeze. 'But we need to get moving,' he said as he rose to his feet and reached down to help me up.

In minutes the breeze was a strong wind.

'I'm guessing twenty knots. Gusting to twenty-seven. I need to show you something so you aren't afraid,' he yelled to me above the wind. 'Each time a gust comes it will tip the boat onto her side and you'll feel like she's going to roll right over and dump us in the water. But we'll be fine because I'll let out on the jib sheet and the main sheet that I'll keep in my left hand, and I'll spill the wind and the boat will right herself. Okay?'

I nodded.

'Or,' he went on, 'I'll nudge her bow up into the wind like this – you see the wind fall out of the sails like I taught you?'

I nodded again. But by now I was scared.

A moment later he shouted, 'Here comes a gust. Can you see it on the water there? It looks like the water is boiling!' He had barely finished speaking when it was upon us and I could feel the boat rolling out from under me. 'Don't be afraid!' he yelled as he let out on the lines, and the boat became level again.

We were nearly halfway home when the bay filled with whitecaps, and waves began breaking over the side of the boat, soaking each of us.

'I'm sorry!' he yelled. 'I have to keep our point of sail straight for home!' He nodded into the distance and I turned and saw the lighthouse at Elie. 'We're ploughing straight for it,' he assured me. 'Just take that tomato can and bail for all you're worth!' It was then he took his St Christopher medallion and placed it between his teeth. Each time I looked up at him he was smiling like he was having the time of his life.

And I wanted to take him in my arms and kiss him again.

'I know her name!' he shouted to me above the wind.

'Whose name?' I shouted back.

'The woman Johnny's been waiting for. Elizabeth! I've heard him talking to her! I think she must be a ghost!'

I threw another can of sea water over the side. 'She's not a ghost!' I shouted back at him. 'She's real!'

chapter thirty-five

pram

This happens often. I see a girl like the one I saw this morning as I waited for the 95 bus to take me from Elie to Marks & Spencer in St Andrews. She's no older than seventeen or eighteen. She could be younger. And she is pushing a baby in a pram. And I am suddenly so ashamed of myself and I can feel something cold churn through me, and it takes all my willpower to turn away through the heaviness that descends on me so that she will not catch me staring, because if she looks back at me, if our eyes meet, she will know at once exactly how foolish I am, how foolish I was to agree to Liam's terms that we wait until we were married to make love. I had opposed him but only half-heartedly at first and then with mounting determination as our days together were coming to a close. His argument was that if something were to happen to him in the war, and he left me pregnant, he would not want to place that burden on me to raise our child on my own. He would want me to forget him and to get on with my life. Those were his words – 'If anything happens to me, Rosie, I want you to get on with your life.'

He told me that this would be so much harder if I had his child.

'We'll have children someday, Rosie,' he had insisted.

'And they won't have to be haunted by a dead father.' It was the same argument against getting married before he left.

But this wee girl with her baby knows. I can feel her watching me as I walk away. I can feel her derision. We have the same anatomy, but there is something about the way I walk, with my shoulders erect and my head held up while she is bent over her pram and struggling to steer it through the crowds on the pavement, maybe only a few coins left in her pocket after buying another bundle of nappies with money she once was free to spend on herself. Her long sentence is only getting started. How many more years will it be before she can take a leisurely walk into town on her own? But look at me. I had an old-fashioned boy who wanted me to save myself for our wedding night. An old-fashioned boy who finished top of his class at Sandhurst and went off to war as a first lieutenant and then got himself killed while I was saving myself. *The joke is on you then, isn't it,* I imagine the young mother thinking. *Maybe you'll keep saving yourself and you'll end up a spinster so young girls like me can laugh at you when we see you on the street. Saving yourself for what, exactly? Someday you'll be old and no one will want to touch you or even come near that place of yours that you saved.*

I remember my da's sister, Auntie Joan, talking about the girls at St Cecilia's school when it was in the news that the Americans and the Russians were going to start a nuclear war that would destroy the world. She said the girls were lined up behind the back wall of the church, doing it with whatever boys they could find, doing it with their clothes on, hiking up their pleated skirts and unbuttoning their coats and holding them out to their sides with their hands like curtains for a little privacy. Just to see what all the fuss was about before the world ended, Auntie Joan had said.

* * *

When I stepped off the bus in Elie, Billy was waiting there, sitting on the bench in front of St Michael's church. As soon as he saw me he stood up and when he said nothing, and just looked deeply into my eyes, I could tell there was something he wanted to say to me, and I just waited.

'His name was Liam Pierce,' he said.

I nodded. He took my hand and I followed him through the small cemetery until we came to the headstone. We stood there in silence for a moment.

'Liam H. Pierce was a lucky man,' he said to me.

'It was bad luck,' I reminded him. 'You said it yourself.'

'He was lucky to have you, is what I mean, Rosie. The time he spent with you wasn't as long as it should have been. But I can swear to you that he was grateful for what you had together. He would have been thinking of you, I mean, his last thoughts would have been of you. How many people get to say that?'

'I think he took a part of me with him,' I said. 'And honestly, this is the first time I've come here since the funeral.'

'It takes time,' he said reassuringly.

'I think I've tried to believe that by staying away, he might still come back.'

'He's never left you, and he never will,' Billy said. He took a kitchen knife from his pocket. 'With your permission?' he said. I had no idea what he meant, but I nodded. He knelt down and dug a perfect square out of the ground. He lifted it out of place with great care. Then he took something from his pocket. 'It's my purple heart.' He held it up for me to see. It was a gold profile of a man's face and a purple ribbon outlined in white. 'It's George Washington,' he said with a wry grin. 'Once the great enemy of England.'

He placed the medal into the ground with great care and set the square of earth back so perfectly you could not tell that the ground had been disturbed.

'Sit with me,' he said.

And I did. I sat just beside him, looking at Liam's name on the granite stone.

'Why don't we talk about him?' he said. 'But first a toast.' He took a small bottle of whisky from his pocket, unscrewed the top, raised the bottle into the air and said, 'Here's to you, Liam H. Pierce. Lest we forget.' He handed me the bottle to take the first drink, then drank some himself. 'Now,' he said. 'Take me back to the beginning. Tell me how you first met. Tell me everything you feel like sharing. I want to know who he was and how he cared for you.'

'You want to know this?' I asked.

'Yes, I do.'

'Why?' I asked.

'Well,' he began slowly, 'because I've never learned how one person properly cares for another. I've only ever looked after myself in this world. And I haven't exactly done an exceptional job at that. I don't know where we're supposed to learn how to care for someone else. You lost your mother so it must have been your father who taught you?'

'Yes, I guess it was.'

'By the way he cared for you?'

'Yes. He's a very kind man. He was always very thoughtful.'

He laughed to himself and took another drink. 'Those words – kind and thoughtful – don't really describe Martin and Donna.'

'So, you never had anyone to teach you?' I said.

When he answered this his voice took on a solemn tone. 'No, I guess not. But it's never too late to learn, is it?'

I shook my head and smiled back at him.

'I wonder who taught Johnny,' he said. 'I mean, to care all these years for people he never really even knew.'

'I don't know who taught him,' I said. 'But that makes him a very special person in my book.'

'Not crazy like some people think?'

'Not crazy at all. Steadfast. Loyal. He kept his promise,

Billy. He told the girl he loved that he would love her for the rest of his life. And he has. That has to count for something in this fucked-up world.'

It was the first time I swore in his presence and it seemed to delight him. Before he took me in his arms I noticed his face was sunburned. I felt him kiss my hair as he said, 'That's more like it. Hearing you swear. I admire a girl who can curse properly.'

I looked down at Liam's name again on the granite stone. I closed my eyes and first it was Liam holding me. And then, it wasn't. 'So much of life is about waiting, isn't it?' I heard myself say.

'What is it that you are waiting for, Rosie?' he asked, and with each of his words I felt his lips moving against my hair. I almost told him then. I almost told him that I was waiting for him to know that he had found his way home.

chapter thirty-six

money

Early October and the days were getting shorter now. In another two months we would have just six hours of sunlight a day until the solstice when we would begin to pick up a few more minutes of light in every twenty-four hours.

As summer drew to an end, and autumn began, I had come to an understanding. I knew that I had fallen in love with Billy, but we had not been together long enough for me to *be in love* with him. I mean, no longer falling but loving him with my eyes open, knowing who he was. It was something that Billy had said to me that made me realise this. He had told me that until we know what a person is afraid of, we don't really know that person. We were driving up the coast of east Angus to the Royal Marine base in Arbroath. He wanted to try driving on what he called the wrong side of the road and I agreed but only after he gave me his flask to hold, and except for the roundabouts, he mastered it in no time and we were both relaxed and enjoying our spin across the countryside.

'You never asked Liam what he was afraid of?'
'No.'
'Well, whatever it was, it was going to define your life together. Our lives are always defined by our fears. I'm pretty sure about that, Rosie. If you really want to know someone

well, look him in his eyes and ask one question. *What is it you're afraid of?* Bingo. Unless he lies to you, you'll have him figured out.'

'What about you then?' I asked.

'Me?' He smiled and turned and winked at me. 'I'm not afraid of anything. You're looking at the one person on earth who has no fear.'

'Go on,' I said.

'You don't believe me?'

'You're a lousy liar.'

'All right then,' he said. 'I'm afraid of money. You need a lot of money just to survive in America. My monthly cheque from the government would barely cover rent and groceries. And I already told you – I don't see myself as a *real* man. Out there in a suit, selling or doing whatever real men do. I have no education. I haven't prepared myself to survive in America. Do you know how much it costs to put kids through college?'

'You're thinking about having kids?'

'Sure. By the time they go to college it will be around one hundred and twenty thousand dollars a year.'

'It's free here in Scotland,' I told him. 'Anyone who is clever enough to be admitted gets one degree free, no matter how much money they have.'

'That's what I call a civilisation,' he said. 'Here's my bottom line on America. Any nation that squanders her wealth on weapons of mass destruction and puts her young people in debt for life for an education is doomed. Period. You can't argue with that, right?'

'So, why don't you stay here in Scotland?'

'The only money I can earn here has to be under the table or I'll lose my monthly benefit. Johnny persuaded the golf course to pay *him* my salary which he then gives to me in cash.'

It was then that I remembered Martin's stock options for Johnny's Aston Martin.

The guards at the gate to the base were expecting us, which

confused me. They gave us directions to a flat in a row of flats opposite a shabby rugby pitch.

'How did they know who we are?' I asked Billy.

He waited until he had pulled the car to a stop in front of the flat before explaining that in Afghanistan he had been attached to a special forces unit that included two Royal Marine Commandos. 'I made a few phone calls,' he went on. 'The Marine who lives here knew your Liam.' He paused and looked into my eyes. 'He'll answer all your questions. He'll tell you everything you have a right to know and were never told because you were not his wife, or formally part of his family.'

He took my hand in his and held it very gently.

'It's up to you, Rosie,' he said just above a whisper. 'We can turn around and go back to Elie, if you want. You don't have to do this.'

I knew at once that I would go meet this Marine. I was out of the car, walking towards the front door of the flat when Billy called to me.

'Shall I come with you, Rosie?'

I stopped, turned back and shook my head.

* * *

He could not have been more gracious. His name was Simon Jones. He came from Liverpool and his words were carried on the music of a thick accent. He had curly black hair and the widest shoulders I had ever seen. He was missing his left arm, his right ear, two fingers on his right hand, and I could see below the cuffs of his trousers where his legs, just narrow metal poles, were fixed in plastic moulded feet inside his trainers. He apologised that he had not been on the mission with Liam. 'I was meant to be,' he said, 'but at the last minute, a friend of mine was chosen to take my place. He was the only one to make it out alive. He told me what happened and I will tell you if you want me to.'

I nodded. 'Yes, tell me,' I said.

'It was an IED. Liam was in the lead. He died instantly. He didn't suffer.'

He reached across the table where we were sitting and took my hand and told me how sorry he was for my loss.

* * *

All the way home Billy let me remain silent. We didn't utter a word as we passed his whisky bottle back and forth. I kept wondering if I could have loved Liam if he had come home to me as broken as Simon was. And I felt guilty for even wondering this.

chapter thirty-seven

torch

Sometime in the middle of that night I awoke suddenly as if a voice were calling to me through the darkness. I sat up in bed and felt anger rush through me that seemed to heat my blood. I kept seeing the young Marine's broken body, the way it had been torn apart and put back together, and thinking about how perfect his body must have been when his mother first held him in her arms and marvelled at his beauty. Why was this boy's body any less sacred than the part of my own body that I'd been told to save for the man I married? It was all so outrageously stupid and so cruelly ridiculous that my anger mounted until it felt like someone had set fire to the roots of my hair. It took only a few more moments for me to know what I wanted to do.

* * *

I marched with a torch up one side of the mountain and down the other, across the golf course to Johnny's cottage, into the baby's room where I sat down on the daybed and shone the light at Billy until I woke him from his sleep. 'You knew,' I said accusingly. I climbed onto the daybed and straddled him with my knees, pushing down into the mattress as I struck him again and again across his chest with both fists. It all came pouring out of me. 'How could you ever be part of such a monstrous thing? How can you men do those things to each other? What gives you the right? You knew what had happened to that soldier. You wanted me to see that... nightmare. How dare you!'

Billy didn't defend himself. He never said a word until it was all out of me and I was just glaring into his eyes which he closed as if he were trying to pretend I wasn't there, or maybe he was trying to fall back into sleep. I pried one of them open.

'No you don't,' I whispered. 'You don't get to shut me out.' I pulled my jumper over my head and then unbuttoned my shirt and grabbed both his hands and placed them on my breasts. 'You're going to make love to me until I'm finished with you.' I stood up and pulled off my trousers. I tore his blankets back and lay on top of him, waiting for what would happen next. When I took his hand and placed it between my thighs I felt the air rush from my lungs.

That was when I heard him say that he had wanted me to know that Liam hadn't suffered. 'And I wanted you to see that there are worse things in war than being killed.'

Soon I wasn't listening to anything he said. I told him in no uncertain terms what I wanted him to do to me. 'Show me something that men are capable of besides butchering each other.' I was telling myself to feel everything so that I would never forget any of it. So that I would have the memory to console me through the rest of my life. But in truth, as I was carried beyond the margins of my known world, nothing struck me more deeply than the stillness of it all. It was as if a trapdoor had opened beneath me and I had fallen through to a silent point defined by neither time nor memory, but only by the sensation that I had come to rest in a place of calm – and something else. Gratitude. Yes, an immense gratitude that flooded through me like a drug, altering my cells. And with it, a new understanding of what life was about. *So, this is how the world is held together*, I thought. *This is how we sail through storms of doubt and hopelessness and fear. And even despair. This is how our hope is meant to be renewed and how we are meant to recover from all that is taken from us. It is the memory of this that has sustained Johnny all these years.*

It went on and on, which both surprised and comforted me. And the whole time I was just hoping that what Billy was doing would make me pregnant so that in another nine months after he was a million miles away from me, I would be pushing our baby in a pram up the High Street where my baby would be known as Johnny Cooper's grandson or granddaughter. Everyone would know this and I would be the one to tell Johnny. We would have become part of his old story that would live on in the town's memory, passed on from one generation to the next.

* * *

Billy and I lay still, catching our breath. 'Did Johnny and his girl have a chance?' he asked as he picked up the whisky bottle from beside the bed.

Before he could open the top, I took the bottle from him and rolled it under the bed. He raised one eyebrow at this.

'I'm the kind of guy that someone like you would grow to disapprove of,' he said as if he were stating a proven fact of life.

I was thinking, *Not if you do this to me every single day.*

'And the reason men do it,' he went on, 'the reason they go to war is to find out if they're cowards. Some men need to know this about themselves more than others. Men who are insecure and who have these terrible doubts about themselves.'

'He was just a boy,' I corrected him.

'Well then, boys,' Billy conceded. 'Some boys need to find out if they have courage so that they don't spend the rest of their lives wondering.'

'Well, if you're right, then they need to come up with

some other way. Some other type of contest that doesn't tear so much from their lives.'

'It's part of the warrior mentality,' he went on. 'The warrior must prove his courage in battle before he believes he has the right to do this to a beautiful girl like you.'

'Yeah? Well, that's just about the most stupid thing I've ever heard,' I argued. 'What about the poet or the artist?' I asked him.

He thought about this for a moment, then said, 'Maybe they have a different way of proving their courage. They prove it by living a different kind of life than the rest of us live. By seeing things the rest of us don't see because we're too frightened by things that don't really mean anything. Like me, and money. They take their vows of poverty and solitary confinement. They follow their own lights. That takes courage.'

I was listening to him but not really hearing him. I burrowed under the blanket and reached down until I felt his injured foot where his toes had been sheared off. I cupped what was left of his foot in the palm of my hand and felt his pulse there which was steady and strong.

'Are you hiding from me?' I heard him ask.

Maybe I didn't answer because I was hiding. Not from him, but from Liam, who, for some reason, I was certain was looking on from wherever it is we go after we die.

'What about you then? Why did you go?'

'To war?'

'Yes,' I said.

'To prove something.'

'To whom?'

'To myself.'

'What?'

'That I wasn't worthless. I thought I might help those people who'd been persecuted for so long. Especially the girls and women. That's what I thought at the beginning. But it was all worthless.' Billy stared at the window a few moments in silence before he came under the blanket with me. He took my face in his hands and whispered, 'Thank you.'

'For what?' I asked.

'For this gift you just gave me.'

'A gift?' I said. 'Is that what it was?'

'Of course,' he said.

'Is it always that way? I mean with every girl you—'

He cut me off by placing a finger on my lips. 'No. It's almost never a gift. More of a bargain, I suppose. A transaction.'

'I could thank you as well,' I told him.

'I don't think that would be appropriate.'

'Why not?'

'I've never felt like more than just a burden on people.'

'A burden?'

'I'm not the kind of horse one should bet on, Rosie.'

'Are you telling me this so that I won't get my hopes up?'

'Maybe. Maybe I am.'

And then, as if to eradicate this possibility completely, he wrapped his arms around me and slowly made love to me once more. This time I was aware that it was only the two of us; Liam was no longer hovering above us. 'I'm incorporating you,' I heard myself saying. 'Not just into my body. Into my soul. Into my whole self.' His lips were pressed against my forehead when I told him this. 'I mean deep inside me,' I said. 'Don't move. Please. Don't move at all.' For some reason I thought again of the shares Martin had sent Johnny and I almost told Billy that he didn't need to be afraid of money any more. But I didn't want to break the silence. The spell that had been cast over us.

It was Billy who spoke next. 'This bed,' he said. 'Can you imagine how Johnny must have wanted to do this with his girl?'

I wondered if perhaps Billy had been conceived in this same bed.

'Her name? I've forgotten her name, I'm sorry.'

'Elizabeth.'

'Like the Queen,' he said.

'I'm sure she made him feel like a prince,' I said.

He kissed my nipples gently. 'You've made me feel like I'm king of the world,' he told me. 'Like I can fly.'

And though it seemed unlikely to me, I believed him, not because I thought he was telling me the truth, but because in those moments of stillness I would have believed anything he told me.

chapter thirty-eight

god

After that night with Billy, I struggled to understand precisely what had changed. I was trying to come to terms with what it all meant. Or if it meant anything at all. There were moments when I first opened my eyes to a new day and I felt like I was in possession of a dream. Or that a dream possessed me. And the only way I could describe this dream to myself was that it felt, not like the beginning of something, but like the end. The end of loneliness perhaps. And not just my loneliness, but Johnny's as well. Because of what had transpired, even if there was nothing holy about it, and it had been simply – to use Billy's word – a transaction of some kind, my fate and Johnny's now seemed to me to be inextricably connected. I would have argued with anyone who dismissed this idea. I would have fought for the truth inside it, fought with my last breath because I believed it with such determination. Or perhaps it was desperation. Maybe I was only a silly girl, desperate to find something I could take hold of. But I was certain that Johnny and I had somehow found our way to the same path below the stars and that this path was leading us to something that had been decided long before. A destination neither of us had chosen but one we had both been moving closer and closer to our whole lives. I also felt there was some public quality to it, though I may have only been imagining that people looked at me differently. Katherine in the bakery. Gillian in the deli. They seemed to have a knowing expression when our eyes met. *You're one of us now*, they seemed to be acknowledging. *You will now remember for the remainder of your life, or for as long as your memory holds up, exactly where you were when it happened. You will never forget, just like you will never forget when you first learned to ride a bicycle. It will stay with you, and if you're lucky the memory will hold equal measures of lust and tenderness. And maybe, years from now, you will have learned enough about yourself and the coldness in the world to finally be certain that there was real love in attendance there as well.*

One thing is for certain, whatever it was that Billy and I shared in the little daybed in Johnny's cottage, neither of us seemed to be able to get enough of it. But we never held each other in that room again, not simply out of fear that Johnny might discover what we were up to. But out of respect for what the room had represented for him for so long.

And because we had found the most perfect place on earth to be alone together. The lighthouse at the end of the pier. Of course it was padlocked but it took Billy only seconds to pick the lock with a fork he had fashioned for the purpose by snapping off all but one tine with a pair of wire cutters.

'Something a special forces guy taught me,' he announced proudly as we made our way inside the first time.

We climbed the iron stairs in the light of a match that he cupped in one hand as he led the way, his other hand gently holding mine as I followed just a step behind. We were careful at first and only went there at night, entering and leaving in the darkness. But we gradually grew more bold, intoxicated by the beauty of watching the sun set and rise from beneath the glass globe that was not large enough for us to straighten our legs completely, and so inspired us to invent new ways of holding each other.

'That's God, right there,' Billy would say as the sun appeared just above the water with a sudden burst of light.

'I'm not sure I believe in God,' I told him.

'I'm not talking about religion,' he said. 'Religion only divides people. I'm talking about the mystery. God is the mystery. We can't even look up at the sky and say how far it goes. How many galaxies? Maybe millions. And take a look at bees. Do you know anything about bees? Oh God, we've got to raise some bees together. This would be a perfect place for them to thrive! One queen bee can produce millions of bees who build the hive. And they live all winter off the wax they've created, beating their wings to create enough heat in the hive to keep from freezing to death. They're the most mysterious and incredible creation on earth. I find God in these mysteries. In what we can't possibly begin to comprehend.'

His enthusiasm was as meaningful and transporting to me as his physical touch. It was as if he were coming to life right in front of me. Maybe, I thought – maybe this is how he was before war changed him. Maybe this is who he is meant to be. Alive and excited with the possibilities of life.

He went on. 'God is what we don't know or can't comprehend. Like right now,' he said as he gently lay his palms on my breasts. 'What were the chances I would ever be in a lighthouse as close to you as this? And you feel the mystery, don't you, Rosie? Like an electric spark running through you. Running through both of us. That's the spark that keeps the world going. One couple after another, drawn together this way to feel that spark. Just like the drones are drawn to the queen bee. They fertilise her and the queen stores up over one hundred million sperm that she uses to fertilise her eggs and produce the hive. She can lay two hundred thousand eggs each year. It's all just incredible. Tomorrow we'll get started and you'll see. I've always wanted to raise bees.'

'So we're like the bees then?'

'No,' he said with a broad smile. 'It's just pure genetics with them. Each bee the queen produces is an exact replica.

A clone. So they are programmed. Not us. Because we have souls, Rosie. Our souls hunger for meaning. They long for meaning. Everyone's soul does. Think about it, these days you can buy whatever you *want* at the mall or online. You can even buy whatever you *need*. But not what *you long for*. That's a different kettle of fish.'

'How do we get what we long for then?'

He kissed me playfully on the tip of my nose. 'Ah, that's where the mystery comes in.' He nodded to the sun lowering itself in the last threads of pink light sewn just above the water. 'We don't want to know the answer or it would no longer be a mystery. And what is life without mystery? Look at the mystery that brought us together. It's all a mystery, Rosie. Atoms in our bodies trace to the remnants of exploded stars. That's something Donna once told me.'

If he hadn't kissed me then, I might have told him that it wasn't a mystery at all that had brought us together. I might have ruined his notion of God. But I found myself quite content to take into my heart every word he said, and to begin to see the world in a new way.

chapter thirty-nine

thief

Of course, it was only a matter of time before Johnny caught on. He had followed us and seen us disappearing into the lighthouse. And he confronted me and was not pleased when I explained that Billy had picked the lock.

'So, he's not only a drunk, he's an experienced thief as well,' he said with disdain.

I defended Billy by recounting that he had learned to pick padlocks in the army.

'I was in the army,' Johnny said adamantly. 'No one ever taught me how to pick a lock.'

'Well, that was some time ago,' I argued.

'Why are you defending him?' he asked impatiently before he said, 'I guess I already know the answer to that question.' Then he asked me what exactly I thought I was doing with myself. Those were his exact words – 'What do you think you're doing with yourself, Rosie?'

'I'm trying to live, Johnny,' I told him.

'We're all trying to live,' he said.

'No, no, we're not,' I argued. 'Some of us are holding on to things that no longer exist. That's not living. That's dreaming.'

What is life without a dream, he wanted to know. 'If you're not believing in some dream, what is there to believe in?'

'Well, you can start by believing in what's real. Your son is real. Billy is real.'

He bowed his head and I immediately felt that I had trespassed on to territory where I had not been invited and had no right to be. 'I liked him better when he was just a dream,' he said. 'When I didn't know if he was a son or a daughter. When I didn't know he was like me.'

I pushed the point. 'Why did you drink, Johnny?' I asked.

'Sorrow,' he answered. 'It helped me escape the sorrow that was crippling me.'

'It might be the same for Billy,' I told him. 'And why did you stop?'

'Because I thought it might make me worthy of having Elizabeth back.'

'Worthy in whose eyes? Martin's? His wife's?'

'Yes, at first. And then it was the idea that I was going to be a father. No father should be a drunk.'

'But all these years,' I said. 'Why didn't you just give up and start drinking again?'

'Because I wanted to live long enough.'

'For what?'

He turned away for a moment. 'You know what for,' he said.

'For the chance that they might find you here,' I said. 'And Billy has. Your son has found you here. It's a gift, Johnny. It's what you've waited for.'

'Be careful what you pray for, they say,' he said under his breath.

'You don't mean that,' I told him. 'He has something very special running through him. It's this fascination with the mysteries of life. His soul is alert, Johnny. The soul he inherited from you.'

'And from his mother,' he said. 'Mostly from his mother. I see a great deal of her in him when I look past the parts of myself. Parts that I don't want to see.'

'And your trees, Johnny. You had your trees to look after.'

'My trees,' he said with incredible sadness in his eyes. 'I wanted to grow something. Something beautiful. Something to make up for all I'd seen and done that was far from beautiful. And I wanted something to care for. Maybe the way people want to care for a dog. Or a cat. I don't know.'

'Yes, you do,' I told him. 'The way you and Elizabeth would have cared for your son. You would have nurtured him and watched over him and kept him safe. You would have been damned good at it too, Johnny.'

He looked into my eyes for a moment and then looked away. 'Maybe. Maybe not.'

'No,' I insisted. 'There is no *maybe*. It's a certainty. You and Elizabeth longed for that chance. It would have filled your souls.'

He looked up at me when I said this and I could tell by his acquiescent expression that he knew I was right.

'Well,' he said softly, 'life went on. It has a way of doing that. Look at you. After all that you lost, your life is going on in a whole new way now. I can see it in your eyes. You've found something with Billy. Something that's deep, and true. I'm happy for you, I really am. But I have to warn you that for him to drink the way he does there's something broken inside him. There's some part missing. And you shouldn't convince yourself that you can be the one to fix that. Remember what I told you – some things that are broken can't be fixed.'

'Some things,' I agreed. 'But not everything. He believes that one of life's mysteries has brought him here. He told me that. Why don't we just sit down with him and tell him that it wasn't a mystery at all? I saw the letter Martin had written to you when he sent the shares. I got on a plane and went to America and found him. And then he led me to Billy and I brought him here. There's no mystery there. It's a simple line of logic. Cause and effect.'

'Then what happens?' he asked.

'I don't know what you mean,' I told him.

'When he finds out that he's been fooled. Then what happens?'

chapter forty

bees

Together we built the boxes. Johnny, Billy and me. We built the little trays that slid into the boxes. It was all on YouTube. Actually, *together* is not the correct description. Right from the start in the wood shop, Johnny was out of sorts. First he insisted on measuring each piece of wood that Billy had already measured. 'Measure twice, cut once,' he said, sounding aggravated. 'Didn't anyone ever teach you that?' And then he refused to allow Billy to use any of the power tools and insisted upon making all the cuts himself. 'Whisky and table saws,' he complained. 'Can you not go anywhere without your damned bottle?'

Johnny seemed to think Billy was doing it just to annoy him. And he may have been right. Billy toasted Johnny before he took his next drink. 'Here's to you not screwing it up, Pops.'

'Don't call me that,' Johnny said as he turned on the saw's motor to drown out whatever Billy said next. I observed all this, wondering how they had managed to keep from killing each other for the months they'd been together.

We bought two queen bees in a shop in Dunfermline for a hundred pounds each, and placed one inside each box where they explored for a few minutes before flying off into the bright sky. We had chosen a hollow just off the fourteenth green to stand the boxes where the high dunes would protect them from the gales and Johnny fixed poles at all four corners of both boxes and drove the poles two feet into the ground to anchor them.

'They're off looking for some action,' Billy declared happily, shielding his eyes from the sun as he tried to follow the queens in flight. 'They'll be back in a few days with enough sperm in them to last for years and to produce enough females to build the colony. The females do all the work, Rosie. They build the hive. They manufacture the honey. They protect the queen. It's like a miniature Ford Motor Company in each box.'

'Why do you know so damned much about bees?' Johnny grumbled.

Before Billy could answer, I intervened and asked about the males. 'What do the males do?'

'They only make up about ten per cent of the population and they spend their whole lives eating honey and waiting for a virgin queen to appear somewhere. They mate with her, and then die. Sounds to me like a pretty good way to go, don't you think, Pops?' Billy quipped.

'Call me by my name,' Johnny insisted. 'That would be the mannerly thing to do.'

Billy held his ground. 'Did anyone ever tell you that you're not very good company sometimes, old man?'

Johnny glared at him. 'Who do you think you are, kid?'

'Who do I think I am?'

I could feel the molecules in the air heating up.

'You heard me,' Johnny went on. 'Who are you without your crutch?'

'What crutch?' Billy asked. And then he got it. 'You mean this?' he said, holding his flask up in the air. 'It's my Winston Churchill impression,' he joked.

Johnny was not amused. 'Don't give me that,' he said to Billy. 'Why don't you try being honest for a change?'

'All right,' Billy said. 'Let's make a deal. I'll be honest with you when you start being honest with me. Why don't we start by you telling me why it is your wife left you?'

At that, Johnny let the hammer he was holding drop to the ground. When he tried to speak, he couldn't. Then he took half a step towards Billy before his knees buckled and he fell to the grass. While I just stood there, frozen with fear and astonishment, Billy rushed into action. He lay his face close to Johnny's nose and mouth.

'He's breathing. But it's shallow. Call an ambulance, Rosie!'

'I don't have my phone,' I told him.

By then he was taking Johnny's pulse. 'It's faint. We need to get him to a hospital. Help me,' he said.

Together we got Johnny into a sitting position so that Billy could drape him across his shoulders. He stood up and began to carry him.

'You go out ahead and see if you can find one of the maintenance crew. Find someone with a car or a phone!' he yelled to me as I ran off towards the clubhouse. The whole time I was thinking that Johnny was going to die before I found anyone to help us. And that it would be my fault.

I was running, and looking back over my shoulder at Billy as he carried Johnny up and over the mounded ground like a wounded soldier. I kept hearing Johnny's words – *Some things that are broken can't be fixed.* And Billy telling me that God resided in the mystery, in the things we didn't understand. It crossed my mind that all of this was somehow meant to be. I mean, that I had managed to bring Billy here so that Johnny could meet his son before his life ended.

Off in the distance I saw the rubbish truck making its Friday morning rounds and I ran straight for it as fast as I could.

Johnny was breathing on his own but the crew who arrived with the ambulance believed he had gone into cardiac arrest and there was no time to waste. They had to get him to A & E in Kircaldy straight away. Billy insisted on riding in the back with him. He called to me as one of the attendants was closing the doors. 'Meet us there, Rosie!'

I noticed something then. There was something new in the way he said my name. It was more than familiarity. There was an intimacy now that I found deeply reassuring even in this moment of crisis. I stood there as the doors were closing and though I couldn't have known any more than any of us ever knows how our lives will unfold, I felt certain that we were meant to be together and that all our lives we had been moving closer and closer to each other. Pulled together by a force like an undertow in the sea that had its point of origin on a Christmas Eve in Paris, so long before.

This thought was with me as I drove to the hospital. I think most of the time it is our own fault when we lose people in this life, especially those people who matter so much to us that we want to believe we will not end up wishing we had loved them better when we had the chance. I was thinking that there ought to be a place, some far-off place, where we turn a corner and everyone we've ever lost in our life is waiting for us, and they will understand that we never meant to disappoint them, and if it is our fault that we lost them, they will find some way to forgive us.

* * *

Billy stood in the hallway of the intensive care ward. He informed me that Johnny was on a ventilator. The doctors were describing his condition as critical but stable. 'Whatever that means,' he said with exasperation.

'Well,' I said, 'I prayed all the way here, to whatever God there is, that he would be alive when I arrived.'

Before I finished, I remembered that this was the same hospital where my mother had given birth to me and then died. I was thirteen years old before my father told me any of the details about how she had haemorrhaged when delivering the placenta. My father was waiting in some corridor here like this one while the doctors were administering her a transfusion to try to save her life.

When I told this to Billy he took me in his arms. 'He might have been standing in this hallway,' I said.

He just kept holding me. I didn't want to move. But that was when I was certain that it was up to me now to tell him the truth. *No more lies*, I thought. *No more deception. No more waiting. All I have to do is tell him that the man lying in bed, behind the closed door that separates us, is his father.*

Suddenly Billy said with a deep shame in his voice, 'I shouldn't have been giving him such a hard time. I just got tired of him constantly pestering me about my drinking. I've been with him for months and I've never missed an hour of work. Why is my drinking any of his business? And it's not just that. It's something else.'

'What?' I asked.

He didn't answer right away. Then he told me. 'It bothers me that Martin set this whole thing up. He's always had to have his fingers in every pie. I get myself in some trouble and Martin bails me out by hitting on his old pal in Scotland to give me a job? What right does he have to do that? And what right does Johnny have to play a part in it? It's my life, isn't it? And I feel bad thinking about myself right now instead of the old man.'

'Pops,' I said. 'You've been calling him Pops.'

'Because he hates it. Anyway, maybe you should call Martin and tell him his friend might be dying.'

This sent a chill through me and I felt my body stiffen in his arms. He felt it too and asked me what was wrong.

Another lie, I thought. *Not a new lie. Just the same old lie.*

'Nothing,' I told him. 'Do you have Martin's number?'

'I don't,' he said. 'Last time I saw him, well, let's just say I never wanted to talk to him again. It didn't go well. Actually, it never did go very well between us. But if he and Johnny were friends—'

I stopped him and said I didn't think they were friends, only acquaintances from Martin's golf trips to Scotland.

'He's never really cared about anyone but himself anyway,' he said. 'Whatever they were to each other there must have been something in it for Martin or he never would have kept in touch with him. He used people. That's what he was best at. He used Johnny to get me here. The first time I ended up in jail he told me he was going to find some way to get me far enough away from him that I didn't embarrass him.'

'But we're together,' I said. 'So we owe him something, don't we?'

* * *

It was hours before we were allowed into the room to see him. I went in just behind Billy and watched as he walked purposefully to the bed, knelt down beside it and took hold of one of Johnny's hands in both of his own. 'You're a tough old fellow and you're going to pull through,' he said. His tone was reverential. I just stood in the threshold for a moment and I was so deeply touched that I couldn't have moved even if I'd wanted to. It was such a beautiful moment to observe. Beautiful and strange. There was a young man holding an old man's hand and not knowing that this old man was his father. There was a timeless quality to what I was witnessing. It was almost as if I were looking at a painting hung from the wall of some gallery or museum. Hung there for generations to gaze at, and to wonder about. I felt transported in those moments. It was as if I had no past now. As if I had just arrived from some other world, for one purpose and only one purpose. To bear witness to this. And then to wonder – *Why me?*

Why had I been so privileged to observe two people who belonged to each other and had never been permitted to be together, now still and at rest in one another's company as if it were the most natural thing in the world? What could be more ordinary than a son sitting by his father's hospital bed, holding his hand?

I don't know how much time passed before Billy rose to his feet. There was a chair in the room but both of us stood at the foot of the bed listening to the beeping and watching the digital lights on the monitors.

When a nurse came in, Billy asked her if he could spend the night. 'I'll sleep in the chair,' he said. 'I won't bother anyone.' She asked if he was family and before he could respond I answered for him and told her that he was.

* * *

The last light had fallen out of the sky when Billy asked me if I would make a run to a pub and fill his flask for him. 'That's all I'll need for the night,' he said. 'And if you can, would you get the photograph from his bedside table? The picture of his field?'

I returned with the photograph, the whisky and a couple of sandwiches as well. And I stayed there with him until I was sure that he had eaten.

chapter forty-one

seeds

When I was a little girl and I would ask my father about my mother he always told me that she was in heaven and that one day I would meet her there. He wasn't much of a talker really, but I can remember one evening over our tea that he had a far-off look in his eyes – and when I asked him if he was okay he said he had done a lot of thinking and he was sure that when we die, we go on and live again. He laughed at himself after he said this, dismissing it as foolish. But it had stayed with me and I took comfort in the memory after Liam was killed. And during the week when Johnny remained in the intensive care unit, barely seeming to make any progress at all. Billy and I visited him each day, and though we could never be sure he knew we were there with him, Billy insisted on talking to him, giving him a rundown of what he'd done each day at work, I think just to reassure Johnny that everything was in order so that he would not worry about his precious ground that meant so much to him, and so he could rest and recover his strength.

* * *

One night when I was visiting him alone, Johnny began speaking in French, his native language, as soon as I stopped talking to him. I had never heard him speak French before. He was speaking just above a whisper and, understanding no French at all, I quickly held my iPhone close to his lips to translate into English what he was saying. Soon it became apparent to me that he was telling his story. 'My name was Jean before it became Johnny. I grew up in a flat in the 18th arrondissement of Paris on Rue de l'Abreuvoir until soon after my father died and my mother fell in love with Jerry Hudson. We moved to La Seyne-sur-Mer, on the Riviera so Jerry could attend the Eglise episcopale libre there. When Jerry and my mother were killed in a boating accident I joined the Legion and proved myself to be a coward in the Zaire in the Battle of Kolwezi. I deserted and became a drunk on the streets of Paris, living most of the time under the Pont de l'Alma along the Seine. I was forty-one years old, panhandling near a theatre on Place du Châtelet one Christmas Eve. An hour later I stopped Elizabeth from stepping into the path of a speeding bus to end her life. We were taken by a private driver to her parents' seaside house in Honfleur. I stole a key to the house and moved in there during the winter when they were gone. I wrote letters – love letters to Elizabeth at an address that she had put on a piece of paper and slipped into my pocket. I got a job working for a printer in Le Havre. Elizabeth found me there after she ran away from her parents. But they found her and took her away and within a year her father, Martin, sent me a plane ticket to San Diego, although I thought it was Elizabeth who had sent it to me. He met me there and put me on a plane to Scotland. Elizabeth found me there. We were married and then I lost her. She went home to get her parents' blessing and I never saw her again.'

He was suddenly silent. If only Billy had been here, I immediately thought. Or if only I had recorded it on my phone, then Billy could have learned his story from his father, the one person in this world who was entitled to tell him. And then I wondered why he was telling his life story now. Did he believe that he was dying? Maybe we know when we are about to die. Maybe we know when it is our last chance to tell our story.

* * *

After the danger passed and Johnny regained enough strength to return to rest in his cottage, I began to spend days with Billy. Essentially I took Johnny's place and worked alongside him, mowing and raking and walking like farmers seeding the divots torn from the ground, with trowels we filled from canvas sacks strapped around our waists like aprons. The mixture of seed and fertiliser was Johnny's invention and it was remarkable to me that even at this time of year – late October – when the nights were quite cold, it was only a matter of days before new shoots of grass would appear in the torn earth and the ground would replenish and repair itself.

I was happy. Billy was happy. We prepared meals for Johnny. We cut peat for his fire that we burned against the nights' chill. We made love under the lighthouse globe. We tended Johnny's trees and took turns speculating which one would be chosen for the Christmas lighting in the town square this year. We held hands and walked along the shore. It was all very magical and yet *satisfying* is not precisely the right word to describe those days because there was sewn through them my continuing desire for Johnny to tell Billy the truth about who he was and what had happened. And yet I must admit that this part of Billy that was missing, this empty place, was where I gained entrance to him and so I was grateful for it. I still wonder how you can ever enter another person except at the place where they are broken. Don't you always remain an outsider to someone who is fully complete and has not been cut open or had something torn from them? No matter how well you come to know this person. No matter what you share. In the candlelight, in the glass globe of the lighthouse I would marvel at Billy's physical beauty and give thanks for the part of him that was broken and his own story that he didn't know, that had made him perfectly imperfect and that had left an empty space for me to fill with whatever I had to give him, and I gave him all I had in me to give. I gave him myself completely. Sometimes when we held each other after making love I would say to myself – *There, you have all of me now. There's nothing left of me.*

Of course I worried that it would not last. What ever lasts in this life?

I worried so much about how Billy would react to the truth that a part of me began to hope that Johnny would never tell him. Because I didn't want anything to change between us. It all felt so delicately balanced. Balanced on a razor's edge of a lie. I was afraid what the truth might mean to him.

Johnny and I talked about this one morning when I'd been so distracted by this fear that I went to his cottage to share my apprehension with him. He sat in the armchair with his face turned to the sunlight. The weeks indoors had robbed him of his normally ruddy complexion and this made him appear to have aged and weakened. But he assured me he was feeling fit again and would soon have his doctor's clearance to return to work.

'Well, that's wonderful news,' I told him.

'Yes,' he said eagerly, 'and I'm planning on taking up the golf course's offer of a chariot to get me about. A motorised buggy. And a sit-down, gas-powered mower for the greens and fairways.'

'So you're making some concessions,' I said, smiling with pleasure.

He told me that tests showed some damage to his heart and that he now realised he had no choice but to slow down a bit. 'It was a wake-up call,' he said. 'I suppose we all need those from time to time. I mean just to remind us how fragile our hold on this world really is. We're just barely holding on, Rosie.'

It was as if he had read my mind.

'Actually,' I said, 'that's what I came to talk to you about.

I feel the same way about Billy and me. You know how I feel about him?'

He nodded. 'I'm not blind,' he said. 'And I can see there is something about him that a young woman like yourself would love.'

'What exactly?' I asked, which seemed to catch him by surprise. 'No, really,' I said. 'I'm not sure what it is myself. I haven't asked myself that question. I wanted it to remain a mystery.'

'Well, then,' he said, 'maybe I shouldn't try to answer it either. He's obviously a beautiful boy – maybe we should just leave it at that.'

I nodded and thought for a moment. 'The thing is,' I went on, 'you see... I don't want to lose him. That's the only thing I'm certain of. After Liam died I didn't think I would ever be close to anyone the way I am to Billy. To your son.'

'To my son,' he repeated softly. 'It's still impossible for me to think of him that way.'

'How *do* you think of him then?' I asked.

'Like I said, as a beautiful boy with a good work ethic and a problem with the drink. He's trying to drown out some pain. And if you're planning on staying at his side for the long haul, this will be like an anchor tied around your ankles. You won't be able to bear it forever.'

'Nothing is forever, Johnny,' I said. And I reminded him that he had beaten his own problem with alcohol.

'I had a reason,' he said.

'Maybe Billy will have a reason someday,' I said.

He looked deeply into my eyes. 'Not even love?' he asked.

I didn't understand, I told him.

'Well, you said that nothing lasts forever. You don't believe love can last forever?'

'I would like to think so, but no, I don't think so,' I said. 'In fact, especially not love. It's too vulnerable. It's too fragile.'

'Tell me why you think that.'

I didn't have to search for my answer. 'My mother,' I said. 'Liam.'

'Ah,' he said. 'Of course. But you need to keep your faith. Believe in what you feel. Believe that your feelings will last. Never stop believing that.'

I asked him then if he had always believed he would meet his child someday. He said no.

'But Elizabeth?' I said.

He nodded his head in silence.

'You still do?'

He looked up at me. 'Maybe not today. Maybe not in this minute. But when I put my head down tonight I will believe it again.'

'How?' I asked.

'I don't know how,' he said to me. 'I only know why. But you didn't come here to talk about me and my ghosts. And I think I know what's troubling you. You're afraid if I tell Billy his story, if I tell him that I'm his father, he will change. He won't be the person you're so fond of.'

I admitted that he was right.

'Well,' he said, 'don't be afraid. I've already decided that I'm not going to tell him. I've decided that it would be selfish of me.'

I didn't understand at first. And then he explained that as grateful as he was that I had brought Billy here, and as much comfort as it might bring him to have a son now after all these years, he was not entitled to this.

'Billy is his own man now,' he said to me. 'He seems so much older than twenty-two. It's strange but in some ways he seems like he's already lived one life. And he doesn't need a father to suddenly appear from the shadows. What good would it do for him to know that he'd been lied to all his life? And what right do I have to inflict the sad story of his past on him? He's an innocent in all that happened to his mother and me. No, I could never do that to him, and I never will tell him,' he added sorrowfully. 'We'll just be two people who worked together in a beautiful and peaceful place. Two people who got on each other's nerves from time to time. But I'll always be grateful to you, for giving me the chance to meet him. And who knows, Rosie, maybe what makes some things so precious *is* that they never last.'

chapter forty-two

monument

To surprise Johnny, Billy made a lovely sign from a cedar board and painted in gleaming white letters:

J o h n n y C o o p e r ' s F i e l d

He attached the sign to a stake with bronze screws and drove it into the ground in front of the trees on top of the hill. When Johnny first saw it, Billy said to him, 'It's your monument, Pops.'

Johnny tried to make light of it. 'You mean you thought the old guy was going to kick the bucket so you'd be free to make a proper mess of things on your own? You can't get rid of me that easily.'

He walked to the sign, reaching for it and withdrawing his hand before he reached for it a second time and ran his fingers over the letters. When he turned back there were tears in his eyes. I thought to myself, *He's going to tell Billy. Despite his apprehensions he's going to tell him that he planted the original trees in this field for him and his mother.*

He thanked Billy. Then he said, 'More than twenty-two years now. That's how long it's been since I planted the first trees here.'

I remembered him giving me the count when we'd first spoken of how long it had been since Elizabeth was here with him.

'Why would you keep track of the days?' I heard Billy asking.

When I turned to look at Johnny he was staring straight into my eyes. Then he smiled. 'It's just a silly thing I've always done,' he said. 'Kind of like the way some people take comfort counting their money.' He paused for a moment before he finished by telling Billy exactly how many years, months and days it had been since he'd had his last drink.

There was a moment of silence before Billy said, 'I heard you were something of a legend around this place.'

'For the wrong reason,' Johnny said.

'It was because of the girl who left you, wasn't it?'

Johnny didn't answer right away. I felt the three of us were moving closer to a line we would cross and then never be able to go back again.

'No, actually,' Johnny said. 'It was for her that I stopped the drinking. It was just in my genes. I guess I inherited it from my father. It's not very interesting, I'm afraid.'

'No, tell me,' Billy insisted.

'I guess the drinking helped me cope with the fact that I never had any self-respect. The drinking numbed me. For a long time it worked and then it stopped working. It won't work forever for you either, Billy.'

'For me? What does this have to do with me?' Billy asked with a sharp blade in his voice.

'Nothing, I suppose. It's just that you remind me of myself a little.'

'My drinking?'

'Yes,' Johnny said.

And Billy must have seen what I saw. That Johnny was waiting for him to share his story with us, in those moments, right there on the hilltop.

Billy looked off into the distance, then at the ground before he said he didn't have a story. 'At least, not one that's worth telling,' he went on. 'I drink because it makes everything easier. When I drink, nothing is too hard. Too difficult. Like talking with you. Like getting through the next hour. The next day. To tell you the truth, when I don't drink I feel like I'm not real.'

'What does it mean to feel real?' Johnny asked gently.

Billy's voice softened and I could tell that he was comforted by Johnny's concern.

'I can't really describe it,' Billy said. 'Not feeling haunted, maybe.'

'Haunted,' Johnny repeated. 'What are you haunted by?'

Billy looked up into the sky as if he might find the answer there. But then he changed the subject. 'Do you know what we have to do with the rest of this day?' he exclaimed with excitement. 'We need to get out on the North Sea. It's a perfect day to sail. It could be the last perfect day.'

'I can't swim,' Johnny said, a lie to conceal his fear of being out on the water after what had happened to his mother and Jerry. Even the thought of it terrified him, but he didn't want to let Billy down.

'Trust me, Pops, you won't have to,' Billy assured him.

* * *

An hour later we were out on the water being blown gently across the bay on a southern breeze with Johnny at the helm, following Billy's instructions, steering us with the tiller in one hand and the main sheet in the other. He looked completely relaxed and his eyes were filled with wonder.

'I guess you can teach an old dog new tricks,' Billy joked.

Johnny was enthralled. He was like a kid with a new toy. When he saw a gust of wind moving towards us he pulled in the sheet to stiffen our sail so we could pick up speed.

'There you go!' Billy called to him.

'I never imagined it was this simple,' Johnny said. 'I mean just a sheet of canvas and a little wind and rope. It's so...'

When he paused, Billy finished for him. 'Elemental. You're undertaking an ancient art. One of the oldest in recorded time, Pops. You're now connected to the first seafarers from Crete who sailed around two thousand BC with a little wind and a sheet of canvas and some rope.' Billy moved to my side of the boat and put his arm around me. 'Have you ever been happier?' he called to Johnny.

'Maybe not,' Johnny called back.

'Well, think about it,' Billy pressed. 'When were you the happiest in your life?'

He didn't have to think about it. 'When I had Elizabeth here with me,' he said.

My eyes had been closed and I was drifting away with the rocking motion of the boat until I heard him speak her name. When I looked at him, he seemed to have left Billy and me behind and was in his own world.

'The day we were married,' he went on. 'She wanted to bake me an apple pie. I climbed up into the branches of a tree. She stood below me holding out her wedding dress for me to drop the apples into, one at a time.' He paused for a moment and gazed off into the distance. Then he said, 'I wonder if we're meant to lose the people we love best.'

Billy's voice startled me when he asked him why.

'So that we can measure how much they meant to us in the way we remember them,' Johnny said.

I felt Billy pulling me closer to him. He held me that way for a long time. I suppose he believed that I must have been thinking of the way I had lost Liam. But I was thinking only about how he had lost the two people who would have poured their love for each other into him.

chapter forty-three

button

Billy and I were holding each other in the glass globe of the lighthouse when he said he wondered what Johnny's girl had been like.

'What have you heard?' I asked him.

'Well, I didn't want to hurt Pops' feelings in the boat when he was telling us how he climbed the tree and dropped the apples into her wedding dress, but I'd heard that a few times before.'

'Everyone knows his story,' I reminded Billy.

'Is that true?' he said. 'I mean, do you think anyone can ever really know another person's story?'

'I'm not sure,' I said.

'People think they know,' he went on. 'I heard she was crazy. She tried to step in front of a bus and kill herself, someone told me. She was living in Paris and Johnny was waiting for a bus or something and he stopped her. She had a rich father, I guess, who she was running away from? Maybe that's why she wanted to kill herself. Anyway, she and Johnny ran away together to this place. I suppose they thought the father would never find them here. But he did. And he took her away. Is that what you've heard?'

'Yes, essentially.'

'What else have you heard?' he asked.

'They were married here by a young priest from St Andrews. But the father hired a lawyer and had the marriage annulled. He took her away.'

'Back to France?'

'No. By then the girl's parents had moved to America.'

'So, did Johnny grow up in France then?'

'That's what I've heard, but he's never spoken to me about it.'

'And he never went looking for her?'

'I don't think so.'

'Why not?' Billy said impatiently, and I felt his body tense before he sat up. 'I should climb down the stairs right now and go and confront him. If he loved her so damned much why didn't he try to get her back? There's no excuse to just give up and then spend the rest of your life regretting.'

'Waiting,' I said, as I recalled what Johnny had told me. 'He was waiting for her to *come back to him*. That would have been the proof, you see?'

'Proof of what?'

'Proof that she loved him as deeply as he loved her. Proof that she found him worthy.'

'Worthy,' he said. 'Are any of us worthy of being loved?'

I sat up then and took him in my arms. 'I'm not sure, Billy,' I said.

For a while neither of us said anything. Of course I wanted to know if Billy thought I was worthy of his love. I certainly hoped he did.

Finally he said, 'What about their baby? The crib he kept in the cottage? There was a baby, someone told me.'

I told him that this baby was all part of the story everyone knew but I couldn't be sure of the details. I was very young back then.

'There must be someone in this town who knows for certain,' he said. I thought he was going to say more about this but instead he took a deep breath as if to clear it all from his mind and then said, 'People come together through a series of incidents and events that are completely unrelated except by chance. Think of it, Rosie. What put Johnny on that sidewalk in Paris at the same moment his girl was there, preparing to step in front of a bus and kill herself? Imagine all the small and unremarkable things that had to happen in order for that to happen. I mean at that exact moment. You can imagine it, right? Let's think of ten things together right now. Ten things that happened in just the hour before their lives coincided on that sidewalk. I'll start. So, the hour before Johnny meets Elizabeth on that sidewalk he is shaving. It is a ritual that normally takes him ten minutes at most. But he cuts himself just above the left side of his lip and he has to hold a cold, wet washcloth on the cut for three minutes before the bleeding stops. Okay, your turn.'

'All right,' I said. 'Elizabeth is painting her nails. She only has one nail left to paint when she accidentally tips over the bottle of polish and it takes her five minutes to clean up the mess.'

'That's one. Let's keep going,' Billy said. 'Johnny climbs down the stairs of his apartment. Normally that late in the afternoon the foyer at the bottom of the stairs is empty, but today a fellow named Owen Fitzgerald has left work early and hurried home to check on his wife who is very sick. They speak for two minutes about his wife's condition. Your turn.'

'Elizabeth stops at a dressmaker's shop to pay her for the dress she has had made. But there is a note on the door that the shopkeeper had to run an errand and will be back in ten minutes. She waits at the door until she returns.'

'Right then, here's the third one,' Billy said. 'Johnny never reads the newspaper but this afternoon he sees something on the front page of a newspaper stand. It is a photograph of a soldier whose face looks familiar to him. He lingers there, staring at the face for thirty seconds before he continues.'

I picked up the story from there. 'So, Elizabeth comes upon three little girls playing hopscotch. It was something that had fascinated her when she was that age and so she stops and spends two minutes watching them jump and skip. She turns to walk away but then stops when she notices that one of the girls has the bluest eyes she's ever seen. She stares into the girl's blue eyes for another fifteen seconds.'

'Good. That's good, Rosie. Meanwhile Johnny stops in front of one of the big department stores where there is a Christmas display of a train going around and around a track, passing through the miniature village. He's dreamed of having a family someday and setting up a train set like this one under the Christmas tree. He stands there for six minutes and can barely tear himself away from the window.'

'It is getting cold and when Elizabeth stops to button her coat the top button comes off and falls into the snow at her feet,' I said. 'She kneels down and searches for it for four minutes but she never finds it.'

'And then Johnny is passing a barbershop when he stops for just ten seconds to watch the barber giving a haircut to a man who is completely bald. He marvels at this before he walks on.'

'Elizabeth approaches a church where she watches six men carrying a coffin up the granite stairs. One of the men slips on one of the steps and drops to his knees and the coffin tips to the side and it almost falls over. That takes another five minutes.'

'Okay, meanwhile Johnny stops at a liquor store and goes inside and buys a pint bottle of whisky. He pays for it and the man at the counter opens his cash drawer and discovers that he doesn't have the correct change, so he goes into the back room for more money. While he is gone Johnny opens his bottle and takes a long swallow. Another six minutes pass before he leaves the store.'

'How many more do we need?' I asked.

'Four more, I think. But maybe it doesn't matter.'

'Yes, it does,' I insisted, because I had begun to see the point Billy was trying to convince me of. 'Elizabeth loves chocolate,' I went on. 'So she stops at a sweet shop and one heart-shaped chocolate catches her eye. Outside the shop she pauses and eats the whole heart before she walks on. That takes another three minutes.'

'Without all that happening, Johnny would have been at the sidewalk by now. But he loses a bit more time when a couple who are new immigrants in France ask him with a kind of sign language for directions to a shelter where homeless people might spend the night. This takes nearly fifteen minutes before they go on their way.'

'She has a letter in her pocket to send to her mother and father. A goodbye letter. She stops at a post box. The mouth of the box is so stuffed with letters – Christmas cards, I suppose, given the season – that she has to push them down inside to make room for her own letter.'

'How far is she from the sidewalk now?' Billy asked me.

'Just a few blocks.'

'Same with Johnny. He is walking straight for it when he is delayed ten more seconds by a pigeon that lands just at his feet. He stops and waits for the bird to walk out of his path.'

'By now he has spotted Elizabeth in a long pale blue cashmere coat,' I said.

'What is she doing?'

'She's just walking towards the edge of the pavement.'

'All right. When she stops, Johnny walks to the sidewalk and stands about four feet from her. I think we've done enough, Rosie.'

'What does all this mean?' I asked him.

'It means if we take away any one of these small and completely insignificant and unrelated incidents out of the timeline, Johnny would not have been there to save her as she began to step in front of the speeding bus. If her button hadn't fallen off, just think.'

'Yes,' I said. 'But what does it mean?'

'It could mean that in all the years of my life and yours a thousand small incidents happened that brought you to see me in jail. Maybe ten thousand. We'll never know. Maybe there were a dozen incidents that happened that caused Johnny to lose his girl and their baby. Take away just one of them, and they would have had a life together.'

A storm had moved up into the bay with dark clouds sailing above us and rain that sounded like small pebbles being poured from a jar against the glass of the lighthouse.

Billy touched my face and turned me so that we were looking into each other's eyes. 'Even if nothing lasts,' he said solemnly. 'Even if you and I don't stand a chance. I want to remember us just as we are now. May I make love to you, Rosie?'

He had never asked me this before. I felt desperate, thinking how long it would take for us to remove enough of our clothes. 'Yes,' I said. 'But hurry, please.'

chapter forty-four

elizabeth

By now it was early November and though Johnny always waited for the first full moon of December to choose which of his trees would be in the town centre for Christmas, on a brilliantly clear evening when the moon lay a perfect path of light across the harbour, and up the side of the hill, he and Billy and I followed the light to the stand of trees, and to one tree in particular that stood directly in its path. 'The moon's position will change slightly by the time it's full again next month, but it looks like that's our tree this year,' Johnny said. 'I'll let you do the honours of cutting it down when the time comes,' he said to Billy.

At that Billy sat down beneath the trees, which surprised both Johnny and me. 'I want to know who she was,' he said. 'This girl. This Elizabeth who you planted the first trees for. Sit,' he said to both of us, and though it seemed quite unreal to me, a moment later we were all sitting together in the path of moonlight as white as paper while Johnny seemed to be weighing in his mind whether or not to grant Billy's request. After he was silent for a few moments, Billy said, 'When was the last time you had a chance to talk to anyone about her?'

'I can't remember,' Johnny said with a great sorrow in his voice.

'I think we have a duty of care to talk about the people we have lost,' I said. 'I've told Billy and you everything I ever knew about Liam. That's how we keep alive these people we've cared about and lost.'

After I said this, Johnny began with these words: 'I couldn't have cared more.'

Billy and I both waited. A gust of wind caught itself in the branches of the trees above us. 'Why did she want to kill herself?' Billy asked.

Johnny turned and looked at him. 'That was at the beginning,' he said. 'The very beginning. All I knew then was that she was confused. Anyone who tries to end her life before it's even begun has to be confused. She didn't think she had any value. She had given up on herself.'

'Why?' Billy asked.

'Because she had never been able to measure up in her father's eyes. I believe that was the reason. He drove a hard bargain. He was one of those men who walks through the rain without getting wet. He didn't tolerate anything but perfection.'

'Did you know the man?' Billy wanted to know.

Johnny looked at me, perhaps trying to recall the details of the lie I had told Billy.

'No,' Johnny lied. 'But whoever he was, he was a blind man. Blind to his daughter's perfection. She never asked for anything for herself. She cared about the world and everyone in it. I remember her telling me that everyone was fighting one kind of battle or another and that they all deserved to be treated with respect and compassion.'

'But why did you let her go?' Billy pressed him.

'Her father took her from me.'

'After she was your wife?'

'That didn't matter to him. He saw me the same way he saw his daughter. I was just another person who didn't measure up to his expectations. It isn't any more complicated than that.'

'But you'd saved his daughter's life?'

'He did thank me for that.'

'Well, I'd say he had a pretty screwed-up way of thanking you. He took the person you loved from you.'

Johnny was quiet for a moment. Then he said he didn't think they should speak any more about Elizabeth's father. 'But I want you to know that I've always believed if I had never taken my first drink when I was sixteen years old… if I'd made something of myself, I would not have lost her.'

'But you stopped drinking. For her.'

'I did. But it was too late, Billy. I had already lost her.'

'People don't just vanish in this world,' Billy argued. 'She's out there somewhere, and for all you know she's kept on loving you just as you have kept on loving her.'

Johnny placed his hand on Billy's shoulder affectionately and thanked him for saying this. 'That means a great deal to me,' he said. 'And I'm going to remember you saying that. She was the most splendid person I've ever known. I wish, more than anything, that you two had known each other. I believe you would have been close friends. Very close. And there's something else I need to say to you.'

I wondered then if Johnny was just going to come out and tell him.

'I've always tried to live in a way that she would be proud of. I want her to be proud of me. And if she were here now she would want me to ask you something. Something I have no right to ask you for. Will you do something for me? As I said, I have no right to ask, but still.'

'Just ask,' Billy said.

'Do you have debts back in America from gambling?'

'A few.'

'How much do you owe people there?'

'Around thirty thousand dollars.'

'All right. I'd like to pay off those debts of yours.'

'Why?'

'I already told you why. I think it's something that Elizabeth would be proud of me for doing. But first you have to do something for me.'

'What's that?'

'You have to let me take you to get some help.'

'Help with what, Pops?'

'I'd like to help you with your drinking so that you don't end up losing the people who matter the most to you, the way I have.'

chapter forty-five

serenity

I had not seen Billy or Johnny for several days as I had taken to my bed with a terrible cold that had me waking up coughing through the night. It was quite late when Billy came to see me. He was very agitated and paced back and forth across the floor of my bedroom, raking his fingers through his hair with one hand, and not even saying hello to me before he started describing the AA meeting he had just attended in the local community centre. 'We're all sitting there in a circle in these little wooden chairs and each person, one after the other, is telling these terrible stories about their problem with booze, beginning with the same confession – "I'm an alcoholic". It was horrible. One after another. Pouring their souls out to each other. I'd seen some of these people around the village but I didn't know any of them by name. All I wanted to do was run from there as fast and as far as I could. But Johnny was sitting beside me and I didn't want to embarrass him. And, I mean how crazy is that? I'm there because he's brought me because he feels it's what this girl he hasn't seen or heard from in over two decades is supposed to be proud of him for doing? Where did he get such a crazy idea, I'd like to know? When it was my turn, I didn't say a word.'

I let him calm down. He finally slumped in a chair. I

watched him drink from his flask and then I asked him what Johnny had said at the meeting.

'It was sad,' he said softly. '"I'm an alcoholic and it made me unworthy of the girl I loved." How does someone live in the past that way? I mean, without going mad. Completely mad.' He stopped and thought for a moment, then asked me if I thought he was mad. 'I'm beginning to wonder if maybe he's made up the whole thing. Do you think there ever was this Elizabeth? Do you think he really stopped her from killing herself? Everybody in this place knows his story, but where did the story originate? Did anyone ever try to find out if it was real?'

'The trees,' I said. 'The way he planted and cares for the trees.'

'Anyone can plant a bunch of trees,' he said dismissively.

'You think he's a liar then?' I asked.

He looked at me for a long time before he bowed his head and said no. He went on speaking barely above a whisper. 'There was so much remorse in his voice when he spoke at the meeting. And pain. I saw the pain in his eyes.'

'What did you feel when you listened to him, Billy?'

He shook his head and I thought he might not answer. 'I'm not sure what I felt. I was so uncomfortable there. I was mainly thinking about myself. But there was a moment when I did see his pain. And it was real.'

Then I asked him if I could go with him to the next meeting.

'The next meeting?'

'Yes.'

'You think I can ever go back there?'

I told him I did. 'I know you can,' I said.

He took a piece of paper from his pocket, unfolded it and read to me. *'God grant me the serenity to accept the things I cannot change. The courage to change the things I can. And the wisdom to know the difference.'*

He folded the paper, put it back in his pocket and said he didn't want to change anything about himself and that he felt lucky just to be alive. 'What have I got to complain about, Rosie? Look at me. I'm living in a beautiful and peaceful place. I've got you to hold on to.'

'Well,' I said, 'if you won't go back for yourself, maybe you'll go back for Johnny. And for me.'

He looked up at the ceiling and told me he hadn't gone through a single day since the war without having a drink. 'I don't know what it would be like,' he said. 'And I don't think I want to know.'

This was one of just many moments when I looked at Billy and it hurt. It just hurt. Maybe it hurt because I was sorry that I loved him.

* * *

For three nights straight after that I was tormented by the same nightmare that left my hands shaking and something cold and damp blowing through my ribs when I finally awoke. In the nightmare Elizabeth didn't lose the button from her coat. It didn't fall to the ground. And so she reached the kerb ahead of Johnny with just enough time to spare to step in front of an earlier bus that ran her over and crushed her. My hands were still shaking when I put the kettle on and made tea.

In my mind I became certain that Johnny had lied about his story and that the lie had spread through the village for more than twenty years. On one of those mornings I was determined to return to America and confront Martin. I went online to find out when the next flight from Edinburgh was scheduled. I began to pack my bag for the trip so that I could learn the truth and tell Billy so that he wouldn't have to go through the rest of his life with scraps of a lie settling into the empty parts of him, the parts that had been hollowed out by whatever had been torn from him by the war.

But I didn't leave. I couldn't make myself leave. I guess I stayed for both of them. For Billy and for Johnny. Or maybe I stayed just for myself. Or maybe I stayed because

I didn't want Johnny's story to turn out to be untrue in any aspect. I wanted each part of it to be exactly as I had heard it all through the years, exactly as I had told the travelling salesman and the anaesthetist on the plane that fell and rose and fell and rose again in the night sky. Exactly as I had always believed it. How do we ever know what's true anyway, I kept asking myself as the November days shortened and the nights grew colder and people in the village began to wait for another Christmas.

chapter forty-six

soldier

I think of it as something of a small miracle that Billy began attending the AA meetings again with Johnny each Thursday evening. At one of those meetings Billy introduced himself and told the strangers in the room that he was an alcoholic but that he didn't intend to stop drinking because the drinking gave him a way to hide from himself and to get through each day. 'I'm not like the rest of you,' he said to the others. 'I plan to keep drinking until the end of my life. I plan to keep it under control so that I can function and so I'm no different from the thousands of businessmen who wear suits made of steel and pass around the world's money between themselves all day long and return home and throw down three double bourbons so they can face their wives. Or from the women who have to have two Martinis in order to get into bed with their husbands. Or maybe I am different from those men and women. Because I am going to be honest about my drinking. I'm going to admit that I need it. And if anyone ever wants to know the truth about me I'll tell them the truth. I'll tell them that I'm an alcoholic. And if it ends up killing me, well, we all have to die from something. We all have to let go someday.'

I had never known Billy sober, but to be honest I loved him the way he was. If it was the whisky that made him smile at me then I was grateful for his whisky. And if it was the whisky that made him speak so sweetly to me, then I was grateful for the whisky. And if it was the whisky that kept Billy working at Johnny's side, then I was grateful for the whisky. And most of all, I was grateful for the whisky because it kept Billy from leaving me. In fact I was afraid if he stopped his drinking that he would be just another soldier too crippled by his wounds to ever touch anyone or to be touched by anyone. I was right about his drinking from the start. His drinking was an act of benevolence. He drank in order to dull his pain just enough so he could touch people the way he touched me. The way he had made me feel calm and at peace. He had that gift. And for this, I was exceedingly grateful. More grateful than I could ever explain to anyone. Even Johnny. Though I tried. 'Aren't there much worse things?' I said to him. 'Much worse things than needing to drink to get through each day?'

chapter forty-seven

choice

I ended up going to spend a few days with my father in his flat in Guardbridge. He had called to tell me that he wanted to speak with me about something. I felt that I needed some space from everything in Elie and so his invitation could not have come at a more appropriate time.

He greeted me in the front garden. It had only been perhaps two months since I'd last seen him and though I knew his health was failing from a series of mini-strokes, one which had left him blind in his right eye, I was not prepared for how thin he looked. When I hugged him I could feel his ribs through his jumper. And his shoulders were oddly pitched forward now. He looked far older than his sixty-five years.

I helped him in the garden and we went on walks about half the distance we would have done before. We repotted his houseplants and put a fresh coat of paint on the dark green trim around the front windows. I cooked him big meals with lots of potatoes and pasta. 'I need to fatten you up,' I kept telling him, though he only ate a small portion of what I put on his plate.

We ended up doing all of our important talking with him sitting on the end of the bed I had slept in as a little girl, exactly as he had when I was his little girl. I told him about Johnny and Billy, except the part about my feelings for Billy. I didn't need to tell him that; he had me figured out. 'I knew as soon as I saw you that you had met someone,' he told me the second night of my visit. 'I could see the glow around you. I'm so happy for you, Rosie.'

In truth I felt a little ashamed for him to think that I had managed to replace Liam so quickly when he had gone his whole life without remarrying after my mother died and left him with me as a newborn baby to look after. When I told him this he said it was completely different.

'You see, with each passing month as you grew older, you were more and more like your mum, and so it got to the point where I felt as if she had been reinstated in my life. As if I'd never lost her. Plus, I was very shy around women. I was always just following your mother's lead,' he said. And when he said this, he bowed his head. 'You might be right about Johnny Cooper's story,' he added. 'What people know of another person's story is often incomplete.'

I could tell there was more on his mind. Something more he wanted to tell me. 'What is it?' I asked.

'It's something I never told you. But I think I have to tell you now.'

When I saw how anxious he was, I sat up in bed and took hold of his hand.

'No, no,' he said stalwartly. 'It's nothing terrible. I'm fine. And if I were to die tonight, well, you know how I've always known that I would see your mother again in heaven. If they let me in,' he said, laughing in his self-deprecating manner.

'What is it you want me to know, Dad?' I asked, still holding his hand.

'I want you to know that your mother had a choice. She was in her fourth month when her kidneys began to fail. She had the option of an abortion and at first Tess agreed. But then she couldn't do it. She told me that what she worried about most was that because she had chosen her baby over me, over the love story we shared, she was afraid that I might not be able to be a good father to you. That I might resent you.'

I wasn't completely shocked by this news. I think deep down I had always suspected it. My first reaction was to reassure him. 'You never made me feel that way,' I told him.

'No, I couldn't possibly resent you. I only wanted to become the kind of father she would be proud of. Just like you told me about Johnny Cooper living all these years. Trying to put together a life his girl would be proud of. But you, are you all right, Rosie? I mean, do you think I was wrong to keep this from you all this time?'

'Honestly, Dad, I don't know how I feel. I don't know if it changes things.'

'No,' he said. 'It only shows you how much your mother wanted you to live. And to be happy. That's all that it means. That's all that matters. You know this now. Believe it. You must never stop believing it.'

* * *

In the morning when I first opened my eyes, the world felt different to me. Or at least my place in the world felt different. It did make me feel guilty that my mother had chosen me, her baby, over the life she would have had with my father. Who knows how much happiness she denied them both by her decision? Who could ever even guess at that? She was so young. She could have saved her life and perhaps gone on to have more babies with him.

I started to wonder then what I would have done. What choice I would have made. And about the hundred things, or thousand things, that had happened to her from the time she was a little girl that led her to make the decision she had made. Maybe the fact that she was only nineteen years old made her believe that she would not die and that the doctor was wrong. No one that young believes they could possibly die, or ever grow old. *I have to find a way to live with this new part of my story,* I told myself. *I have to make peace with it.*

But, beyond the guilt I felt, what struck me most deeply was that now I had some new common ground with Billy. Each of us had lived all our lives not knowing that a part of our story was missing. It was something I believed would draw us even closer.

* * *

It was my last night with my father when he and I talked about this. 'Most people have no choice at all how their lives end,' he said. 'How or when. And how many people are there like your mum and Liam who risk their lives for someone else? And this Billy, who you are so fond of. He risked his life as well as a soldier.'

I told him that Billy talked of the war as a waste. And that I had tried to make him see that he had done an honourable thing. 'I told him that the soldiers who went to Afghanistan gave the young girls there a chance to live. A whole generation of young girls got to learn to read and go to school. Liam and Billy made that possible.'

'Make him see this,' my father said. 'Don't stop trying to make him see this.'

I told him that I would try. And then I told him what Johnny had decided – that he had no right to tell Billy he was his father. 'Because he's never really *been* his father,' I said.

'But he's looking after him now,' he said. 'He's taking him to AA meetings. He's taught him how to tend the ground. They've worked side by side. That's more than many fathers ever do. He's the missing piece, Rosie.'

He paused then. In the silence I heard the train rush through the station close by. Often this was the last sound I heard at night before I fell asleep, and I loved imagining the passengers on board and where they were going, and the people who were waiting to welcome them.

'I think Johnny should do whatever he believes Elizabeth would want him to do,' my father said. 'That should be the only thing that matters. He'll have to decide what she would want her son to know. Just as I had to decide.' I hugged him goodbye and just as I turned away to walk to my car he said, 'No matter what happens, you found Johnny's son for him. That's something your mother would have done.'

chapter forty-eight

winter

With the cold weather setting in we covered the bee boxes with black roofing felt that would block out the freezing winds and absorb the sun's warmth for the hives. The morning we chose to do this, the wind was howling from the east and the task seemed to take hours. We'd get everything in place and then before we could strap it securely and properly, another gust of wind would tear it off. I suggested we give up and wait for a calmer day but Billy seemed to be enjoying the challenge. 'The old sailors always said if you wait to reef your sail in a storm, you've waited too long!' Billy hollered to me rather triumphantly.

Eventually we prevailed and huddled down in the dunes below the gale. The one thing I noticed about Billy's drinking was that he often repeated himself. While we worked he told me the same story again about how the bees all cluster together and the worker bees vibrate their bodies to create enough heat to keep the queen warm.

'Yes, you told me that before,' I reminded him.

He seemed completely surprised. 'I did?'

'Yes, you did.'

'Funny, I don't remember telling you. Did I tell you that they work in groups? One group vibrates and creates the heat while another group rests before they switch places. To keep their strength up and the heat at a constant temperature?'

'Yes,' I told him again. This time there must have been an impatience in my voice because he turned on me.

'You think it's my drinking, don't you?'

At first I denied it. But then I said, 'I've wondered if you would want to be with me if you didn't drink. I admit it.'

'What?' he said with great incredulity. 'You can't mean that, Rosie. Being with you, making love to you is the greatest gift anyone has ever given me. It's something I will always remember. It's one of the last things I'll be thinking about at the end of my life. I'm sure of it. And it doesn't have anything to do with my drinking. You have to trust me, Rosie.'

I tried to put an end to this by telling him that I did trust him and that I would trust anyone who cared about bees the way he did.

But he pushed on and told me that he hadn't missed a single AA meeting. He'd taken on the task of making the coffee at each session. And he'd got to know some of the people and found them to be genuine and decent people who seemed to care about him. 'There's a community there,' he said. 'I suppose it's an openness that I've missed since the war. I mean, in combat you form these close relationships. You miss that. I've missed it, but I didn't realise until I'd been to a few meetings.'

I told him that I was glad to hear this. He smiled at me and took his flask from the pocket of his waxed jacket.

'Here,' he said, handing me the flask. I tried to decline, but he insisted. So I took a sip and was surprised to find that it was filled with cranberry juice.

'Cranberry juice,' I said.

'And a splash of tonic water,' he said. 'I'm growing fond of it. I don't think it will kill me, do you?'

'Hardly.'

'It's got to be the most expensive cranberry juice and tonic water anyone ever paid for. Johnny gave me a cheque for thirty-seven thousand five hundred and eighty dollars to pay off my gambling debts. I mailed it to the fellow who runs the jail that had become something of a boarding house for me. He's a very decent guy. I trust him. But tell me, how do you think Johnny came upon that much money he could afford to just send away?'

I lied again. 'A lot of years of pay cheques, and nothing he needed to spend them on?'

'Well, I plan to find some way to pay him back someday,' Billy said. 'I'm giving him a portion of my weekly wages and in about a hundred years we'll be even. I'll find some better way. One of the guys on the maintenance crew told me you can work as a caddie in St Andrews in the summer and earn two hundred pounds a day. Two hundred pounds sterling is about two hundred and eighty US dollars. Divided into thirty-seven thousand five hundred and eighty dollars is only one hundred and thirty-four days' work as a caddie. The season is a hundred and eighty days long.'

I didn't want to discourage him though I wondered how he would manage to walk so many miles each day on his wounded foot.

'So, you're serious about this,' I said.

'I am. I'll want to find myself a place of my own, but even after paying rent, in two seasons I should have enough to pay Johnny back every dollar.'

I tried to conceal just how relieved I was. And then I gave up that concealment and suggested that he could live with me in my cottage. He looked at me and thanked me gratefully.

'I wouldn't want to inflict that on you,' he said. 'You'd evict me after a month. Remember, I have it in my history. I ended up with Martin and Donna because my mother and father couldn't stand me.'

'You don't know that,' I said. 'They might have had problems of their own.'

'Possibly,' he said. 'But what kind of problems would be made worse by having a baby?'

I could have let it go then, but I wanted to undermine his verdict that he had been responsible. 'It could have been simply money. The father might have lost his job, for example. You just don't know and—'

'What's your point, Rosie?' he asked, cutting me off. And then he laughed at himself and told me that after he was adopted he'd spent hours and hours looking at people and wondering if they were his parents. 'Wherever we went I was always on the lookout,' he said.

chapter forty-nine

sorrow

We were spending most of our nights together by then and I enjoyed packing his tuna and sweetcorn sandwiches in the morning and filling his flask with the precise measure of cranberry juice and tonic water he taught me to mix. Often after seeing Billy off at the front door, I would hurry up the stairs to my bedroom, to the window beneath the gable where I could watch him make his way along High Street toward the golf course where I knew Johnny was waiting for him. I would stand at the window for at least five minutes watching until Billy turned on to Ferry Road and out of my sight. A deep and perplexing sorrow always seemed to be waiting for me at the window on those mornings. At this distance Billy's small struggle with each step of his wounded foot was apparent and he looked like the most lonely and vulnerable person in the world. I always fought against the desire to run after him and walk hand in hand beside him to banish the vision that would overtake me, the vision of him as an old man, alone with no one to look after him. That was just one part of the sorrow I dealt with that seemed to have several dimensions to it. There was also the sorrow I felt now that I knew I was responsible for my mother's death and that I had not accomplished anything in the life she gave me other than a degree in hospitality from the university in Dundee. I had chosen hospitality without any real passion for the field and only because in Scotland where tourism was a key industry, such a degree came with the assurance of always finding work. But from the moment I fell in love with Liam, I envisioned a completely different life as a wife and mother. A life that would consume my empty hours and give me the satisfaction of being of use. Of having a purpose.

I was aware, of course, that on those mornings I was feeling sorry for myself to a degree that I would have found entirely unacceptable in the life I had before I lost Liam. The only way I can even come close to describing the paralysis that would overcome me on those mornings was that the strongest impulse in me was to disappear from the world. It took all my strength to fight against this impulse. Some mornings while I watched Billy walking up the street I was already composing the note I would leave on the table for him, telling him goodbye and wishing him well and thanking him for everything we had shared. I knew where I would go, and this only made the impulse more difficult to resist. I would go up into the Highlands, to Uist in the Outer Hebrides. I knew the islands and their locations on the map. Berneray. Baleshare. North Uist. Grimsay. Benbecula, South Uist and Eriskay. There were also the Isles of Lewis and Harris, Barra and Vatersay not far away. I had only seen photographs of these weather-beaten places, and I'd never met anyone who had spent time there except on summer holiday, but those far-off outposts represented to me the fulfilment of my desire to disappear. And to be of use. In college I had met an enterprising girl from Glasgow called Emily Hutchinson who was determined to revive the wool industry that had vanished over the past ten years, once the merino wool from Australia and New Zealand that was so much easier to care for had completely taken over the market. Sheep farmers in the Hebrides had to pay more to shear their sheep than they could sell the wool for. The wool was completely worthless.

Soon before I met Liam, Emily had asked me to join her in a plan she had to change this by processing it for insulation in the walls of houses. It was perfect for that purpose, blocking the wind as wool does so naturally, and the moisture content in each fibre making it fire-resistant as well. Emily had done her research and she was certain that the two of us were going to put the sheep farmers back in business. It seemed like a heroic enterprise to me and if I had not met Liam, I would have set out on that path with her.

One morning, after heading back downstairs, I actually considered contacting the university to see if I could track her down. But then I let go of that notion and wondered how and why I had lost the resolve and the determination that led me to climb on board the plane to America to find Martin. I had thought of myself as the person who could join the broken ends of Johnny's story together. Why did I no longer feel that way? All the years I had heard Johnny's story, and even as I flew across the Atlantic and then across America to California, I hadn't even known if Johnny's child was a son or a daughter. So was it Billy who had changed me? Had I lost my resolve because of my affection for him? Because I didn't want to tip his world onto its side by telling him that Johnny was his father? Or was it simply because it was out of my hands now? It was in Johnny's hands. And his hands alone. And if that was the case, then it was my helplessness that had changed me and made me feel so unspeakably sad. When you are doing something you are at least doing something. But when you are doing nothing you can be preyed upon by any number of demons. And there are too many hours, far too many hours to just sit and wonder what is going to happen next, and how things will turn out in the end.

I began taking long solitary walks as November came to its end, purposefully avoiding the ground where I knew I would see Johnny and Billy in the distance, carrying on as if they were not even part of the story that was churning away inside me and that had changed me so profoundly.

chapter fifty

meeting

We had our full moon hanging in a clear sky on the night of December 7. Billy told me the next morning over breakfast that he would cut down the tree that afternoon. 'You haven't been yourself lately,' he said with concern. 'Is it Liam?'

'No,' I said. 'Maybe it's just that I seem different to you because—'

He finished the sentence for me. 'Because I'm no longer drinking?'

I nodded shyly.

'No way,' he said. 'I like you better since I've been off the sauce. But I also can see clearer, and I see something in your eyes, so why don't you tell me what it is?'

'Maybe I'm just a silly girl who wants to know what happens next?'

He stood up from the table and walked around and hugged me from behind. He kissed my hair and said, 'It's part of the mystery. Remember? It's the mystery that makes life worth living. It's what we don't know that matters. Remember me telling you what Donna told me when I was a boy? That atoms in our bodies trace back to the remnants of exploded stars.'

'Is that true?' I asked.

'You mean you didn't believe me? Yes. Yes, it's true. But

I can tell you one thing that's going to happen next. Tonight you're coming with me to my meeting. Will you come with me, Rosie?'

He hugged me tighter as he asked me this, and I told him that I would.

'But first,' he said, 'I need you to take a short walk with me.'

* * *

We went together to the pub and the deli, the only places in town where alcohol was sold, and I stood beside him while he did exactly what his father had done all those years earlier when he found out that Elizabeth was going to have their baby. He instructed the owners to tell their employees to refuse to ever sell him any booze. 'That's that,' he said to me as he kissed me goodbye and went off to work. I told him that I was proud of him, but I did not let on just how remarkable this seemed to me that he was retracing the steps his father had taken so long ago.

* * *

That evening Johnny and I walked to the community centre. 'Billy always goes early to make the coffee,' Johnny said. 'He seems to have found something, and I've noticed a change in him. Have you?'

I wasn't sure exactly how to answer that question. Billy had always been sweet to me. 'Maybe he seems less restless,' I said.

'Yes, it's this place, it's worked its magic on him, I think, Rosie. And I have you to thank for this. You're the one who set all this in motion.'

'But how does it end?' I asked.

'Oh, I'm not sure,' he said. 'I'm just trying to be grateful for now.'

* * *

Their stories were heartbreaking and though the details varied, they were essentially all about loss. A woman I'd passed on the street a thousand times had lost her only child to booze. The vicar from the church had lost his most important post in India to booze. The joiner who once built some of the finest summer houses in Elie had lost his reputation and his customers to booze. The banker who had got drunk and missed a train that was to take him to his wedding to a bride who never forgave him and married someone else. What struck me was how open they all were and how calmly they shared their stories, and without any trace of self-pity or bitterness. I suppose they had been rendered quite indifferent to all that they had lost by the gratitude they felt for having just endured one more day without a drink. It all seemed terribly unfair to me that so many people in the world could drink with impunity while others became helpless slaves to alcohol. Billy was one of the last to speak. I was surprised when he took my hand before he began. I had rather thought he had forgotten I was sitting beside him. He began with the same confession. 'My name is Billy Stoddard,' he said, 'and I'm an alcoholic.'

He went on to tell everyone in the room that he had spent his life running away from himself because he always knew from the time he was a little boy that he failed to measure up in the eyes of his father whom he admired and wanted to be like, just as any small boy wants to be like his father. He said all this, with Johnny sitting beside him, his head bowed.

When Billy had finished and everyone in the room had thanked him, it was Johnny's turn to tell his story. He began on the pavement in Paris when he stopped a young girl from stepping in front of a speeding bus. Every detail of his story matched precisely the story I'd heard and everyone in the village had heard for so many years. He told it with a solemn and steady voice and in a manner of such emotional honesty and modesty that none of it sounded rehearsed. In fact, it sounded like he was telling his story for the very first time. 'I've never lost her,' he said, as he had told me. 'She's been with me every hour of every day, so that I'm never alone.'

I could tell that it comforted him to be relating all of this once again. And I wondered if perhaps he needed to tell his story to make it feel real to him after all these years.

* * *

The meeting ended early so that everyone could join the others in the town square to string lights on Johnny's tree that he and Billy hauled from the hill in the back of a pickup truck. The moon was just a thin sickle resting on its back in the east over the harbour. But the stars were so bright and clear they looked near enough to reach out and touch. Carols were sung, among them my favourite that my father always sang with me each Christmas Eve, with that last verse –

What can I give Him
Poor as I am.
If I were a shepherd
I would bring a lamb
If I were a wise man
I would do my part
Yet what I can give Him
Give my heart.

The voices of the town's people were still in my head when I lay in Billy's arms in the lighthouse. Snow had begun to fall and it was as if we were lying inside one of those snow globes that had fascinated me since I was a child. Billy asked me to sing the final verse of the carol for him, which I did as best I could. And then I decided that there was no point in waiting any longer. Something told me that Billy and I would never be closer and that we would never have a moment filled with more beauty and mystery. And so I just told him that Johnny was his father. 'The cot next to the daybed was meant for you, Billy. Elizabeth is your mother. And she and Johnny did not give you up for adoption. Martin lied to you about that. He believed his daughter could do far better than Johnny for a husband. And because she was ill, he took you from them.'

How did I expect him to respond? Now, when I think back on it, I can't be sure. And I don't think I was sure then either. He said nothing at first. He just let go of me, put his coat back on and left. When I called his name he kept climbing down the iron stairs. I heard the door swing on its rusty hinges behind him, and whatever hope I had in my heart for us vanished in that moment.

BOOK IV

chapter fifty-one

knitting

He never said goodbye to me, but when he went to tell Johnny that he was leaving he said these words to him: 'How could the two of you have tricked me like this?'

Exactly as Johnny had predicted he would react.

And then he left Elie. And I assumed Scotland. I pictured him at the airport in Edinburgh, waiting for a flight back to America, intent upon putting as many miles between us as he could, and as quickly as he could. I imagined him already walking through the airport with that barely perceptible rocking motion on his wounded foot, trying to forget me as he flew from light into darkness across the Atlantic Ocean. A few days passed when I never left my phone, hoping against the hope I had lost that he might call, but knowing that he wouldn't.

And then I left too. I drove four hours north to Mallaig, left the car in the car park of the ferry that took me to the Outer Hebrides, and which docked in the town of Lochboisdale in South Uist where the Vikings had once invaded, and where only sixteen of the three-hundred inhabitants spoke English instead of Gaelic as their primary language. It might not have been the end of the world but you could certainly see the end of the world from there. I hitched a ride with an elderly man in a van with three muddy dogs in the back.

He was delivering eggs and milk to the Polochar Inn, seven and a half miles south in the village of Kilbride. The inn was modest in appearance, with white stucco painted walls, four handsome gables on its roof of black slate shingles and four brick chimneys. It stood just across a narrow strip of marshland and just beyond a lovely white sand beach that overlooked the Sound of Barra with its collection of small islands and the lime-green glens and the dark mountains of South Uist rising up in the distance.

Inside I borrowed a sheet of paper and a pen from the woman behind the bar, sat at a table, and before I even took my coat off I began writing what I believed would be the first of many letters to Johnny, putting down the exact words that I had turned over and over in my mind on the journey from Elie.

> *Dear Johnny, I cannot tell you how sorry I am that, because of me, you have lost your son who you waited so many years to meet. This long-lost son whom you and I had just begun to build a world of dreams around. I have run away to South Uist. I have my phone with me and I have been waiting every minute for it to ring with some word from Billy. I would ask that you write to me from time to time to let me know that you are looking after yourself, and post it to the Polochar Inn in Kilbride. I'm going to try to find some way to be useful here, Johnny. And to believe that someday we will see each other again and then I will be able to tell you just how terribly sorry I am for what has transpired, and ask you to please forgive me.*
>
> *With love, Rosie.*

I paid for a month in advance for a room on the second floor of the inn. The bed and Queen Anne chair sat in front of a double set of windows that looked out at the Isle of Barra. Then I went for a walk, aware that in those first hours I was looking for someone to save me, or at least, I needed someone to make me feel welcome here so that I would not give in to the powerful urge to take the next ferry back to my car and return home.

Her name was Sally Wallace, a widow in her mid-thirties, who was out walking a border collie named Gus. Best of all, she spoke both Gaelic and English and we sat in her cottage drinking tea and talking like old friends. She lived alone, though a pair of black wellies far too large for her stood in her hallway, so I suspected she had at least one close male companion. Her days were taken up with knitting, with wool sheared from local sheep, jumpers and caps and socks for the fleet of local fishermen. When I told her that the rest of Scotland seemed to be using merino wool from Australia and New Zealand, she informed me that when it came to blocking the freezing cold wind at sea that was useless in comparison. She had a loom in her front room where she burned peat in a fireplace attached to a back boiler that heated the four rooms of her cottage.

'So, let me guess,' she said with a wry grin. 'You've come here to run away from a man who either broke your heart or treated you poorly one too many times, for his own good.'

'The former,' I admitted.

'I was hoping so,' she said. 'That's a road I've travelled, so I can be of some help to you.'

* * *

And that's how our friendship began. She taught me how to knit and the first thing I made was a pair of socks for Billy with one two inches shorter at the toe to accommodate his wounded foot. When I finished them, I wrapped them in blue tissue paper and put them in the drawer of my bedside table. When I closed the drawer I told myself that I was closing a door against that part of my life and that I was going to build a new life here.

chapter fifty-two

gratitude

They were uncomplicated days, battered by the most horrible weather I could ever have imagined. Nights when the windows in my room at the inn never stopped rattling and the wind thundered across the roof. Days I spent knitting with Sally in her cottage and waiting for the mailboat to deliver a letter from Johnny. Each night when I closed my eyes I imagined myself making love to Billy with snow falling on the glass globe of the lighthouse. I could remember every single thing he had ever said to me while we held each other there, and as the days and nights in the Hebrides passed, I realised that my life was beginning to resemble the life Johnny had lived for so long. A life *alive* only in the past. But I lacked the one element that had carried him through his years alone. I lacked hope. I didn't dare hope for Billy's return. I declared a prohibition against any kind of hope and just passed the hours with a deep gratitude for what I had shared with Liam and Billy and Johnny in the past, though it was receding from me so steadily that I was often unsure any of it had been real. And I was grateful for what I shared each day in Sally's company.

I felt comfort too, in the early hours before dawn each morning, wrapped in a blanket, sitting in the Queen Anne chair, writing this story as the first slanting light of day reached my windows. Writing all of it down, from the beginning, on the plane to California to find Martin, to now. Over my month at the inn I did my best to get it all down as it happened, and to tell the story truthfully. All that is missing now is an account of my time here, of the days I am living, as opposed to the days I have lived. And so I have decided to keep a diary.

January 21

I feel like I am meant to start this diary because this afternoon, while I was at Sally's knitting, my first letter from Johnny arrived. It was waiting for me when I returned to the inn and was written on stationery from the golf club.

> *Dearest Rosie, the most important thing I can say to you is that you have nothing to apologise for! You found my son and you brought him to Scotland. This was a gift for me. You should be proud of yourself for all that you did. And you must look after yourself. Billy will have to find his way just as we all must. Do you know what it means to me that I can now sit in my cottage and go to work each day with the memory of my son beside me? This is the gift you gave me, Rosie. God bless you. I will hold only good thoughts for you up in the Highlands. I've always wanted to see the Hebrides. And I promise I will write to you often. Love, Johnny.*

January 23

This is what living a real life means. It means walking along the beach, collecting the scallop shells and then asking Erik, the maintenance man at the inn, to let me use his electric drill to bore a tiny hole in each shell just large enough to run a length of fishing line through them, and then tying them to a piece of driftwood that the tide has carried into the shore to make a mobile to hang above the wicker crib of the new baby who was born during the terrible storm three nights ago. Sally has taken me to meet the mother, who is younger than me by two years, and now has the most beautiful baby girl I have ever seen. The mother speaks only Gaelic and named her daughter Kassity, a name I had never heard before, which means 'She is full of love'. Later Sally let me treat her to a sherry in the pub and I told her that when the mother placed Kassity in my arms it was the first time in my life that I had held a newborn baby. I didn't realise that there were tears running down my cheeks when I told her this until she reached across the little table and wiped them away. I have told her Johnny's story. I have told her about Billy. I have told her about Liam and my mother. And I have told her how much it means to me to spend hours each day knitting with her, and talking. There is something about knitting that makes talking easier for me. We have a fleet of thirty-two fishermen here who are in constant need of our work, either knitting them new jumpers, caps, socks and scarves, or repairing their old clothing. Sally has invented a pattern that is unique to this part of the world. At this point I am very much a beginner and cannot keep up with her, of course. However, I am beginning to pick up speed and I find comfort in the repetition. I feel like I am mending myself as I mend the fishermen's clothing. Maybe we can only mend ourselves, and to depend upon someone else to mend us is a great mistake.

February 3

I lay in bed that night thinking of the one thing I had sworn never to think about again. The sound I made when I drew Billy inside me. As hard as I tried I could not banish that sound from my mind and memory. Finally I got up, dressed and walked out into the gale where a gust almost knocked me to my knees on the gravel lane. When I went to bed I fell asleep and dreamed of the girl pushing her pram in front of the Marks & Spencer store, trying to picture precisely the expression on her face as she looked at me.

February 5

My letter to Johnny.

> *Dear Johnny, I have discovered there is a golf course here and people actually play in the awful weather. It has the same lovely crumpled ground as the Elie course with mounds that catch the afternoon shadows off the dunes. If you do come and visit me here, we will walk the ground together. Here is a mystery we must solve: you wrote and told me that you went to visit my father and that you found him to be terribly thin. But when I spoke to him just a week ago, he told me that he's put on half a stone and is doing well. I suspect he is not being completely honest with me and is trying to protect me. I don't want him to think that I am spying on him, so I don't really know what to do or how to interfere without seeming to interfere. In any event, I need you to find someone with a tape measure who can measure you for a jumper I plan to knit you. Across the shoulders. Down the length of your arms. And from your Adam's apple to your waist. I have already chosen the colour and won't spoil the surprise by telling you any more. Much love, Rosie.*

February 9

Today Sally walked me to the strand of beach where she walked for weeks waiting for the tide that had carried her husband's empty boat to shore to bring his body back to her for a proper burial. But he was gone and lost at sea. Acknowledging this was the most difficult thing she ever did, she told me. He was twenty-seven years old, the oldest in a family of four boys. One of the brothers was named Cameron. He spent a great deal of time with Sally, comforting her. And then, in Sally's words – 'He comforted me the way a man always thinks he can best comfort a woman.' She broke it off and she was greatly ashamed of what she'd done in her grief. 'But did it help?' I asked her. She knew exactly why I was asking her this. 'It did help,' she told me. And she said she knew at least two young men who would no doubt love to comfort me, to help me get over Billy. But when I told her that he was not only the first but the only one I had ever slept with, she told me rather sadly that it would be impossible for me to ever forget him completely. 'He'll always be alive in some part of you,' she said. And I feel that this might be the truest thing anyone has ever told me.

February 14

How suddenly life can change for a woman, or a girl. I mean, how her whole entire world can change like a sudden turn of the wind. In some ways it takes something like war to change a man's life forever the way Billy's war had changed his anatomy or the way it had killed Liam. But for a girl, it can just take making love at the right time, or the wrong time, depending how she feels about becoming pregnant. I am up against two problems today. First, there is no pharmacy anywhere near here to buy a pregnancy test. And second, because my periods have never been regular, I had no idea I might be pregnant until an hour ago when I slipped into my jeans and noticed that I could hardly button them. When I let my breath out the button popped off under the strain and rolled across the floor. I remembered the story Billy and I made up of Elizabeth searching for her button in Paris the night Johnny saved her life.

Tonight I feel the need for Billy.

February 17

I spent most of this day sitting at Sally's bedside, making us tea and watching over her as the tablets she took carried her off to sleep and relief from the depression that overcame her from time to time and that she named her 'black dog', in honour of Winston Churchill, who had given that name to the mental depression that plagued him as well. 'Hold my hand please, Rosie,' she would say as she drifted in and out of sleep and drowned in the nightmares of her young husband's body dragged by currents across the bottom of the sea, apologising to me again and again for being such poor company. 'It will pass,' she told me. 'It will pass,' I told her. By dusk she was able to sit up and eat some of the soup I had warmed while she told me that she had been suffering this ordeal since she was a girl. She always felt like she was missing the layer of skin normal people possessed to protect them from sorrow. 'My James,' she said, 'was so patient with me. But I know there were many days when he was grateful to be able to escape my darkness by going out to sea. It becomes a terrible burden on the people who care most about you. And we often lash out at each other in our frustration.' She, because this boy who loved her could not stop her pain. He, because he was unable to stop the pain for this girl who he adored. 'But we carried on,' she told me. 'And there were many more good days than poor ones. Until James was lost.' That is the word she always uses to describe his death. Lost. Lost, as if he might still be found. She explained that what she found most unacceptable about her condition was the burden it placed on others and the way it made her so self-centered. 'It's like a blindness,' she said.

'You become blind to anyone else's pain but your own. You can't see beyond it.'

Finally, as I was getting ready to leave and I could tell that she was more herself again, I told her I thought I might be pregnant. She placed her hand against my belly and explained that she and several other women in the town had been trained as midwives to help deliver babies in this remote place where there were no medical facilities and doctors were not always available. Before she withdrew her hand I asked her how far I would have to travel to get a testing kit. She smiled at me and said, 'My medicine cabinet.' She had ordered three from Amazon after she and James had begun trying to conceive. I thanked her but admitted that I didn't think I was ready to find out just yet. 'When you are ready, I'll be here with you,' she told me.

I came to this place to disappear from the world and now I find myself being drawn deeper into the centre of it. Closer to the mystery that so inspired Billy.

February 18

I took a walk in blowing snow this morning, nearly blind and only able to see about a foot in front of me to take the next step. I wondered if I were to suffer from depression like Sally, if I might have just walked into the sea until I was soaked through my clothes to my skin, and then laid down in the dunes to wait for hypothermia to kill me as Johnny had planned to do. I wondered if I was a strong person or a weak person. Each step I took required me to overcome the fear that some harm would come to me. That I might fall into the sea or be lost in the storm and unable to find my way back to the inn. I thought of Liam at war and afraid and trying to overcome his fears there. I thought of Johnny as a young boy too frightened to fight with the Legion and pretending to be dead in the battle before deserting. I thought of Billy who had told me that he was not afraid in the war because he had learned a trick. The trick was to tell yourself that you were already dead. That there was no chance you were going to make it out alive. 'Once you believe this, the fear evaporates,' he had told me.

February 20

Sally was feeling better today and she had retrieved a pregnancy test from her medicine cabinet. It was sitting on the table right next to me while we knitted. 'It's yours whenever you want to use it,' she said, without looking up. We talked a little about her depression and she told me that the Valium she took was prescribed by a doctor in Mallaig who renewed the prescription by post. He was young and handsome and he fancied her, she could tell, but she knew it would never work between them because he needed to be in a real town and she could never leave here. She had read somewhere that Valium was the drug of choice for American housewives in the 1950s and 1960s when they were stuck at home every day with kids who were driving them crazy and no car to go anywhere because no one owned more than one car in those days, and the husband took it with him to work. She liked the idea of being connected to this band of women on another continent in another century, though she had longed to be a wife and a mother and could not imagine ever being discontented in this role. 'I pictured myself with a small army of children, teaching them all how to knit, the boys as well as the girls,' she told me.

'So,' I asked, 'do you just let go of all that now?'

'I let go of that, or I let go of James,' she said. 'I can't keep them both.' She said this with a sombre tone, but then she smiled and said maybe she would start visiting the doctor in Mallaig each month instead of receiving her tablets through the post. 'At the right time each month,' she said, and we both laughed at this. She asked me how I had managed to let go of Liam and take Billy into my arms. I told her I hadn't planned it. Everything had just happened. I confessed that at first I had imagined it was Liam in my arms. But then it was Billy and only Billy. 'And does he love you the way you love him?' she asked.

'I don't think so,' I heard myself say. 'Or he wouldn't have left and I wouldn't be here.'

Sally told me that it would all sort itself out. She thought maybe Billy just needed some time to grow accustomed to what had fallen in front of him. Before I left she asked me to stand with her outside her cottage. And as we stared out at the sea that was as calm as a mill pond she took hold of my hand and asked me to tell her something that no one else had been willing to tell her. 'Tell me that James isn't coming back,' she said. And I did this for her. And after I had said the words, I asked her to say the same for Billy. She turned and waited until I was looking at her. She shook her head once, very slowly, and said, 'Not yet, Rosie.'

February 22

I told Sally today that I believe I am turning my life into an impenetrable web of dreams or lies because I am caught in the space between how we imagine our lives will turn out and how they actually do. And I've yet to make the accommodations that we all must make in that space in order to carry on and to find contentment there. Or, if not contentment, then... Then what, precisely? Resignation? Acceptance? Indifference? Sally thought acceptance was the most accurate description. But when I told her that we were both standing on the same middle ground she insisted that I was wrong. She had lost James and she had to accept this. 'But,' she said, 'it's different with your Billy. You don't know that you've lost him.' I told her that it felt just as it had when I learned that Liam had been killed. She told me that it was not the same. Liam was never coming back, but I could not be sure about Billy. Still, I felt sure. And there was nothing that Sally could say to me that took away that feeling. The feeling of being left behind again. It was only then that I realised I had felt the same way about my mother. All my life I'd had this empty feeling that I could never define or describe to anyone. But now I knew it was the feeling of being left behind.

February 27

To give you some idea just how ignorant and unprepared I was for what was happening, it wasn't until Sally was helping me try on the body of a jumper we were finishing when she pointed out that my blouse was stained. Colostrum, she said, which meant that I could be three or even four months along. This shocked me, even though it had been almost four months since Billy and I first made love, and of course my belly kept swelling no matter how determined I was to deny it. My first reaction was to think, *So this is my fate then, to which I must resign myself. The life of a single mother.*

I was too stunned to say much of anything to Sally who was on her phone in minutes, calling her doctor friend in Mallaig for an appointment. She told me that most women had their babies at home but she thought it wise for me to have a thorough exam, to know when this baby was due. And because of my history – my mother's death due to complications in her pregnancy – I should speak to the doctor about having the baby in a hospital. And then she said with great tenderness, 'And if you don't plan to keep the baby, we can see where we stand.'

I do feel like she is standing beside me in this adventure and that we are somehow in this together, and the thought has crossed my mind that maybe this baby should be given to her to compensate for the baby she and James never had the opportunity to have.

March 3

A certain measure of my modesty is gone now after the examination in Mallaig this afternoon. Apparently there is no room for modesty when it comes to pregnancy and giving birth. I surrendered mine in less than fifteen minutes. I took off my knickers, then lay on my back on the examination table, and spread my legs wide with my knees raised. I kept my eyes shut. Thoughts raced through my mind, though they were incomplete and never approached any degree of real coherence. When I felt the doctor's fingers inside me, I concentrated on the way Billy's wounded foot had felt in my hand, feeling his pulse there. His vulnerability made my own more acceptable. Sally made the journey with me. On the way in, for all four hours we talked away like we were on holiday. The trip back was different. There were spaces of silence that neither of us seemed eager to fill. From time to time as I drove, Sally would lay her hand on my knee and tell me that everything was going to sort itself out and that I was a strong, young girl who was going to have a healthy baby, and become a wonderful mother. The nearer we got to South Uist, the more I realised that the place had captured me. The faraway feeling had comforted me in the weeks I'd lived there. The weeks since I'd disappeared there. I could actually picture myself now, walking the strand of beach across from the inn, with a baby wrapped inside my jumper. I could see my whole life rolling out ahead of me there until I was an old woman, waiting for this grown-up child to visit me. The way Johnny had waited. How strange, I thought, if my life turns out the way Johnny's has. One of Billy's mysteries: where God resided. I was heading for the great unknown.

The doctor says that I am three months pregnant.

March 10

It's official. I'm going to have a baby in late August or early September. Which seems like a lifetime away. One year after I flew to America and found Billy in jail. A letter from Johnny arrived today, handwritten on both sides of a single piece of paper. Before I read the letter properly I searched both sides for Billy's name. It wasn't there.

> *Dearest Rosie,*
> *I hope you are looking after yourself and keeping well. Have you had a chance to walk the golf course? I meant to ask if you go there if you would take a few photographs for me. I've heard so much about the ground there over the years. And did I ever tell you that I was planning to take Elizabeth there before she left Elie to return home to tell her mother and father that we were married? I thought that I might find work there and that we'd be safe and no one could ever find us. I might come and see you, depending how long you plan to stay. I can take a coach to Mallaig and another, and then the ferry out to where you are. I wonder if it's beginning to feel like spring there? Here the weather has been good to us and I don't think we'll see any winter temperatures again. I wish you and I could have talked before you left. But there's nothing I would have said to try to stop you from running away. I actually believe that running away has its place and that the people left behind should understand. I do understand, Rosie. One day you might see my old face at your door. I've made arrangements with the bank to wire you money. I have no need for it and young people always need more money. Love and best wishes, Johnny.*

Running away has its place, I read aloud in my room, and then I gazed out of the windows and counted seven bright stars in the night sky, pierced with light. I thought then that I was going to have to find some courage somewhere and get a lot tougher than I'd ever been. I was going to have to become someone new. Someone who wasn't waiting for anyone to show up at my door and rescue me from all that I was afraid of. Our fear is what defines us, Billy had said to me. I don't want to be defined that way as a mother. I don't want my child to think of me as a frightened person and I don't want to pass on my fears to her. Or him. But what if it is already in the DNA? My fears are already her fears, or his fears. All that I am afraid of has already been imprinted in the cells of this baby that is now the size of a lemon. However, I am encouraged by the thought that Billy's fearlessness has also been imprinted on this baby's DNA. I take comfort in knowing this.

March 17

I should be writing every day, keeping a record of this time, but I am taking naps instead whenever I am not knitting with Sally. I've never felt so exhausted in my life. I lay my head down and drop into the deepest sleep. And often I have this recurring dream that I am sleeping in a London Tube station during an air raid during the Second World War. I am sleeping with this lemon in my belly, determined not to get us both killed by one of Hitler's bombs. I have been reading books from the little library at the inn and learned that if Hitler had not wasted his bombing on the cities of England and had bombed the RAF airfields instead, he would have defeated us and we would all be speaking German now. He made a tactical error, you might say. I must try not to make any errors in my life going forward. I must become a stalwart mother for this child. The money that Johnny wired is such excess that I was deeply embarrassed. Fifty-two thousand pounds. So much money. Martin Stoddard's money. I must not spend it on this room. I must find a small cottage of my own and live for far less than I am paying here. I have seen a notice tacked to the church door just down the road for a one-bedroom cottage for two hundred and forty pounds a month. At that rate I could live here with the baby until she is eighteen years old and heading off to college.

In the library here there is a book of American artwork and I have been drawn to a painting of Cyrus Dallin's statue, *Appeal to the Great Spirit* – a Native American on horseback, his arms outstretched, his brave face turned to the heavens. I must try to surrender as this brave Native American has surrendered. I must try to let go of everything that I am afraid of and to surrender to the light and shadows, to the wind, to the scent of the sea.

March 19

I have been to the Askernish golf course today. I took photos for Johnny and then realised that I have no way to print them and send them to him. I told him this in my letter.

> *Dear Johnny,*
>
> *You're going to have to ask the club if I can send the photographs of the Askernish golf course to them by email or text so you can see them because I have no place to print them here in South Uist and I know they have a printer in the Elie clubhouse. This is a land that time forgot. I so appreciate your letters. But you have not mentioned your heart. I would like to know if you are looking after yourself and not trying to do too much. I must tell you that I pictured you and Elizabeth walking the golf course here. Such lovely and peaceful ground, though I would not want to be out there during a gale.*

I have nearly finished knitting your jumper and I shall post it to you by the end of this week. The wool here comes from many breeds of sheep. Cheviot. Blackface Texel. Suffolk. Hebridean. Lleyn. Zwartbles. And Shetland. Yours is all Hebridean. You must remember to never put it in a washing machine or a tumble dryer or it will shrink to nothing. I am keeping track now and your days have lengthened from just over six hours of sunlight back in December to nearly twelve hours now. I hope this doesn't compel you to be working all those hours each day. I don't know if this will make any sense at all to you, Johnny, but I feel that coming here was the best thing for me to do. I have found myself at peace here. Though I must tell you that barely a single hour passes when I don't think of Billy and long for his company. I believe the best part of him he inherited from his father and mother. God bless you for this, Johnny. Love, Rosie.

March 23

I told Sally today that I sometimes feel like I have been separated from my body. It's an odd sensation. Rather like riding a bicycle that is moving on its own, without me pedalling. I am fourteen weeks now and I am moving along one train track at my normal speed, and in the opposite direction my body is moving along a parallel track at a much faster speed. What I mean is I am moving toward what was already my past. My time with Billy who set the other train in motion. After all that Sally has been through I don't want to burden her with my own sorrow. But I am sad, almost constantly sad, that Billy is not here with me to marvel at the mystery of it all. In four weeks I will be going back to Mallaig for my ultrasound at which time I can learn if this baby is a boy or a girl. But I have decided that I prefer not to know. This morning when I arrived at Sally's she presented me with a Moses basket where the baby will sleep for the first few months, beside my bed. It's beautiful and it's made of woven seagrass by a local woman called Aisling, which means 'Dream'. It strikes me that it would make a wonderful name for a baby girl. And Sally has a pattern for a hooded baby jumper that I will soon be working on. I have thought of writing to Martin to ask him to help me find Billy. For twenty-four hours, right through my sleep, I thought of nothing else.

March 24

I know what it is now that is making me so sad. Being pregnant has connected me to my mother and to Elizabeth. To their sad stories. The stories of their pregnancies that no longer belong only to them, but to me. I could be a girl who dies in childbirth like my mother. Or a girl who carries her baby without the man she loves at her side like Elizabeth. It struck me tonight that I have never seen a photograph of my mother in her pregnancy. And of course, the same is true about Elizabeth. I thought about this. And wondered if there was some way I could write to my dad and ask him if he had a photograph and if he could send it to me, without telling him that I was pregnant. Thinking about all of this, I was unable to fall asleep and so I called my father and asked him, and he told me that he had not kept any photographs from those days. He said, 'I grew up with people who had been through the Second World War, and I adopted their way of dealing with sadness. You simply closed a heavy door against it. I'm sorry, Rosie. In my time we just never spoke about sad things. I remember your mum and me – and how we were in all our glory, and how lovely she was when she was carrying you. She was radiant. And always so calm. I remember how calm she was. Serene is the right word, I think. But I've no pictures to show you. Except the one of us on our wedding day which has always been above the fireplace and which you and I often looked at together.' He didn't ask me any questions. But he told me that Johnny had visited him and told him why I had run off. He told me how sorry he was and that Billy must have been a great comfort to me after all that I had been through with Liam's death. We talked like old friends and before I fell asleep I told myself that all the loss and sorrow were going to end with me. I found my defiance and told myself that I was not going to lose Billy. I would not be content to wait for him as Johnny had waited for Elizabeth. I would not accept that he was lost at sea as Sally had her James. I would find him. No matter how long it took. No matter what was required of me. I would find him.

March 27

Sally and I flew a kite today in the field overlooking the bay. It is a tradition here when a wife loses a husband or a mother loses a son at sea. We ran through the tall grass like children and then in a solemn moment Sally walked a little way away from me and let go of the spool of string. There was a strong wind and it only took a few minutes for the kite to unravel all the string on the spool and to go sailing off, free of us, above our heads. 'Well, there's that done now,' Sally said to me. I took her hand and we walked slowly back to her place. I asked her what it meant. She told me she was meant to move on with her life. To meet someone new. To get on with living. When I asked her if she thought she was ready she told me that she wasn't sure. Life is for the living, her friends had kept telling her, but a part of her wished that she and James had perished together in the storm that took him. I tightened my grip on her hand and told her that she must not feel that way. But I understood. She told me she wasn't sure if it was the waiting for James to come back, or the knowing that he wasn't coming back that had taken the greater toll on her. She told me that she couldn't really remember what she was like before it all began. She felt certain she had lost a part of herself that she would never get back. She turned for one last glimpse of the kite before it disappeared over the sea. We were quite a pair, I thought.

I told her that I was thinking about writing to Martin at the home where he was being cared for in California. It was my only way of trying to reach Billy. And though I knew that Martin would be the last person Billy would contact, in spite of his frailty, he had known Billy's whereabouts before and that had enabled me to find him, and so he might know where he had gone now. He's that kind of man, I explained to Sally, who has his hands on the levers and switches. But I assured her that I would not say anything about the baby. If I were to ever manage to reach Billy, and if he were to ever write back to me, I didn't want it to be prompted by sympathy.

March 28

I finally wrote the letter. But not the letter I had intended to write. Instead, I followed the anger that was rising in me and condemned him. First I began with *Dear Mr Stoddard*. Then I changed it to *Dear Martin*. And then went on. *I have no idea how you ever believed you had the right to destroy the lives of Johnny and Elizabeth. How does anyone ever consider himself better than someone else? Such unpardonable ignorance. And don't think that just because you came to Scotland to apologise to Johnny, that you atoned in any way. You didn't. And everyone in the town of Elie where you once played your beloved golf has nothing but contempt for you and for what you did. You will leave this world with that knowledge. Soon, I hope. For the world will be far better off without you. Just another selfish man who was blinded to the important things in life by privilege. I damn all privileged men. Every last one of you.*

And then I remembered Johnny's words and assured him that in his next life he would be a beggar in Calcutta.

When I finished, I folded the letter, placed it in an envelope and took it straight to the front desk where I purchased an international stamp and left it to be posted the next day.

March 30

For the first time this morning since I knitted them and wrapped them in tissue paper then placed them in the drawer of my bedside table, I held Billy's socks. The room was dark. I could see the first gold light of dawn just above the water way off in the distance. I have become that part of the one sock that is missing. I have become another part of Billy that he is missing. But I have no idea if it even matters to him. Or if he has already become as accustomed to me missing as he has to that part of his foot. I wonder if he is a person who just moves on and never looks back at what no longer exists. This is becoming hard for me now.

April 4

I have begun watching *Call the Midwife* on iPlayer on my phone. One episode every morning. I am eleven series behind but I am determined to catch up. Each time a new baby is born, it makes me cry. I can't help it. When there is a close-up of these newborns they all seem to have the same expression of surprise as if they are thinking, *Oh my, back again so soon*. What a mystery it is. Perhaps this life is only the shadow of another life and what Billy told me is true – 'Atoms in our bodies trace to the remnants of exploding stars.' I confess that the distress that these mothers must endure to bring their babies into the world, despite the compassion and the expertise of the midwives attending them, has convinced me that Sally and the doctor are right. I will have this baby in the maternity hospital if I can make the four-hour journey in time. And if the weather is not so poor that the ferry cannot run. In which case I could have the baby in my car – something which I have now seen on one episode of the series and it left me wanting no part of that experience. These mothers bringing babies into the world is very much an enterprise that has nothing to do with men. With the fathers. They are outside the room. Outside the house. In the pubs. But there is a part of me that wants Billy at my side. Sitting with his face by mine. Holding my hand. Telling me that all of this great mystery was set in motion long ago and that it just took twenty-odd years for everything to coincide so that the three of us were finally together. The three of us who had always been meant to be together.

And here is another mystery that would appeal to Billy. Each time one of these newborn babies cries on my iPhone, I can feel the colostrum leaking from my breasts as if it is my baby that my body is preparing the milk for.

I do not speak of Billy when I am with Sally because I am afraid that this will only make her loss more difficult to bear. I think one of the reasons she and I have become so close is that we have both lost the men we loved. We have both been left behind to fend for ourselves. And we draw strength from each other because of this. And I must admit that there are times in her presence when I feel that I could go on this way quite well. On my own, I mean. Taking care of a baby on my own. Actually, I believe Sally thinks she is preparing me for this. I can tell that she no longer believes there is any chance in the world that I will ever be reunited with Billy. To her, he is just someone who found his way inside my knickers. Not that she sees this as an issue, given when it comes to birth men play such a minimal part in this business of bringing babies into the world. 'Three minutes!' she has said with a sly smile. 'That's about the extent of it.'

April 6

It was all hands on deck the past two days as Sally and I and a few dozen other residents went from farm to farm with a vet and his sonogram machine in tow. From the O'Connor farm to the O'Murchadha farm to the O'Ceallaigh farm to the Breathnach farm. We helped wash the ewes in tubs of warm water then held them down so the vet could apply gel and then press his wand at the hairless area around the ewes' udders. Then on his screen we saw the outline of the baby lambs' spines. Each ewe who was carrying one baby got a dash of blue paint across her back. Ewes with twins, a dash of red so that the farmer knew to double her nutrients through the remainder of her pregnancy. Those sheep who had failed to produce a lamb were called *yelds* and they were set aside for someone's tea. I received an education today about the raising of sheep. Ewes were mated with a tup. The tups were fitted with a harness which has a coloured crayon block. Once the tup covers the ewe it leaves a crayon mark on her rear. Depending on the size of the flock, the farmer would swap out a tup for a new one two or three times during the mating season. It was all described to me in very clinical terms, and I suppose it marks me as a sentimental fool that I found it all rather sad. Particularly that the ewes who failed to produce babies were slaughtered. But it was simply mathematics. Essential in order to keep the flock expanding. I wondered at my own ignorance in these matters, having grown up on an estate with a father who was gamekeeper. I suppose my father knew my nature well enough to do his best to protect me from as much of the world's harsh reality as possible. Mostly because I had already lost my mother. It makes me wonder how many other aspects of life he protected me from and if after my mother died he set out determined to protect me from all of life's misfortune. If so, I am not convinced that he wasn't doing me a disservice. If I had been raised differently and had been exposed to life's hardships rather than protected from them, I might have been tougher. Tough enough to deal with Liam's death and Billy's departure from my life. Both events carried such a degree of suddenness that they left me reeling in a way that I have felt like a girl chasing after her hat in a gale. I need to find my way to steadiness now. And I need to hold tighter to my defiance so that I can proceed with determination. I have always admired people who have this quality of determination. Billy has it. And despite his wounds, he appeared to me from the first moments we met and talked as someone who the world could never destroy or bring to his knees. Where does it come from, I wondered? And then I decided if it is not poured into you by your parents, then you acquire it on your own as Billy had.

April 15

I have been thinking about the part of Johnny and Elizabeth's story I heard when I was sixteen or seventeen. The part where she told him, or he told her, that they were each able to see in each other what no one else could see and what they could not see in themselves – their value. Where does our value come from? I mean, what is it that gives us value? What is each one of us worth and what are any of our accomplishments worth in the end, if nothing lasts as Billy believes? If he were here with me I would try for all I am worth to convince him that love lasts. That what I feel for him today I will feel until I take my last breath. But then what? Will my love for him no longer matter when I am not here in this world to bestow it upon him? It won't matter at all unless it is passed on. Unless someone tells my story so that the love I had for Billy is carried across time. Maybe that is why I have bothered to write this. Because without a story there is nothing permanent. We are all just transients. Just passing each other like the strangers we are. Just passing through. I am thankful that I have a story now to write down. It began as Johnny's story and now it has become mine as well. I am living it each day and I am sharing it with Sally so that there is at least one person in this world who might pass my story on to someone else, just as I am passing on Johnny and Elizabeth's story to you. And I think if I ever see Billy again, the first thing I will do is sit him down and tell him every detail about their story, their love story that carried him into this world, so that he will be able to pass it along to someone someday. Perhaps to a young man or woman sitting next to him at a bar. A stranger who is interested enough to listen. So far I have written all these pages into two spiral notebooks. I am going to start typing them on to my iPad now so that if I never see Billy again, but can find some way to send them to him, I will be able to do this. And I may leave out these diary entries so that my part of the story is not included. I wonder if this might be the best way to convey Johnny and Elizabeth's story to him, without my own story to dilute theirs. Maybe I want my story to belong only to me. I read somewhere that Native Americans never wanted their photographs taken by white men because these photographs that you could hold in the palm of your hand only diminished them. Maybe the same is true of our story when we share it with someone else. Maybe the thing to do is to protect our stories by keeping them in our hearts.

April 24

Sally told me today that when she finally accepted the fact that James was dead she began to build walls around her heart to protect her from ever being hurt this way again. She felt the walls first at the funeral service, she told me. It was her way of coping. I told her that I had begun to do the same thing when Liam was killed. But I was unable to do it. And I asked her if she thought any of us could live without love, and if we are all looking for the same thing – someone who will cast a light over the walls of our heart. Even as I said this it struck me that this was the answer I was looking for from Johnny when I had asked him to please tell me the difference between just being alive and living. 'It doesn't have to be a man though, does it?' Sally said. 'Your baby could be the one who casts a light over the walls of your heart.'

She was right, of course. But it was still too unreal for me to grasp. This baby is not real to me. But Billy is. Maybe it will be different once she or he is born. Maybe it will be the end of loneliness. And then I thought of Johnny and how he had his heart broken but had refused to build walls around his heart. Why? Because he must have believed that one day Elizabeth would want to enter his heart again? Or because he had kept her alive in his heart across all the years? Maybe he had built up walls but she was still there inside those walls. Taking walks with him to the bakery to choose their bread for the day. Standing beside him while he did his work each day from dawn until dusk. I wonder where his belief in Elizabeth came from. Maybe just desperation. Maybe he had no choice but to believe in her in order to keep from giving up. But he must have known just how unwise it was to believe in someone who didn't believe she had any value. Until she met Johnny. Before then she must have felt like she was on an island with a father and mother to whom she could never measure up. Just who did they think they were to have the right to cripple their own daughter that way? Why couldn't they have told her that they were proud of her, imperfection and all? Lying, if they had to. I mean, even if they weren't proud of her. 'Someone will come along and cast a light over the walls of your heart,' I told Sally. She looked at me and I thought she was going to say something about this but instead she changed the subject and told me she had found the perfect pattern for my baby's jumper. It was cable-knit with a hood. When I looked at it, that was the first moment when my baby felt real to me.

April 27

Today I sat with an elderly man on a bench, talking under dark clouds sweeping across the sky above us. Talking about fear. He had escaped the Russians when they invaded Poland and he was captured in the Second World War. And then he escaped the Germans when they invaded and captured him and sent him to a concentration camp. He managed to make it all the way to London and to join the British Army where he finally got his revenge on the Nazis when he invaded Germany, serving under General Montgomery. He told me that when the war ended all he wanted was to find a peaceful place in some corner of the world and so he came to South Uist and fished for fifty-two years until he retired. I told him that I knew how he had survived. I told him what Billy had told me. That he had convinced himself he was already dead. When I said this, he pulled his shoulders back and closed his eyes for a moment. I told him that I had learned this from a soldier. He told me that he fought as hard as he had so that there would never be another war and so that there would never be another boy who would have to pretend he was already dead like that. When I asked him when he had last been to Poland he told me that he had never been back, but that he had a sister just a year younger who was living in Warsaw. She had survived another concentration camp by working as a seamstress repairing the uniforms of dead German soldiers so they could be reissued to new conscripts. He dreamed of seeing her again. And of seeing the city as well. He had visited Warsaw once when he was a boy, ten years before the war began. He had studied the timetables and knew that from the ferry dock in Mallaig the train trip took two days and eighteen minutes. 'Why don't you go?' I asked him. He was far too old, he told me. And he thought that he had waited too long and was too old to make the journey now. I could tell how badly he wanted to go, but he kept coming up with one excuse after another. First it was the expense. I asked him to wait for ten minutes and I would be right back. When I returned I gave him three hundred pounds. He tried to stop me from putting the money in his jacket pocket. 'Go to Warsaw,' I said. 'See you sister.' Then he said he didn't want to go without something special, some gift to give her. That was the first time I took off the engagement ring Liam had given me since he slipped it on my finger. It was a simple ring of silver with a small diamond set between two small sapphires. 'Give this to her,' I said. 'It will make me very pleased if you give this to her. And it will make me happy to think that you and your sister are together again.' I was certain that I had convinced him. He leaned forward with his elbows on his knees as if he was going to go straight home and begin packing for the trip. He had tears in his eyes when we said goodbye. I fell asleep picturing him on the train. Sleeping and waking. Sleeping and waking as the train pulled into Warsaw. But some time in the night he returned the money and the ring to the clerk on duty at the inn.

April 28

I put the ring back on and then took it off and folded it in a piece of waxed paper and put it in a pocket in my backpack. I had decided that I would bury it at Liam's grave where Billy had buried his medal. Call it wishful thinking or just ignorance on my part, but I had a powerful sense that Billy would be with me, to help me do this.

As I walked to Sally's this morning a spring snowstorm was upon us. I watched big, fat flakes like scraps of paper falling and disappearing into the sea as if the waves were eating them. I wondered if it was snowing in Elie and what Johnny would do to pass the time if he couldn't be out on the golf course working.

As I was beginning to knit the baby jumper, Sally told me a true story that I will never forget about a doctor named Helena Wright. At the end of the Great War she set out to help the wives of soldiers who had been left too crippled by physical wounds or shell shock to make love to them. There were hundreds of women who came to the clinic. They wanted to conceive and have babies more than anything else in the world. This was their greatest desire and they had spoken with their husbands and persuaded them to allow them to conceive with another man. A million British men had been killed in the war which meant that by 1921 Britain had more than one and a half million women of childbearing age without men who could make this happen. Some called them the 'mateless multitude'. But Helena answered to no one. She was ahead of her time and she made her own rules when it came to morality. She set up a secret, underground fertility service, and began searching for a man or men who would be willing to father children for the women she was trying to assist, without any emotional ties or claim to the children these women conceived. She wanted a man who met her specific requirements. He must be good-looking, physically strong, intelligent and of a good disposition. It went without saying that he also needed to be extremely virile. Who she found was a fellow named Derek who was now thirty-one years old. He had spent the war working on his family's rubber and tea plantation in Ceylon, though his younger brother had been killed during the Battle of the Somme. After the war, Derek married a nurse and it was she who introduced him to Doctor Wright, who in turn told him about her desire to help these women to become mothers. Sally blushed when she told me that though Derek had a happy marriage, his wife had confided to Doctor Wright that she could not begin to satisfy his sexual appetite, and she agreed to allow him to impregnate the doctor's clients – each of whom had to sign a confidentiality agreement and pay a small fee to a trust that the doctor established to cover all prenatal care in her clinic. Doctor Wright decreed that there would be no meetings between Derek and any of the women before the assigned conception date in case anyone got cold feet. Instead the women were to track their ovulation and then notify the clinic by telegram of the dates that they were most likely to conceive. And then the assignation would be arranged. Over the course of the years Derek fathered almost five hundred children, the last when he was sixty-one years old with a woman who had tried for twenty years to persuade her shell-shocked husband to make love to her. She had come to Doctor Wright, as many other women had, as a last resort. She was forty-eight years old and gave birth to a perfectly healthy baby girl.

This strange story of Doctor Wright is playing over and over in my mind. And I seem to be growing more and more confused. There is Sally, telling me that her greatest regret was being on the pill for the time she was married to James. 'I could have filled this cottage with babies,' she told me. She believes it is too late for her now, though she is just thirty-one years old. She can't seem to imagine having a baby with another man. And here I am well into my pregnancy and yet I feel none of this deep desire for a baby. When I think of those thousand-odd women who went to Doctor Wright for help to conceive a baby with a stranger, it makes me think there might be something wrong with me. Perhaps some part of me is missing. The mateless multitude. Am I not one of them now, though I have, growing inside me with well-defined fingers and toes now, the very thing they desired most? And how could it ever work? How could a man accept a baby fathered by another man, a complete stranger?

May 1

Maybe I am losing my mind. When I am with Sally I feel like my life is centred and on track. But when I am alone I am increasingly desperate about everything. Especially about returning home. What is home? Where is home? I keep asking myself. And I have begun to believe that I am unsuited to be a mother and that I will stay here, deliver this baby and give him or her to Sally to make up for the baby she never had the chance to have with James. Is this crazy? Am I crazy? It is the first thought in my mind when I awake each morning, and the last thing I think about before I fall asleep. Something else has happened to me lately. I will not allow myself to open the drawer where I put Billy's socks. I don't want to look at them or touch them. I believe it is because they will make Billy seem real. And he isn't real. If he was real, he would be with me, with one hand on my belly next to mine, to feel his baby fluttering like a tiny bird. Is it his baby? Or is it our baby? Or is it just my baby? There are too many questions I seem unable to answer these days.

May 18

I've lost my friend. Sally had to go to Glasgow to look after her mother. I can't remember precisely when she left. Or how many days I have spent without talking to anyone. I am taking my breakfast in my room now. Mostly I only eat the toast and drink the coffee and then I don't eat another thing until the next morning when I do it again. I have not left this room. I have the baby's jumper here with me and the yarn I need to finish it but I have put it on the shelf in the closet and left it there. At night I dream that someone sneaks into the room and steals it and takes the baby from my belly. But when I wake, the baby is there. Before she left for Glasgow Sally gave me a copy of D. H. Lawrence's *Lady Chatterley's Lover*. Constance Reid takes a lover because her husband, Sir Clifford Chatterley, is one of those soldiers from the Great War who cannot make love to her the way Billy made love to me without even trying. So naturally. So effortlessly. I read it in two days and then began reading it again from page one because Constance called herself a half-virgin, the same thing I called myself when Liam was killed. I feel fat and sluggish. Today I never took off my nightie. I never got dressed.

May 21

Dear Billy, I have read that it only takes six days without food or water to starve yourself to death. And your baby. I have made it through two days so far and, except for cramps, I don't feel any different. I don't want to sound mean, but since I can't post these letters to you because I have no idea where you are, I am writing them to hurt you a little because I am still right here and you are somewhere else. I remember everything we ever said to each other. What have I become, my dearest friend? Am I anyone you would recognise now?

May 22

I have no idea why, but I went looking for a sharp knife today. I thought about it for hours. Each time I managed to get it out of my mind, it returned. And then it took me a lot of time, waiting around the pub until the barman was not looking so I could take the serrated knife he uses to cut his lemons and limes.

May 24

Dear Billy. Dear Billy. Dear Billy.

May 26

I called The Homestead in California today. When I asked to speak to Martin Stoddard, the woman on the phone asked me if I was family. I lied. She told me that Martin died yesterday. Yesterday was my twenty-ninth birthday. Sally knocked at my door and called my name. But I pretended I wasn't in and didn't answer.

May 28

When I sit in this chair at the window and look out on the beach where I have walked a hundred times since I first arrived here, I cannot imagine walking there again. Martin is dead. If only he had died when Elizabeth and Johnny were at the beginning. At least they had a beginning. I had no real beginning with Billy. I came into his life in the middle and tried to give it the right ending. But nothing lasts. Nothing ever lasts.

May 29

I knew where I wanted to cut myself first. I sat in the chair pushed up to the window just after dawn. I stripped off my tights and rested my bare left foot on the windowsill. I lay the steel teeth of the serrated knife against my foot at the place where Billy's foot was missing. Something like contentment came to me as soon as the faint line of blood appeared and I wondered if it had been this way for Elizabeth when she was a girl, cutting herself with her father's letter opener. I felt very little pain. Much less pain than I had wanted to feel. Or maybe the pain was there and I just didn't feel it. I don't know what I feel. I don't know what I am supposed to feel. Except this. That it would have been better if I had died and my mother had lived.

May 30

Sally got the manager of the inn to open my door this afternoon. When I heard her calling my name and then when I heard the key in the latch I felt like a trapped animal. I lay down in my bed and pulled the covers over me, pretending to be sleeping. I didn't fool her. Nothing I said fooled her. And it only took a few minutes before she glanced across the room and saw the knife on the windowsill. I told her that I had been trying to get a splinter out of my foot. She pulled the covers aside and saw for herself the thin line of blood. She was very calm. She took hold of my hands and waited for me to tell her. I explained that I hadn't felt anything for days and I just wanted to feel something. She understood and told me that after James had been missing at sea for three weeks she had begun to feel numb. Too numb to feel any pain. There was a storm and the rocks leading to the shore were covered in ice and she walked down over the rocks hoping she would fall and crack her head open just so she could feel the pain. She didn't want to die, she told me. She just wanted to feel the pain. The pain had been her companion while she waited for word about James, and then while she waited for the tide to carry his body on to the shore. When the pain stopped she was lost and it made her feel more alone than she'd ever felt before. 'So, is that where you are, Rosie?' she asked me. It was odd but when she said my name it made me realise that I had felt so alone, I never expected to hear anyone say it again. Then she told me that she had something very difficult to ask me. She apologised before she asked if I had done anything to harm the baby. I told her that I hadn't and that I wouldn't know what to do in any case. And then I told her that I didn't feel like this was my baby. All I did was hold Billy in my arms and feel him move inside me. I did nothing really. She tried to console me by telling me that I was going to be a wonderful mother. She seemed so certain of this. That once I held this baby I would know everything I needed to know and feel everything I was meant to feel. I told her about the babies I'd watched on *Call the Midwife*. The ones who were stillborn, or born with terrible deformities or hearts too weak to sustain them. She tried her best to reason with me that the mathematics were in my favour, especially because I was so young. She told me that I was standing in the most meaningful time in my life, and that soon I would see this and I would understand what she meant. She told me that she had grown up with younger brothers and sisters. One sister was born when she was ten years old and she practically raised her for her mum who already had her hands full. And then I asked her if she would take this baby when the time came. She didn't answer this question. Instead she gently swept my hair from my face with her hand, and told me that she would be with me in the hospital and that she would look after me and teach me everything. 'You'll get your sea legs,' she said. 'God looks over all expectant mothers.' But I know this isn't true. God was not looking after the mother on *Call the Midwife* who gave birth to a little girl whose arms and legs were only stumps. And if God was looking after me then I don't think I would have lain awake half the night while Sally was asleep beside me in the bed, thinking about cutting off the part of my foot that Billy was missing so that I could put on the socks I knitted for him.

June 14

I am living with Sally now. She insisted that I move into her cottage. It only has one bedroom and one bed, and we are sharing it. We are taking long walks each day and she is making me eat, even though I have no appetite. The baby's hooded jumper is finished and in a drawer with Billy's socks. I'm not sure where Sally is keeping them. She has bought me my maternity wardrobe. Jeans with a wide elastic waistband. Long, loose-fitting dresses that blow like tents in the wind on our walks. This is where I will stay until my labour begins in three months and we go together to the maternity ward in Mallaig. That is the plan. But I am secretly hoping my labour comes on too quickly and too suddenly to make it to hospital. I would like to have this baby here in Sally's cottage, with Sally and the other midwives of South Uist attending me. This baby, is what I keep saying. Not *my* baby. Because it still isn't real to me. I am not real either. I am some imitation of an expectant mother. And what is it that I am supposed to expect? I keep thinking of Johnny doing up the baby's room in his cottage, *expecting* Elizabeth to return to him with their child. What would Johnny think of me hiding here in Sally's cottage? Spending most of my day sleeping in her bed with the curtains drawn. Sally does not hold this against me and is doing her best to make it seem like this is perfectly normal behaviour for a pregnant mother. But I have not told her that I have begun to say the same prayer each night before I close my eyes. I pray that I will not wake in the morning. That I will simply slip away in the night to wherever it is we go when we leave this world to become part of the mystery Billy believes in.

June 30

This morning a letter from Johnny arrived for me at the inn. Sally brought it back to the cottage and we sat on the beach in the late afternoon sun as I read it aloud to her.

> *Dear Rosie, We are enjoying a succession of bright summer days here and I hope the weather where you are is being kind to you. I got someone at the club to print out the photographs of the Askernish golf course that you sent for me and they are on my kitchen table where I look at them all the time and picture you taking your walks there. I've been to hospital at Kirkcaldy for tests on my heart. And all the results came back in good form. I felt like some highly trained mechanics were examining an old internal combustion engine to see if it had any more miles left in it. I don't expect to be conking out any time soon. In fact I feel stronger than I did before my spell. I've been thinking a lot about the day Billy and you took me sailing. It was the first time I'd been out on the water in a boat since I was a boy, living in France on the Riviera, in the boathouse my mother*

and Jerry had converted into a house for us. We had a rowing boat that we took out whenever it was calm and I loved being out on the water. I remember flocks of geese flying overhead and it was so still that you could hear their wings creaking like hinges when they passed. After the squall that capsized the boat and killed my mother and Jerry, I never went out in a boat again until you and Billy and I sailed together last October. Now whenever I see a boat under sail I think of that afternoon. I wanted to tell you that I was notified that Martin died. He left instructions with someone at the assisted living facility to contact me upon his death. I'm not sure why he did this. It confuses me a bit. But maybe he was confused in the end. Or maybe he just felt guilty. I don't know. And I'd rather not think about it. You will find this amusing, but I have been spending time trying to teach myself how to make pastry the way Elizabeth was trying to teach me. It's far more difficult than you might imagine to make it properly. I got someone to google instructions for me and I kept following them but the pie crust was always too thick. I remember Elizabeth telling me that mastering the art of making thin crust was what made all the difference. I know there is something she told me that I am forgetting, but I am determined to keep trying. The next time we are together I'm going to bake you a proper pie. I have not heard from you in a long time and I am taking this as a good sign that you have found a way to pick your life up and are busy and have found peace in a beautiful and safe part of the world.

Love to you, Rosie. Johnny.

'He didn't say a word about Billy,' I said when I put the letter back into the envelope. 'He's trying to help me forget him.'

Sally and I both sat quietly for a long time.

July 1

I don't want to forget Billy.

July 17

I'm in my eighth month now. I have some lower back pain. Pain in my pelvis. I'm having to pee a lot more often. I still wish I had a photograph of my mum when she was carrying me. I keep imagining what she looked like and I feel more connected to her now than at any other time in my life.

July 19

I must have heard the knock at the door because when I woke I was thinking a knock at the door in the middle of the night can change everything. For a moment I thought for certain it was Billy. He had come to find me. Sally was already out of bed opening the door. From where I lay, I could hear the frightened voice of a girl speaking frantically to her, and when I went to the door I could see her with her head bowed. She was crying and Sally was trying her best to comfort her. They were speaking in Gaelic and it wasn't until later when the girl had gone and Sally was dressing that she told me what had happened. Apparently the girl's fiancé had come upon her with another boy. The boy she had pledged herself to had disappeared and no one had seen him for two days. The island was organising a search party. I began dressing in spite of Sally's insistence that I should remain at the cottage in my condition. My condition. I dressed anyway and we were soon on our way with torches to join the others at the dock. When I asked Sally why the girl had taken up with this boy while she was engaged, she explained that the girl had only ever been with her fiancé since they had been at school together. She wanted to be sure before she married him that he was the only one she wanted. It was nothing more than a test. Her fiancé's name was Kane. He was quiet and sensitive and now the girl was concerned that he would conclude that she had betrayed him and might harm himself. Sally had promised the girl that she would say nothing of this to anyone else in town.

We all gathered at the inn and divided the island into sections where groups of two, three or four people began searching just after dawn. Sally and I searched along the eastern shore. When we walked across the rocks, she took hold of my hand as a precaution. She continued to tell me that she wished I had remained at her cottage, but I told her that I felt grateful to be part of the search because for the first time in months I was not thinking about myself and my own predicament, and this was a great relief to me. I kept recalling what Johnny had said to me one morning over tea. That most of us go through life believing that our story is about us, but in truth, the real story of our life is the part we play in someone else's story. I was now playing a part in the story of this girl who had kissed a boy who was not the boy she had sworn to marry. She had allowed him to run his hands under her jumper, over her breasts just to see if what she felt for her fiancé would not be exceeded by what she felt with someone else. She could not have known that this test carried any danger and set the whole island into organised chaos because she had no idea that her fiancé had followed her and was watching. Was she to blame for this? What, precisely, was she to blame for? Curiosity? I wondered what it was about us that makes us believe we can possess someone else, or that we can be possessed by someone. And maybe the difference between being alive and really living comes from giving yourself away. Maybe she wasn't certain that she was giving herself away to the right boy and she had to find out before she married him and it would be too late. Who could blame her for this except Kane, who might have swum out to sea and drowned himself by now because he could not abide the thought that some other boy had touched this girl he believed belonged to him? It made me wonder whom I belonged to and if we ever truly belong to anyone but ourselves. And what does it mean to belong to someone? I thought of Martin who believed that his daughter belonged to him and this gave him the right to decide what he thought was best for her. This gave him the right to deny her life with Johnny. To deny her destiny, perhaps, and Johnny's destiny as well. The whole time I was walking with Sally, searching the shoreline and fields that bordered the sea, my thoughts were scattered. I couldn't seem to line them up in any logical order. And what was worse was that it seemed that I had not been able to think in any reliable way for months. As the hours passed I grew more certain that this young man had ended his life and that Billy had done the same. His life seemed to matter so little to him. There was that. And the way he left without saying goodbye to Johnny or to me. I told Sally that a part of me felt like I was searching for Billy. 'You'll find him one day,' she insisted once again. But I knew she had said this only to reassure me. And when the boy was found alive, sitting alone in the dunes where he had spent what must have been a night of torment, I tried to take this as a sign that Billy was still alive too and that I might find him somehow. But that word – torment – as soon as I wrote it, I knew that I, too, was tormented by the thought that Billy had found his way into the arms of someone else. Someone new. Someone who would help him forget me.

July 29

Waiting. You can wait so long for something that you can no longer be certain what it is you are waiting for. Or what you hope will come from all the waiting. What you hope will happen at the end of all the waiting.

We have come to Mallaig again for me to be examined by the doctor. The ferry crossing was terribly rough, though oddly I was one of the only people not throwing up. Sally and I stayed out on the deck until we were ordered inside, down below. There were only a few passengers on board, one of them with a big belly matching my own. I tried to keep my distance from her but in the cramped quarters it was impossible and she was determined to talk to me the whole distance across the Sea of the Hebrides, telling me how busy she had been preparing her baby's room – everything pink because she had found out it was a girl – and she described everything she had purchased for this child from the style of her pram to the type of bottles she would use to top her up in the event her breast milk wasn't sufficient. Her list was prodigious and yet she went through it reciting everything from memory, a whole catalogue of items that were – apparently – absolutely required for any newborn. I was trying not to listen. I was trying to remember the part of Johnny's story where the woman he met at AA meetings helped him prepare his little cottage for the baby he and Elizabeth would love and protect there together. Sally could tell how uncomfortable all of this was making me. The girl couldn't have been sweeter but her sweetness only made her enthusiasm more maddening. I was trying to calculate how many ferry crossings had been required to transport all this baby paraphernalia to the island. I felt like my skull was going to crack into two halves. I don't have it in me to be unpleasant to anyone. All my life I've avoided confrontation and it would have been cruel of me to do or say anything that would hurt her feelings, but the end result was that she was describing for me in infinite detail the world I was headed for, the world that was waiting for me whether I wanted to inhabit it or not. She was telling me about the cute 'onesies' she'd recently purchased online for her little princess when I could take no more and I interrupted her with one question. 'Tell me about the baby's father.'

<u>July 30</u>

I never had a mother but her history is following me. And so they did another scan and another urine examination yesterday, and the doctor told me that there was more protein in my urine than he'd have liked to see which could be a sign of pre-eclampsia. How ignorant am I to have thought that protein was a good thing? As for the pre-eclampsia, he told me to keep a close watch on swelling of my ankles and to anticipate spending the last five weeks or so of my pregnancy on bed rest. When I complained to Sally about this, she gave me a proper dressing-down. She reminded me of what I'd told her Johnny had said to me – that most of us miss the real story of our lives because we think it is about us, and it isn't. It's the part we play in someone else's life that is our real story. Our real purpose. I had a sense that I had been blind all my life. Blind to the grief others suffered and the pain they endured. I had placed myself at the centre of every hour I had lived. I had been healthy every day of my life. I had never been in any real danger. I had been loved and protected and somehow I had become a person who never acknowledged how lucky I was. I thought of all that Liam and Billy had endured at war. And finally I realised exactly how selfish I'd been these past months while I'd been feeling sorry for myself.

I apologised. 'Think of what you are giving to your father,' Sally said. 'A grandchild. Your mother's grandchild. And Johnny's too. What were the odds that he would ever have a grandchild after all that had been taken from him?'

July 31

This morning I asked Sally whether it was a boy or a girl. I told her that I could tell she had known from the scan; I had seen the expression in her eyes. She wanted to make sure that I really did want to find out. I assured her that I did. And after she told me, and had fallen asleep, I wrote to Johnny. I didn't tell him about the baby. But I knew that this daughter of mine was going to carry the name Elizabeth in honour of the girl Johnny had loved, the girl who was the grandmother she might never meet in this world.

August 17

So I am the queen now, like the queen bees in Billy's hive. With the swelling in my ankles, I am mostly on bed rest, being attended to day and night by Sally and her friends. At first I protested. But I am now so sleepy so much of the time that it's quite nice being looked after this way. Someone always bringing me a cup of tea and biscuits. Plenty of biscuits. And scones. I wrote Johnny another short note today.

> *Johnny, I meant to tell you that I plan to return in two months. I will always be grateful for the time I have spent here at the edge of the world, but I think once I am back in Elie I will never leave again. I'm going to settle down and try to learn to be more grateful for each day. You are the perfect person to teach me how to do this. And I have a favour to ask of you. Will you please plant one new tree in your field and look after it until I am back? Thank you, Johnny. God bless you.*
>   *Rosie*

August 19

I was thinking that every baby deserves to be carried into this world on a love story like my baby – there, I've finally grown comfortable with those words – *my baby*. I've got a stack of books on the bedside table that cover every topic from the physical properties of the placenta to helping the baby learn to latch on to the nipple. My nipples. The books are all written in such a breezy fashion as if they were preparing you for a dance class. I feel as if I have ventured beyond the margins of my known world with a well-worn map in hand that millions of girls and women have followed since the beginning of time. What I am reading now is giving me the dimensions of a new life, a life that will be mine. It will belong to me from the moment my baby is born. And I will never be alone again. It will be the two of us. Elizabeth and me. The two of us against the whole world if necessary. Maybe we'll travel the world together. Her small hand in one of mine. A single suitcase in my other hand, going from station to station, airport to airport, hearing strange languages being spoken all around us, asking whomever we encounter if they have seen a handsome young man with the toes missing from his left foot, a former soldier. On we go this way, for how many years? Will we ever find my baby's father? And if we do, what kind of person will he have become through the years since he held me in his arms? And what will I tell my daughter about him? That he was gentle. And that he had consoled me after I had lost Liam and that I had loved him. All you need is love, I would teach her, as Johnny had said to me. Even if it is not a perfect love. Even if the person you love vanishes and you spend the rest of your time searching for him. Or wishing he would return.

August 22

Dear Elizabeth, you are now only about five weeks from entering this world. And at the doctor's examination I heard your heartbeat. It was strong and each beat echoed in my ears. I pray that your heart will carry you through a long life and will not stop beating until you have done everything you wanted to do in this world and have had many great adventures and have learned all that you could possibly learn. You are already a person. A stranger to me. But not really. And there are things I want you to know, so I am writing this letter for you in case I never have the chance to tell you. In case something happens to me and we are deprived of the chance to talk, the way my mother and I were. Your grandmother who died just sixteen days after she gave birth to me. I hope you will spend your whole life trying to learn. To know all that you can know. And to believe that it is more important to love than to be loved. To understand than to be understood. What I mean is, now that you have become real to me, you have given me the chance to finally move from the centre of the stage, off to the side. You have given me a new story to play a part in, a new story that will replace my own. I think I began to surrender my story the first time I heard your father's, many years ago when I was just ten or eleven years old and my father, your grandfather, told me the story of Johnny Cooper, your other grandfather who had a wife named Elizabeth, who you are named after. They had a son named Billy who was taken from them. And he is your father. You were conceived in a lighthouse in Elie and I think this means that you should feel all your life that you are special because how many people can say that they were conceived under a glass globe, with a sky above that was bright with starlight? I was never meant for anything special like that. I am just a simple girl who has lived an unremarkable life. But it was the story of Johnny and Elizabeth, your grandparents, who opened the door to a larger life than I ever could have imagined for myself. A new life with you at the centre of it. I did not spend long enough with your father but they were the most meaningful days of my life. They were days when your father helped heal my wounds. What better thing can anyone ever do for someone than that?

You should know your father's name. Billy. Billy Cooper. He believes that life is meant to be a mystery and that it is the mystery, and the things we cannot know, that matters most and that defines our lives. He told me one night in the lighthouse that atoms in our bodies trace to the remnants of exploded stars. I would like to have him beside me just now, close enough to feel his heart beating while your heart is beating inside me. There was a part of me that was missing until he came along and filled it. And if that isn't the definition of love, then I don't know what love is. There is also a great deal that is missing from your father's life. Right now, wherever he is in the world, he has no idea that he is going to be a father. Until a few months ago he had no idea who his own father was. And he still has never met his mother. He had about as much chance of ever finding the people he belonged to as a suitcase that falls from a speeding train. He was lost his whole life and had no idea. Maybe you will be lost too in your life, Elizabeth. Maybe there will be times when you don't feel real at all. Or when you feel as if you have no purpose. You must hold on to your father's mysteries then, and you will be reassured that it is fine and natural to be lost in this world from time to time, because we cannot even look up into the sky and say how far it goes. We think we know the answers, but really the answers that matter most are beyond our understanding. I hope you see the miracles in your life. I hope you find miracles in the sunrise and the sun setting over the water. And the stars that are so bright and clear on cold winter nights, they look like they might crack and fall to earth in pieces. And in the band of moonlight that looks like it is ironed across the water in the harbour. I am going to try to make certain that you always live near the sea until it is time in your life for you to decide on your own where it is you wish to live. I hope your father is with me then so we can talk about how your life began. About our love story that carried you into the world. Maybe this is too much for me to hope for. And if it doesn't come to pass, then you are going to have to be patient with me, Elizabeth, and listen politely each time I tell you the story, no matter how many times I need to tell it to you. I love you already. Your mum.

August 25

Dear Elizabeth. We could stay here on this island until I'm an eighty-year-old woman and you are fifty-one with grown-up children and wee grandchildren and you come by to check on me each day to see that I'm looking after myself. You would marry a local fisherman and I could learn to speak Gaelic. We could pretend that there is no world beyond our shores. That there are no wars or rumours of war. That there are no people in the rest of the world who matter to us at all. That everyone we ever knew in that world is lost and gone now. Johnny. My father. Billy. I will sit in a stuffed chair by a window and tell you over and over again what it was like when I first came here. How I ran away from everything and came here without knowing that I was pregnant. Without knowing how long I might stay. I will describe for you my room at the inn before Sally insisted I move into her place so she could keep watch over me. I will tell you how, at first, I thought that I would never make a proper mother because I never had a mother to show me. And that I considered having you and giving you to Sally to have as her own. You would have been the baby that she and James were going to have if the sea had not swallowed him. I will tell you about the socks that I knitted for your father, one two inches shorter than the other to accommodate his missing toes. I wonder if we will know each other well enough to speak about the things that really make up a life. Will we ever talk about what it is like to make love to someone you care about or to discuss the difference between babies who come into this world as a result of love and those who come into this world as a result of lust? Will we be close enough to speak of such things? I wonder. I wonder if my mother and I would have been that close. I have no photographs to show you of my mum when she was pregnant with me. But Sally has taken plenty of pictures of me with my big belly now, so you will never have to wonder about this as I have. You will have answers that I never had.

Maybe our lives are only a collection of moments, Elizabeth. Some moments tell us who we are. Others tell us who we might have been if we had not been so afraid. And what are we most afraid of? Of failing? Maybe. But I think we are most afraid of being alone.

September 2

How do we know where we belong in the world, Elizabeth? I think it must be a feeling. A feeling that we have a purpose. Maybe we belong in the place where we are something to someone. A lover. A friend. A confidante. A colleague. A listener. That is where we belong.

September 5

Sally has insisted that we go to church on Sundays and pray for the baby and for me. We walk there arm in arm, though I feel perfectly steady on my feet which I can no longer see now when I look down. The church is a handsome building built from rectangular blocks of granite. The door is painted glossy red. Every Sunday there is the same collection of people here.

A few elderly men nodding off to sleep. Mothers who have dragged their teenage children here against their will; you can tell by their expressions of bored superiority. *Why are we here?* they seem to be thinking. *We aren't afraid of dying, so what are we here for?*

I remember going to church with Liam before he left for the war and it helped drive away my fear that something awful would happen to him. And now I pray for a healthy baby. I pray that Billy is safe and that he will miss being with me enough to return to me. I counted fourteen women here this morning and I wondered what it was they were afraid of. What fears had brought them to church on this dreary morning when a cold rain lashed against the stained-glass windows? Were they afraid of dying? Afraid that there might be nothing at the end of the journey except the cold grave? Or were they here hoping to be forgiven for something they had done wrong? Perhaps for some pain they had caused someone. Maybe some boy who longed for them and loved them and whom they could not love equally in return. Maybe between them they had left a small army of broken-hearted boys behind them. Some who never found joy with anyone that matched the joy they had found with them. Regret. Perhaps it was regret that brought them to church. I have no regrets. Even if nothing lasts. I began to think this morning that I had met Billy in this life and that I would never see him again until we were in another world somewhere beyond the stars that were too numerous to be counted, somewhere beyond constellations as wide as continents in the sky above us. I had a sense that he and I had only met here to start our long journey together that would continue through centuries of time and beyond the time when time had any meaning at all. I decided something in church this morning while the rector was giving his homily with such earnestness. I decided that though my daughter deserves the proper and elegant name of Elizabeth and I have no doubt that she will grow into it, for now I am going to shorten it and call her Lily. Sally has found her head today and placed my hands there. She believes she will weigh around seven pounds.

September 8

When I woke this morning Sally told me that she had been listening to me carrying on a long conversation with my baby while I slept. She couldn't quite understand what we were talking about but I was definitely telling Lily about Elie. When I woke she was sitting at the end of the bed with a book in her hands. It was *Far from the Madding Crowd* by Thomas Hardy. She told me that she had had a vision in church that Billy and I were going to be reunited and raise the baby together. She had found a passage in the book that she wanted to read to me. It was something a young man said to the girl he loved after they had been parted for a long time. Years earlier he had asked her to marry him and she had declined. But now she saw that she loved him and that he loved her and so they had a new chance. 'She asks him what it is he wants from life,' Sally told me, 'and he says that he wants to sit with her by the fire. Whenever she looks up he will be there and whenever he looks up she will be there too. Who could ever ask for more?' Sally said then, and I knew that she was speaking not just for me and Billy. She told me that she had read these words when she and James were first falling in love.

While she talked she grew very sad. She told me that she and James had loved each other since they were fourteen years old. They both knew that they were meant to be together. They married when they were seventeen and for a while it was all wonderful. When a fisherman comes home from sea he only wants three things. Warm socks. A warm meal. And a warm bed. Especially after fishing in the winter, spending hours beating ice off the shrouds with a cricket bat so the boat won't sink under the weight. It was all so simple and they were both so content. But then she had felt the need to grow and that was when she studied to become a midwife and the work fulfilled her in a way that she had not anticipated. And James grew to resent this because there were times when she wasn't there for him. And they began growing apart. If she wasn't there to cook him a warm meal, he would sit by the fire and drink whisky instead. 'Whisky makes a useful servant but a brutal master,' she told me. He blamed her and told her that he had not changed at all. He still wanted the same things he had always wanted with her. But she had wanted more. 'Why do we always want more, Rosie?' she asked. 'Why did I want more?' I tried to tell her that she should not blame herself for this, that we all change and we are never the same person for very long. The world presents new possibilities. And we are meant to learn as much as we can. I told her that this is what I wanted for Lily. 'Even if it costs her her love story?' she asked me. At first I didn't know how to answer this but then I told her that I hoped she might fall in love with someone who would allow her room to grow and not resent her for it. 'That's asking for a lot,' she said. 'For a man like my James it was far too much to ask for.' And now she wished that she had just loved him the way he needed her to love him. And then she said something that I knew I would never forget. 'I would tear the world down if it would bring James back.'

September 15

Dear Lily, I hope you like me when you are seventeen. I hope you won't resent me if I try to hold you close. If I hold you too close it will be because I love you and because you are all that I have in this world. I must find some way to grow so that you are not all I have or I might try to hold you too close and hold you back from whatever your destiny might be. I must give you the space you need to be free of me. But not now. Not yet. First, I must bring you safely into this world and then fill you with all the love I can summon. Fill every molecule of you with love, from your toes to the top of your head. Love in such quantity that the world can never diminish it, and that it will carry you through whatever troubles fall onto your path.

September 16

Dear Lily, I must tell you that I am not the most academic – more of a tea-and-filing type girl. I can teach you to roll out perfect pie crusts, thanks to Johnny who learned from your grandmother whose name you bear. When they were married in secret, one of the first things she did was bake him an apple pie. You will hear this story, growing up in Elie. I became a part of the story only because I cared about him. Or maybe it was more than that. Maybe I wanted to do something important in my unimportant life. I remember sitting on the plane to America and thinking how fortunate I was to be on the journey to try to find Johnny's child and wife. I felt brave for the first time in my life. And it was also the first time I had any clear idea just how big the world outside Elie was. I wonder how much of the world you will see and if you will be content with your small part of it. What will you want to be in the world? Will you be content with who you are? Some people seem so content. Others like your father have a restlessness about them. I do believe that if you can find joy in simple things that you will be fortunate. And there is something that Johnny once said to me that I hope you will remember. He told me that most of the time when people disappoint us they don't mean to, they are really trying their hardest to do the best they can. And so we must forgive them. We must forgive the people who hurt us. The people who leave us. I was thinking this morning when you woke me that what I want to tell you is that if you ever have something you really care about, hold it tight and don't let it slip from your hands.

September 20

I have been thinking of something else, Lily. I must learn how to tell the difference between what is really true and what we just tell ourselves is true because we need to believe in it. I must learn this so that I can teach you the difference. Because if you don't learn to tell the difference between the two, then you can spend your whole life lying to yourself. Why would we ever lie to ourselves? Just to keep from giving up, I guess. Maybe Johnny has lied to himself for so many years about his Elizabeth just to keep from giving up. Maybe she never really loved him as much as he believed she did or she would have found some way to return to him. Right? Surely, she would have found some way. And surely, Johnny knows this. He must know this. Why didn't Elizabeth find some way to be with Johnny? I guess we can never know another person's story really. We know only pieces of it. Now I wonder what happens if you lie to yourself about something long enough, just to keep from giving up. Does it become the only truth that matters to you? And what does giving up mean? How does someone give up? You can't just lie down and let go of everything, can you? I must tell you that I was giving up here for a while a few months ago. Then Sally took me in and now I have you to live for. And the last thing I want to do is give up. You and I have a mountain to climb together. And someday when you read this, I hope it makes you laugh when I tell you that this mountain we must climb could well begin with an enema. How many episodes of Call the Midwife have I watched now? Several whole seasons – and far too many episodes where this is what the poor mothers have to have. But I think I'll be fine. We'll both be fine. It will be smooth sailing. And thanks to your father, I know a bit about sailing!

September 26

Dear Lily, this morning I am pretending that the hospital part is already over and that you and I are lying beside each other in my bed in my cottage in Elie and that we have the breastfeeding part figured out and that I know you well enough to make you content, and that we are as close as two people can be in this world. You and I will live in a world of make-believe for a while. The world all small children live in, maybe to protect themselves from all that they cannot know or understand. I look forward to being in this world with you, to be reinstated in the world of make-believe I lived in when I was little and when I believed that my mother was looking down at me each day from heaven. Let's pretend that we will never have our hearts broken or lose people who matter most to us. Let's pretend that the storm will pass while we are sleeping and that bright stars will fill the sky above our cottage. Let's pretend that you and I will never be angry with each other for long. Let's pretend that you will always be happy to see me and that each time you leave me, you will soon return. Let's pretend that we'll always have enough food in the cupboard. Let's pretend that I will buy us a little boat with a sail and that the wind will push us across the harbour through the sunlight. Let's pretend that you will learn to sail the boat and when I am old you will take me sailing and tell me stories of our time together when I was young, even though I will always seem old to you. Let's pretend that we enjoy being silly together and that we will always feel free to laugh at one another and to gently point out each other's mistakes. Let's pretend that we have a competition that carries on through all our years together to see who can make the best pastry. Let's pretend that I teach you to knit the way Sally taught me in the Hebrides where I went to disappear on my own, only to discover that I was not on my own and that I would never be on my own again because I had a daughter there to keep me company. Let's pretend that one day you will meet the Elizabeth I have named you after. Let's pretend that one day I will see her son again, the son who is your father. Let's pretend that Johnny was not lying to himself all the years he waited for the person he loved to return to him. Let's pretend that stories like his story never end unhappily. Or unfinished. Let's pretend that the fair has come to town and you and I are riding the big wheel and we're at the very top and can see so far. The whole of our known world. And we will never venture any further from each other than the margins of that world.

October 3

Dear Lily, this afternoon at three o'clock we will take the ferry to Mallaig because Sally has determined that my cervix has begun to dilate and I am having mild contractions. If we weren't on an island and if there wasn't my mother's history, we would stay right here because this mild labour could go on for days, and you would be born in Sally's bed where she has looked after me and kept me company. But we are being cautious. I believe you will be here soon.

chapter fifty-three

elie

In the end, I think, it is the heart that determines our destiny. And though I would never consider myself a particularly insightful person, and I could never find the words to accurately describe the moment I placed Lily in Johnny's arms, I saw straight through to his heart, and the affection that ran through it entered my own and steadied me so that I felt certain of my purpose. His was an open, honest and caring heart. I would need the words of a writer like Thomas Hardy to describe what that moment was like, but it contained an incredible stillness like the moment I first drew Billy inside me. A moment of such stillness, it seemed that all the sound had fallen from the world, and that time had ceased to advance, and had turned in on itself.

After a week with Sally helping me get the breastfeeding down pat, I spent the next sixteen days in my father's flat, exactly the number of days my father had with my mum and me as a newborn baby before she died. It all came back to him and he helped me get my sea legs under me. He knew which kind of crying required my immediate attention, and which kind was Lily just simply letting off the frustration of being a baby and could be ignored for a bit. He, like Sally, taught me the importance of establishing routine for both Lily and myself. Feeding at the same time. Putting her down to nap at the same hour. Taking our walks at the same time. And speaking softly to her each time I put her down to sleep, a little nursery rhyme, the same words each time so that she would get used to being carried away on the familiarity of the cadence of my voice and the sound of those words. *Hey, Willie Winkie, are ye comin' ben? The cat's singin grey thrums to the sleepin hen, The dog's speldert on the floor and disna gie a cheep, But here's a waukrife laddie, that wunna fa' asleep.*

It all came perfectly naturally to me. I felt as if I'd finally found my way to the purpose that my life had been intended for and had prepared me for.

And yet, I was not comfortable telling Johnny right away that this was his granddaughter. I had planned to, of course, but when I saw Lily in his arms and heard him say she was the most beautiful thing he'd ever seen and when he called her a little Eskimo because of her jet-black hair, her fat cheeks and deep-set blue eyes, I did not tell him that he was part of her story. Maybe I just didn't want to break the spell. Maybe because deep down I knew that he already knew. Or maybe it was just that I didn't want to shift his attention from my baby to his broken story and to his own baby he never had the chance to hold in his arms. I'm not sure. I wish that I were sure of more these days. Maybe it is just that I have enlisted in the ranks of all new mothers who must learn to navigate the world as sleep-deprived zombies. The first week was easy. Lily was a sleepyhead who only woke to be fed. And each time our eyes met she seemed to be exhausted from a long journey. And often there was a look of surprise in her eyes as if she was startled to be back again so soon. That's the only way I can describe her expression. Maybe she had come from one of Billy's other worlds. She was certainly not of this world. I would have been foolishly self-centered to claim responsibility for her stunning beauty and her perfection; I knew that there had to be some other explanation for the miracle I had been present to witness. From the moment Lily was born I felt connected to some vast and ancient mystery that I knew I would never fully comprehend.

I have been thinking a great deal about Elizabeth. Johnny's Elizabeth. And wondering how she could have endured having her baby taken from her. I know that she was a fragile bird. A bird with broken wings when she and Johnny fell in love, but how on earth could she have given up her baby? I would sooner have had both my arms cut off than give away Lily. Until Lily was born, I could never have been certain that Martin had given his daughter no choice. Now I believe he must have taken away her choice or she never would have allowed Billy to be taken from her. And now it was too late to fix any of it. Martin was gone. Billy was gone. Elizabeth was gone.

I said those words out loud to myself as I stood at the window of my cottage, watching Johnny walk towards me across the field of tall fescue grass bending in the wind, carrying something in one of his hands. He never came to see me in those days without something more he wanted to give us.

This time he brought a beautiful miniature carousel, carved from rosewood. When he plugged it in, the tiny coloured horses began to go round, and a small light came on and it began to play, *You are my sunshine. My only sunshine.*

We placed it on my bedside table beside the Moses basket where Lily slept.

We talked. I told him what I had been thinking. 'Martin is gone. Billy and his mother are gone. They're all gone,' I said.

He took hold of my hand and said, 'No, Rosie. Martin is gone. But Billy and his mother are only missing. As far as we know they aren't gone. They're only lost to us.'

He looked into my eyes.

'Right?' he said.

All I could do was nod my head. I didn't really believe what he believed, or maybe I just didn't believe it deeply enough, and he saw this and he told me that I must not give up hope. 'Hope has kept me alive for a long time, Rosie,' he said. 'You'll want to fill this beautiful little daughter of yours with hope.'

That is when I knew it was time to tell him. 'Did you plant the new tree?' I asked.

'Of course,' he said. 'The same day I received your letter.'

'I want to go and see it,' I told him.

* * *

I strapped Lily across my chest in the woollen wrap that Sally had knitted for me. And then the three of us made our way to his field together.

I watched Johnny kneel down and remove the basket that was protecting the sapling. 'We had quite a storm blow through here a few days ago,' he said.

I asked him if, when he planted it for me, it brought back memories.

'Yes,' he said. 'I remembered planting the first two for Elizabeth and the baby. It was like it happened yesterday. That's the thing with time, isn't it?' he said, as if he were trying to convince himself of all the years that had passed.

I put my hand on his shoulder. I wanted to say the right thing. 'Think of all that we do not know, Johnny,' I said. Then, 'Is my mother in heaven?' I heard myself say, though it surprised me that this question had come into my mind. 'Is Liam in another world?'

Johnny put his arms around me. We didn't say anything at first.

Then I asked, 'You really don't believe they're gone?'

I felt him shake his head.

'Here,' I said, stepping away and untying the wrap. Lily was fast asleep. 'Whenever I carry her in this, so close to the milk supply, it reassures her and puts her to sleep.' I handed her to him and told him to hold her tight. 'She won't break. She likes to be held close,' I told him.

He smiled down at her and said, 'I guess we never stop wanting that. All our lives. To be held close, I mean.'

'She belongs to you, Johnny,' I told him. He didn't look up at me. He had been swept away by Lily. I couldn't even begin to imagine what thoughts were racing through his mind. I told him a second time that she belonged to him.

'She looks as if she's come from somewhere far away, doesn't she?' he said, still in her spell.

I touched his face and when he looked up at me the stillness was all around us as if we were the only ones left in the world, standing at the place where past and future meet. 'Billy is her father,' I said. 'This is your granddaughter. She belongs to you and no one can ever take that away from you, Johnny. That's why I named her Elizabeth.'

There were tears falling down his cheeks and when I wiped them away he told me he had known, deep down, but he hadn't wanted to acknowledge it in case he didn't get the chance to know her.

'I need to apologise to you,' I said.

'What could you possibly have to apologise for?' he asked.

I told him how sorry I was that I had told Billy. 'He would still be here,' I said. 'It's my fault that he left.'

Johnny raised Lily in his arms and kissed her forehead. 'He is here,' he said. 'He's right here with us now. Everything we do is a choice between darkness and light. You chose light. Just look at all this beautiful light.'

I thanked him for this and then I told him what was in my heart. 'I wouldn't have asked for too much,' I began. 'If Billy had loved me only a little, only as much as he could, I would have been satisfied. It would have been enough for me.'

chapter fifty-four

lochmaben

With Christmas coming round again, it had been over a year since I'd lost Billy, but I still remembered the feeling I'd had in his arms, that there would never be a thing we wouldn't understand together. I was thinking of this as I wrapped Lily against my chest and then walked to the bus stop to take the 95 into St Andrews to do my shopping. We sat on the upper deck of the bus and every few miles Lily would open her eyes just long enough for them to fill with the light glancing off the sea.

In town I bought some foil paper to wrap Johnny's jumper and the scarf I'd knitted my father. I found the perfect silver necklace for Sally with the Scottish cross on it and wrote a card to send with it while I waited in the queue at the post office on South Street. *Let's say that someday we'll be old ladies who spend Christmas together, Sally. I'll travel to be with you, wherever you are.*

* * *

I always did my Christmas shopping before the university students had left town at the end of the term so I could be in their presence and feel their excitement. Today I sat among them in the Rector's Café, drinking a cup of tea to warm up a bit before the ride back to Elie, listening to them talking with excitement about their plans for the Christmas break. They all looked so handsome and clever, and so full of promise. That's the word that best describes them, I think. *Promise*. For them, anything seemed possible. I was in good spirits until I thought about the families waiting for them which immediately carried me away to a dark place. When I was a girl my father's younger brother, my Uncle Tommy, was a mystery to me. He owned a dairy farm in a wee town called Lochmaben. I always loved going there and spending time with my three cousins, hiding in the stone barns and chasing each other through the fields of rye and barley and wheat. But Uncle Tommy was never there. He had been replaced by a fellow named Jimmy Hughes, who Tommy's wife had married by then. When I was old enough my father told me the story of what had happened and it was a story that began right on the campus of the University of St Andrews where I was sitting now with Lily. On the night of December 21, 1988, many students from the university who were on foreign exchanges from America were making their way back home for Christmas when the plane they were flying in exploded in the air due to a terrorist bomb. All 243 passengers and 16 crew fell through the sky and were scattered across the hills and fields. My father had told me all the details of that catastrophe. How they had fallen at over 120 miles an hour. Many of them still strapped in their seats. It took two and a half minutes for them to reach the ground from 30,000 feet and the chief forensic examiners from Edinburgh believed some of them had remained conscious almost until the moment they hit the ground. My Uncle Tommy had joined the search party through the night. On his land, just as dawn was breaking, he came upon a young boy and girl, strapped in their seats, holding hands, planted upright, eight feet deep in the ground of his wheat field. He took it so hard that he was never the same again. He could no longer work his fields, and within a year ended up in an institution where my father and I would visit him from time to time and he would just stare into space with a vacant expression.

Now as I looked at these young students so full of promise, I began to wonder how many of them knew that story and would be thinking of it as they made their way across the night sky toward home for Christmas. And I wished that Billy had been sitting with me to tell me not to worry about such horrible things so close to Christmas, surrounded by these joyful young students, with my lovely Lily sleeping peacefully against me. I suppose because it was all still so new, I had many moments like this that I wished I could have shared with Billy. I told myself again this morning that, in time, I would grow used to his absence, and as the memory of the time we had shared grew dim, things would be easier to bear.

* * *

It was a soft, star-filled night when Johnny and I joined the rest of the town for the lighting of his tree. The wind had fallen off, waves were spilling gently onto the shore and all my fears about how I would ever be able to protect Lily in a world where beautiful young people so full of promise fell from the sky were gone as we sang the old carols together.

It was a perfect night to be outside. Johnny wanted to hold Lily and show her the lighted tree for her first Christmas. The community centre was giving out cups of hot chocolate. At first I was unaware that an odd silence had fallen among the crowd. Rather than the next carol just starting up, there was a hush that caught my attention and when I turned away from the lighted tree and from Johnny holding Lily, I saw them. They were coming straight for me. Billy and Elizabeth walking arm in arm. And in that moment when I saw the joy in their eyes, I knew that Billy had been right about the mysteries in this world. This was a world where young men were crippled by wars, and innocents fell from the night sky, and mothers died in childbirth, and the sea swallowed young husbands, but it was also a world filled with wondrous beauty where a family could be drawn together against long odds, and made whole in their time.

Acknowledgemenats

I am most grateful for my agent, Paul Bresnick, who has been at my side for so many years, and for the people at Legend Press in London, especially my editor Cari Rosen, who is the finest editor I've worked with in my forty-eight years of a writing life. Thank you for Legend Press for their support as I spent the winter of 2024-2025 at the war in Ukraine writing a book about a woman who lost her husband and only brother after Russia invaded her country, so that the five children these two men left behind would one day know who their fathers were, and what they fought and died for. Any reader wishing to contact me can reach me at hancockpt@aol.com